Lichenwald

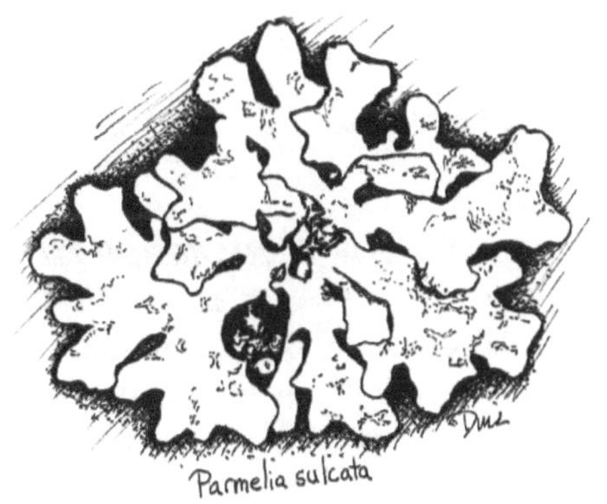

Parmelia sulcata

Also by Ellen King Rice

The EvoAngel (2016)

Undergrowth (2018)

PRAISE FOR *THE EVOANGEL*

'Compelling characters and plot with fungi thrown in! A FINALIST and highly recommended.' *The Wishing Shelf Book Awards*

"Melding together of science and a great thriller . . ."

"This is a great read and with such an unusual plot twist."

"A wonderful read!"

"A delightful page-turning thriller . . ."

"A totally engrossing read . . ."

PRAISE FOR *UNDERGROWTH*

"Nothing says Pacific Northwest better than mushrooms, lush forests and gray, rainy days. . . Rice's multi-generational story combines a murder, mushroom research and disturbing backwoods encounters."

"A must-read for Olympia lovers."

"As compelling and hard to set aside as a box of chocolates."

Dedicated to all who care for the elderly.

Thank you so very much.

This is a work of fiction. Names, characters and incidents are a product of the author's imagination. Biscuit, the dog, is based on a real canine friend who is even more charming than the portrayal in this adventure. The bra shopping scene was inspired by the talented help of "Ms. Dragona" of Macy's. Thank you, dear lady, for all you do to help women feel their best.

The fungal details, including the description of the lichens are as accurate as I can make them.

Cover by Damonza.com

Art by Duncan Sheffels.

Library of Congress Control Number: 2019904790

Paperback ISBN-13: 978-1-7338276-0-7

EPUB ISBN-13: 978-0-9969796-3-4

Mobi: ISBN-13: 978-0-9969796-4-1

Lichenwald

By Ellen King Rice

*A story of mushrooms and lichens
of the Pacific Northwest*

www.ellenkingrice.com

I find that with the passing years my pace is just a little slowed.
I may not go as fast or far, but I see more on the road.
Don Blanding (1894-1957)

"Everything flows and nothing abides."
Heraclitus (circa 535- 475 BCE)

Chapter One

10:30 a.m. Friday, November 21
Olympia, Washington

"Fresh blood. We need fresh blood." Professor Yousef Berbera, the department head, sat back into the cracked vinyl executive chair at the head of the conference table. The Biology Department of Summit College did not budget for luxury office equipment.

Cleaning was a low priority as well. The morning light streamed through grimy windows, illuminating an accumulation of greasy finger swipes on the laminated table top.

Dr. Zinnie Fazail wrapped her rosy-brown fingers around her favorite pottery mug, comforted by the heat leaking to her hands from the chamomile tea within. She let go of the warmth long enough to tuck a lock of dark hair behind her ear. The strand would not stay.

She needed a haircut.

White wiry hairs mixed in with her dark curls to make her look distinguished on good days and harassed on days like this one. Her focus split between Dr. Berbera's official bad news and the urgent tactile messaging from her clothes. Her jeans were ominously tight in the thighs and waist. The band to her bra felt sloppily loose, as if its exhausted elastic had finally decomposed into strands of rubber humus. These unhappy developments correlated with a particularly hectic October and early November. Her plaid shirt covered her drooping breasts and her mature waist, but the straining jeans beneath the flannel were proffering an additional, and rather alarming, body-status update.

Her juxtaposition next to the department's youngest and most ambitious member didn't help. Dr. Laurel Baumgarten quivered with the fire of a thoroughbred at the starting gate. Zinnie's mood soured further as she noted even Laurel's hiking boots were slender. Laurel's long legs reached the floor easily.

Zinnie was so short she perched on the edge of the office chair to keep her feet from dangling like a child's.

Laurel's silk khaki shirt draped smoothly over pert breasts as she continued as the meeting's note taker, with every comment being captured into a document file with adept keyboarding skills.

Laurel's long brown hair rested in a sleek ponytail without any of the escaping tendrils that typically marked field biologists and harried college instructors. Laurel hit Return and gazed expectantly at the department head.

Zinnie shot a look across the table to her lanky colleague, Bridget, who rolled her eyes. Bridget's short-cropped hair spiked in peaks and tufts from her recent hand swipes of aggravation. It had been a long meeting.

Professor Berbera paused to review his notes. Laurel took the moment to reach for her bright coffee cup. She apparently had one from each of her alma maters. In late September Laurel arrived at the first departmental meeting of the year with a purple mug from the elite Williams College. In October she attended with a cup emblazoned with Duke's navy-blue crest. Today Laurel's mug represented her Ph.D.; it displayed the sunburst and twin oak leaves of the Yale School of Forestry.

Zinnie repressed the urge to make a snide comment about the coffee cup collection of the impressively-educated young woman. Zinnie's own greenish-gray pottery mug of uncertain origins was the color of a cheerful *Lobaria* lichen. She'd used it for three decades, and she wouldn't trade it for any college-themed tchotchke, no matter how refined the school.

She struggled to reframe her sour mindset. The scent of vanilla floated her way from Bridget's coffee and creamer. Zinnie inhaled and worked to relax the muscles in her neck and forehead.

As a lichenologist, she should view eager Laurel as the vibrant green alga layer in a lichen. Every lichen had two parts — a tough fungal 'mycobiont' and a green chlorophyll-containing 'photobiont.'

The bigger and often dull fungus section grew into a resilient covering. This stout outer layer allowed the chlorophyll factories underneath to operate under dry or cold conditions. The fragile photobiont partner could be either a green alga species or a dark cyanobacteria or a combination of both. Like creative artists, the delicate photobionts used light. Specifically, the algae and cyanobacteria used sunlight and moisture to create carbohydrates, which, in turn, fed both the photobiont layer and the fungus.

Tough protector and vibrant producer survived together.

This positive framing of a publicly unappreciated life form amused Zinnie. She knew the dull old fungus was always the dominant partner.

It wasn't Laurel's fault she was slim, smart and accomplished.

Zinnie felt the underside of her breasts droop and stick to her ribcage. Her best bra was in the laundry, and her stretched out second-best bra was not up to the task of lifting aging mammary glands. It was time to go lingerie shopping. No bra could be expected to serve forever.

Unfortunately, she had no idea of where to shop for what she needed. The boutique where she'd found her last bra had closed years ago. Her one effort of buying online had been unsatisfactory in fit and a logistical misery to return. Was there a YouTube video showing lingerie shopping for sagging matrons? What would the search terms be?

Her subconscious nudged, demanding a new focus on the work at hand. Yousef Berbera's gravel voice droned on. Dropping enrollment. Rising student debt. Less financial aid.

"We can't depend on past enrollment numbers," he said. "With visa changes, our international student population has plummeted. Canada is more affordable and more welcoming to immigrants. It's a huge loss because our international kids paid full freight. We need something dazzling, people."

He rested his broad forearms on the conference table. "We must become a collegiate Bali of Biology — a destination students choose over other campuses."

"That's a tall order, Yousef," said Bridget. "We're supposed to invent something new without any extra budget, I take it."

Berbera nodded. He said, "I'll be plain with you. If our enrollment keeps shrinking, we'll have to cut staff."

Laurel Baumgarten leaned in and said, "Are there any upcoming retirements?"

Five middle-aged bodies shifted uncomfortably in their inadequately padded seats.

Laurel had the grace to blush. "I just asked," she said, "in case a retirement provided savings for the department."

Zinnie set down her mug and said, "I'm the closest to retirement. I'm sixty, but I worked part-time for several years. I'll be working until I'm seventy."

Laurel's eyebrows lifted. "You have another decade?" she whispered.

Mohan, a large man and a lecturer in plant genetics, rumbled a gentle laugh. "I have three kids in college. I'll be working until I'm ninety."

Bridget leaned toward Laurel and said, "We're counting on you to get us out of this pickle. You're the last hire. You'll be first to go, you know." Bridget's hazel eyes sparkled with an impish glow, earning her a frown from the department head.

"Enough, Bridget," Professor Berbera said. "We're all in this together. We need the smart brains at this table to think of who might want to come to this college for specialty classes next summer, and who we can recruit for next fall. That's two different types of student. Put your thinking caps on, and we'll meet again Monday morning after the Thanksgiving break." He paused. "It's dire, people. I need some help with this. Meanwhile, I've got an eleven o'clock class, so we'll adjourn."

As the meeting broke up, Laurel pursued Dr. Berbera down the hall, no doubt to pepper him with questions and complex suggestions.

Bridget slid into Laurel's vacated chair next to Zinnie. "How's your mother?" she asked.

"Not good. She's easily agitated, and she's speaking in German," Zinnie said.

"That's her childhood language?" Bridget's eyes were direct and stilled with concentration and interest.

"Yes. One I never learned. She also keeps escaping from the house. We've had a wonderful home health aide named Neena, but today's her last day. Neena has a bum knee, and my mom can still scurry in a hurry. It's not working out." Zinnie sighed. "Mom's on a mission. She thinks she can find one of the elusive blue mushrooms of western Washington."

"Blue mushrooms. Which species is that?"

"We've got several, including a few species found to the north and south of Thurston County, which suggests those could be found here. I took Mom to a mycology club meeting in September, and a student asked us to keep an eye out for the 'verdigris' mushroom, which is *Stropharia aeruginosa*. Mom remembers finding a blue mushroom cluster years ago, and she's determined to find more."

Zinnie exhaled and tried not to sound whiney. "Mom really wants to help this student, but mom's 'helping' is a problem. She's been all over the neighborhood, rooting in the wood chips and peering under bushes. She loses the words to describe what she's doing. Other times she speaks German, or refuses to speak. It's crazy making."

"Damn. I'm sorry." Bridget sat back in the chair. She ran both hands through her hair before dropping her hands to her lap with a disciplined effort. "We've got another problem."

"Besides sliding enrollment and my pants shrinking?"

Bridget laughed and said, "I'm not kidding. A real problem. *Beginning Biology for non-Science Majors*. Monday, Wednesday, Friday at three. I can't teach it another term. I'm losing my mind. The jock enrollment is killing me."

"Seriously? It's an entry-level course."

"It's not the students. It's the coaches. They want me to give credit for Friday lab work when the athletes are on the road for games. I can't do it. Our college rules are clear. Other colleges will allow make-ups and do-overs, but Summit College emphatically does not."

"Say that to the coaches."

"I have. They're not hearing me. The football coach was bad enough, but the soccer coach is utterly mental."

"Sic Yousef on them. That's why a Department Head earns the not-so-big bucks."

"I did. Yousef put a stop to coaches emailing me directly. Now the coaches are telling the students to 'negotiate exceptions,' and I can't handle the tears. These kids are under so much pressure. Some will lose their scholarship if they aren't on the team, and they can't be on the team if they earn incompletes."

Zinnie thought for a moment. She said, "From what I've heard, our soccer team this year might actually be a national contender, which means this season is a ticket to fame and glory for some. Passion can unhinge people."

"Lovely behavioral analysis, Zinnie. I need a way to unload this mess. I've rescheduled labs twice, and it's exhausting. There's a rumor that the women's softball team is also going to be stellar. Their coach is wound so tight, she makes the soccer coach look like a comfy sofa. Who can I get to teach this monster after winter break?"

"Not me!" Zinnie leaned back in her chair. "I get it. You were asking about my mother hoping to unload your problem class onto me."

Bridget didn't deny it. "I'm stressed to the max. I've got two other courses, and my monograph on hemlock canopy life is close to submission, and . . ." She lowered her voice. "Chloe is pregnant."

Zinnie felt a giant bubble of happiness rising inside. She smiled. "Oh, Bridget. How wonderful. I know it's been a long road."

"We're both nervous. Getting past twenty-four weeks was huge."

"You must be thrilled!"

"Yeah, nervously so. This time we think it's going to happen."

"You'll take some family leave when the baby comes?"

"For sure. But there's also a real chance Chloe will be put on bed rest, so I'd like to hand this class off. I don't need the stress, and I need to be available."

"Mohan won't take it?"

"No. He's slammed."

"Bridget, I can't. With my mom being as she is, I just can't."

There was a tap on the doorframe. Zinnie turned to see Dr. Berbera's patrician administrative assistant, Margaux. The silver-haired woman said, "Zinnie, I'm so sorry to interrupt. There's been a call for you."

Margaux normally took messages during faculty meetings or routed calls to voicemail.

Zinnie's stomach roiled with a spurt of acid as she asked, "From Neena?"

"Yes. Your mother went out, and Neena can't find her."

"Did Neena say anything else?" Zinnie spoke as she stood and swept her papers into a leather daypack.

"She said your mother was insistent her blue mushrooms are out in the fall." As Margaux spoke, Laurel Baumgarten came back into the conference room.

"How can I help?" Bridget reached out with an intended pat for Zinnie's arm.

Zinnie was already moving toward the door. "Please go on the Mushroom Observer website, and then to the iNaturalist website and see if anyone posted a blue mushroom record today from Thurston County. That might tell me where I can find my mother. I'll go home and start looking. Maybe someone in the neighborhood has found her."

"Got it. We're looking for any blue species?"

"Yes. There's a partial list on my desk. I printed it out this morning."

"I'll go get it," Laurel said, sliding her laptop into a shoulder bag.

"Thanks." Zinnie was almost to the door of the conference room when she heard a crash and a cry of dismay. She whirled around to see Laurel looking down at the shattered remains of Zinnie's beloved pottery mug.

"I'm so sorry!" Laurel's stricken face looked on the verge of tears. Her shoulder bag had connected with the mug.

"You go," Bridget said. "We'll clean up."

"Right." Zinnie took a deep breath and strode down the hall, thighs rubbing. She hit the exit door of the Biology building with tears poised to spill. She sniffed and wiped a hand under a suddenly running nose, lamenting the loss of her beloved mug.

As soon as she found her mother, she intended to have chocolate, then wine and then some more chocolate, ass-size be damned.

Which was exactly the behavior that had gotten her to this weight. Chasing after her mother was going to give her gout or diabetes.

Or a heart attack.

Maybe she should just buy a box of mushrooms from the store, dye them blue and stick them under the rhododendrons edging their driveway.

The problem was her mother knew her mushrooms. Even with a declining mind, a dye job of grocery store *champignons* would never work. Grocery store mushrooms were grown for consistency in size and shape. They inherently lacked the wildness of a woodland fungus.

Zinnie reached the faculty parking lot and fumbled for her keys. Standing in the fall sunshine, she realized she was the rare lichenologist who hated her life.

Things had to change.

From the desk of Dr. Zinnie Fazail

<u>*A partial list of blue mushrooms of western Washington*</u>
Stropharia aeruginosa – Mushroom Observer/iNaturalist – turquoise
Stropharia caerulea – Mushroom Obs – Pierce Co – pale blue
Clitocybe odora –Thurston County near campus – pale blue
Clitocybe nuba – Thurston County,– "Blewit" – pale blue
Arrhenia chlorocyanea – South Thurston County – small
Cortinarius violaceus – mycorrhizal w firs – navy blue to purple
Hygrocybe psittacina (blue-green)
Entoloma nitidum/*Entoloma bloxamii*
Leptonia species – perhaps several – navy blue in this group!!
Entoloma medianox – found near campus! Meaty mushroom. Navy blue.

<u>*Shelf fungus/jelly fungus/blobby things*</u>
Trametes versicolor (also in many other colors)
Osteina obducta – Yes (S.N. pers. Comm.) – pale blue-tinged
Polyozellus –blue chanterelle – dark blue but higher elevations?
Chlorociboria aeruginascens – neon turquoise – found near campus

<u>*Toothed fungi*</u>: *Phellodon atratus* – lovely dark navy with pale rim.

<u>*Maybe*</u>
Another tiny mycena – God, so many in this group – *Mycena subcaerulea*
Milky cap - *Lactarius indigo* – east coast and deep south
Leptonia carnia – largest *Leptonia* – an impressive blue. This would be cool.
Pulcherricium caeruleum or *Terana caerulana* "Cobalt Crust Fungus"
Neoalbatrellus subcaeruleoporus – "Little blue polypore" From Calif./OR
Hydnellum cyanopodium – Bleeding Blue Tooth – found in CA and AK. Why not WA?

Chapter Two

"Marvin, I can't thank you enough," Zinnie said. She stood in the driveway to her home after an hour of frantic searching for her mother. She was speaking to her neighbor, who had found Ursula Fazail just minutes before.

"No worries. She was asleep on my sun porch. I'm glad I came home for lunch." Her balding neighbor removed his thick-rimmed glasses and rubbed the lenses on his shirt front, restoring them to his face a moment later, the right lens still smudged. He was, as usual, wearing jeans and a plaid shirt under an unzipped and pilled fleece cardigan.

Marvin said, "She had her hearing aids out. Which is why she didn't hear people calling."

"Now she's rested and starting lunch with Neena, and I'm a mess." Zinnie sighed. "She was literally next door and didn't recognize our house. That's scary."

"I can see where she gets confused. These houses do look alike."

"Hey, mine is light tan with a white trim and yours is light tan with a dark trim." Zinnie said. "I think your master suite is downstairs, the reverse of mine."

"You can tell the floor plan from the trim color? I didn't know." He smiled. "I'd get lost in this subdivision if I didn't have my name above the house number."

"Don't tell Tilly Chen her house is indistinguishable," Zinnie said.

"She has the house with the neon red door?"

"Yes. Crimson Maple, I believe it's called."

"Right." Marvin raised an eyebrow. "Our one subdivision landmark. How did that color get past the home association board?"

"I heard Tilly bought an eight pack of gift wrap off each band kid with a parent on the board."

"Ah. Shrewd woman."

Zinnie laughed. "She also said we should be culturally sensitive to her family's heritage and a red door was lucky *feng shui*. The HOA board was leaning toward 'yes' and then she brought in hot pot stickers."

"Too funny."

"No kidding." Zinne found herself grinning and decided to dish further. She said, "Her husband is a sweet guy. He told me the pot stickers were from Costco, and Tilly knows diddly-squat about *feng shui*. Tilly wants her bridge group to find the house easily. She built a campaign for a red door from smoke and razzle-dazzle."

Marvin laughed. "Like I said, a shrewd woman."

Zinnie tucked her cold hands into her pockets, enjoying the gossipy conversation as she took in a burst of autumn sunshine. "I like her. She got her way and was nice about it. She's also the one who had the speed bump installed. Our loop was like a racetrack before the bump went in."

Marvin looked up the street at the long row of houses, each an earth-toned, double-storied home, each lawn guarded by a perimeter of azaleas, rhododendrons and fir trees. "I'm embarrassed to admit how little I know the neighborhood," he said.

Zinnie said, "I've met just about all the neighbors, usually under difficult circumstances." She added, "My son, Charlie, was fantastically wild in high school. I heard from neighbors about soaped windows, shaved cats, painted dogs and toilet-papered trees — and most of the crazy driving was his."

"Your son? Dark hair, tall guy? He's great!" Marvin smiled. "Charlie helped me with the sofa and some book boxes when I moved in."

"He's matured a bit."

"A happy ending then. Speaking of which, I have something for you from this morning's adventure. Give me a minute."

Marvin disappeared into his back yard and returned with a stick in his hand.

"I'm supposed to give you this," he said, holding out a foot-long branch of Douglas fir with a silvery mass on one end. "Your mother said this lichen was for you."

Zinnie felt her eyes well up with tears. "Imshaug's tube lichen. *Hypogymnia imshaugii.*"

"If you say so. Or should I say '*Gesundheit*'?" Marvin's green eyes twinkled behind his smudged lenses.

"Was Mom was speaking English?"

"Some of it was in German. I didn't follow her completely. She said something about a gangster and a protection racket. Those words were in English and very clear."

"She was talking about the lichen — a lichen is a fungus and an alga species living together. The fungus grows into a thick layer providing protection — a greenhouse roof, if you will. Meanwhile, the alga is the producer, taking in sunlight and carbon dioxide to make sugars to feed itself and the fungus. The fungus is in the 'protection' business."

"Wow. What a riot."

"It's actually a lot weirder. The name of the lichen is the name of the fungus. The alga partner isn't part of the specimen name. An unnamed slave, some say."

"Harsh!"

"Oh, yeah. And the fungus also determines the shape of the lichen. Often only the fungus reproduces sexually, which it can do by firing off spores like mobsters at a shootout. If it sounded bizarre, then Mom was lucid."

"Interesting." He paused, and said, "She's very proud of you. She told me several times you are a professor and I really should take your class because you are fascinating."

Zinnie's heart lifted. Her mother must have felt really well to have so many coherent thoughts to share. Zinnie cleared her throat and pointed at the sprawling mass on the branch fragment. "We classify lichens by shape. I tell my beginning students, 'spray-paint, salad or twiggy ropes,' which is the introduction to 'cructose, foliose, or fruticose.' This one is a foliose lichen."

"Salad?"

"Right. It looks 'leafy.' Most foliose lichens are bi-colored too. Here you see the bright silver top and the black underside."

"Sounds mobster-like." He lowered his voice to a deep baritone and intoned, "Flashing silver in the sun, inky heart underneath." Marvin smiled. "I may have to use that during National Poetry Month."

Zinnie laughed, feeling lighter than she had in days. "You're a school librarian, right?"

"Yes. Middle School – Do you need to keep this sample?"

"Good heavens, no."

"I'd like to take it for the show-and-tell box at the library."

"Please do! It will dry out to a very brittle piece. You can revive it with a soaking. It's an example of cryptobiosis. I can get you some more interesting things, if you like."

"Always. The kids love stuff like this."

Zinnie's mood lifted further as she recognized the signs of a fellow dedicated educator. Marvin was a good guy.

Marvin cleared his throat and said, "Since we're sharing family histories a bit, I should tell you my daughter is flying in this afternoon."

"I didn't know you had a daughter."

Marvin managed a laugh. "I didn't either." He peered over the top of his bifocals. "Which makes me sound like a total jerk. Look, I'm going to overshare a minute, but you're having family adventures and, as a neighbor, perhaps it's right that you know that I'm having one too. I met a woman at a conference some sixteen years ago and, ah, we had a good time. A pregnancy resulted."

Zinnie blinked. "You're a *children's* librarian?"

His green eyes sparkled as he grinned. "Some of our conferences are all about not being around children."

"Okay." Zinnie knew to be calm. She could see a glisten of sweat emerging on Marvin's forehead. This conversation wasn't easy for him.

"Anyway," he said. "I was told there was a pregnancy, but I was also told that I should butt out, so I did. I didn't know when the kid was born or if it was a boy or a girl. I'm not proud of that. I thought the kid was put up for adoption. Now the kid is a teenager, and she wants to meet her old man, which is terrifying as hell. I haven't told my co-workers, and I'm not sure how this is all going to work out."

"You'll do fine," Zinnie said. "Successful families come in many patterns."

"I know, but thanks for saying it. The piece that may be helpful to you is Allison, my daughter, speaks fluent German. That's where she grew up. Germany."

"Oh!" Zinnie looked at him. "Do you think she'd be willing to talk to my mother? For, ah, pay?"

"I don't know. She's coming here because she says she can't live with her mother, and she wants to know me." He inhaled. "As rough as this morning has been for you, I want you to know it is comforting to hear that you had a teenager that survived some crazy times."

His eyes shifted to the picture window of Zinnie's house where Neena, the home health aide, was waving. "I should get on the road to the airport soon, and it looks like you're needed. Are you okay now?"

"I'm not completely sure," Zinnie admitted. "Today's Neena's last day. I'm not sure how we're going to cope without her. We'll have a different health aide next week."

"Another new thing to navigate." Marvin sighed. "Middle age is not for the young, is it?"

"You are sweet to think of me as middle-aged. Today I am feeling distinctly worn and ancient." Zinnie waggled her fingers in a good-bye, feeling an odd sense of loss as she turned away from Marvin.

* * *

"I feel so bad Mrs. F. got away from me, but I just can't keep up when she gets out the door," Neena said.

"I know," Zinnie said.

"You need a different lock on the exterior doors. You give these doors a pull or a shove, and they pop open! You need a deadbolt with a key on both sides so she can't get out so easily."

"I know," Zinnie admitted. "Our doors have been this way for years. I'm afraid of people being trapped inside. What if there's a fire?"

"If there is a fire and you cannot find a key, then everyone goes out a window," Neena insisted. "Even if you have to throw something at the picture window. You could throw one of your big rocks." Neena waved a hand at a pair of large amethyst geodes on the fireplace mantle. "Those things are heavy. They would go right through the glass."

"Right."

Neena sighed. "I feel bad about leaving. I'm so sorry I am no longer the right person for Mrs. F."

Zinnie hugged the small woman, trying to keep at bay the horror she felt at the prospect of Monday arriving with no Neena. This sweet and efficient health aide had saved her sanity by allowing Zinnie to escape to the sweet bliss of work.

"I have my ticket to San Diego for Sunday," Neena said. "My third grandbaby should be coming soon, but I wish I could be here too."

Zinnie blinked back tears. Winter in San Diego helping with grandchildren sounded wonderful. "I could go, and you could stay here." She tried to make it sound like a joke, but her voice wobbled.

"Come," Neena said. "I heated some soup. You'll feel better after you eat."

Neena led the way from the living room to the cozy kitchen where Ursula Fazail sat at the table, cheerfully alternating between slurping tomato soup from a mug and nibbling on cheese on toast. "*Sehr gut!*" she cried at Neena's return.

"*Danke*," Neena said, stopping to pat Ursula's shoulder. "*Danke schön.*"

Tears welled in Zinnie's eyes. Her tall mother, with her increasingly thin frame, wild white hair and bright blue eyes — now frequently worried — was still her mother who always loved tomato soup.

"Hi, Mom," she said.

"Sweetheart!" Ursula beamed. "I found a huge Imshaug this morning. Truly impressive. I must give it to you."

Zinnie smiled down at her mother. The morning outing followed by a nap had invigorated her mother. This hour was a good one.

"I know," Zinnie said. "Marvin had it."

"Good man. He's a good man."

Neena waved at a chair, and Zinnie sat down, happy to have her mother's mind present. Neena placed soup, cheese, toast triangles and a glass of milk in front of Zinnie, stirring up an appetite that surprised her.

Neena kept up a steady conversation with Ursula, saying, "After lunch we're going to watch the Discovery Channel."

"Ah. *Gut.*"

"Then it will be shower time."

"Okay."

"Your daughter is going to go back to work."

Ursula looked across the table at Zinnie. "Did you sleep in?" Ursula asked. "Why are you here? You come when it gets dark!"

"Right, Mom. Just a quick trip home today to see you." In the space of a moment, Ursula no longer remembered her morning jaunt.

"How is your proposal?" Ursula asked, beaming.

"A little behind." Zinnie's chest tightened, and she focused on taking two deep breaths. She was behind, and she wasn't flexible. She craved sensible systems. The chasms of confusion

Ursula presented between events of clarity were too deep and unnerving.

Zinnie grieved for her loss of a predictable mother. She shoved the grief aside and said, "We're just starting the Thanksgiving break. I'm going back to campus to get some files, then I'll be back. I'll be home all next week."

"I'll check with the agency," Neena said. "Maybe Frank will be here Monday."

"*Nein! Nein!*" Ursula began rocking back and forth. "*Der Bertrunkene!*"

"Mom doesn't like Frank," Zinnie said. "He drinks."

"You're right," Neena admitted. "He's been getting worse." She sighed. "I'm worried, Dr. Z. The other aides I would recommend are all booked and the two new ones . . ." She paused before rushing in with, "They aren't very nice. You want to be careful and keep an eye on them until you are sure they are going to be professional. Maybe it is time to have a live-in oversight person."

Zinnie exhaled. Neena had mentioned this possibility before. Someone could stay in Charlie's old bedroom in exchange for extra coverage for Ursula's needs. It made tremendous sense.

Her stomach clenched in revolt. Somehow a person moving into Charlie's bedroom meant saying good-bye to her little boy. Zinnie sniffed, ordering her body to behave. She was being ridiculous. Charlie was twenty-eight and finishing a Ph.D. in mycology. He didn't miss his high school posters. He was still her son, but he wasn't a baby, a little boy or a teenager. He was an adult. The room could change.

To Neena, she said "I know." Zinnie sighed. "I can't keep putting this off."

"You're a busy professor."

"Thank you — but I've avoided thinking about more help." She smiled. "Sometimes claiming 'busy professor' means I indulge my passions. My brain, as usual, has been on lichens."

She pointed at her toast crusts. "Even this says 'lichens' to me. Lichens have yeast in them."

"Like bread yeast?" Neena asked.

"Different yeasts, but still simple fungi *like* a bread yeast. We're learning yeasts are part of the fungal-algae team making up lichens. It's not just a partnership — it's a threesome or a foursome."

Neena's eyebrows shot up. "Is that legal in Washington?"

Zinnie snorted. "Well, it certainly is occurring. After a hundred years of thinking we knew the basics of lichens, we are now learning more complex systems are at work." She smiled. "Turns out lichens are better at world peace than we are. They blend complicated tribes easily. Start with one fungus and one alga. When a yeast or two is added, it affects color and shape. With each different combination plate, the lifestyle and look changes."

Neena sat down at the table. She reached over and gently patted Ursula's arm. "What do you think? Isn't that interesting?"

Ursula turned and smiled at the home health aide. *"Guten Tag. Ich heisse Ursula."*

"Guten Tag. Ich heisse Neena." Neena looked across the table at Zinnie and said, "Please think about getting a live-in. I think it's time."

Zinnie's heart sank. Neena was right. The clarity periods were getting shorter and the confusion stranger. Despite Ursula's coherent lecture to Marvin, her mother was getting worse. She had to take steps now to keep her mother safe. These disappearances to hunt for blue mushrooms had to stop.

Hypogymnia imshaugii

Chapter Three

Zinnie knew she had limited time to work. As she opened the door to the computer lab, her eyes flew to the wall clock, and a squiggle of disquiet skittered through her stomach. The afternoon was evaporating. It should only take a few minutes to find the images she needed. This didn't quell her sense of unease. There had been something odd last time she had perused her photo files. She'd been too rushed then to do anything more than close the program.

She moved to the back of the lab and sat down in a cubicle, feeling the waistband of her jeans tighten against her abdomen. Her thighs felt like sausages in denim. "What do you expect?" she grumbled. "Your interactions with the environment have changed. Less movement and different food consumption patterns — like putting your face in the pretzels — result in anatomical changes."

Having a clear intellectual understanding of the physiology in play did not help her feel better.

Zinnie stared at the ceiling, her brain whizzing with connections. She ignored the mental nudge to open the photo files. When she was in this zone, insights happened.

Nutritional pathways. It was a different way to think about how lichens and fungi were structured. The algae in lichens functioned the same as algae in ponds or in oceans. Algae used chlorophyll to take in photons from light. Some ninety-nine chemical steps later, the algae had glucose. Algae worked and ate while sunbathing.

Fungi, however, had four different nutritional paths. If she looked up the feeding habits of the blue mushrooms in the area, she could zero in on which, if any, digested wood chips. Her mother was frequently focusing on wood chips in the neighborhood landscaping when searching for the blue mushrooms. It should be possible to sort out whether certain blue mushrooms preferred softwood or hardwood chips. Perhaps Ursula's blue mushrooms grew in cedar chips. The resin from cedars made for a particular micro-climate that only appealed to certain fungi.

This might be interesting to her students. Usually she began fungal identification by teaching shapes. Identification by feeding habits would be different.

Zinnie pulled a memo pad out from her daypack and began making notes.

From the desk of Dr. Zinnie Fazail

<u>*Remember to address "Styles of Fungal Nutrition" –*</u>

Mycorrhizal: A form of commerce. Fungi link with plant roots. Fungi exchange water and minerals for sugars
Lichenized: "Farming" or a "Protection Racket." Algae or cyanobacteria produce sugars and fix nitrogen. Fungi provide housing and protection
Saprophytic – consuming nutrients from dead things
Parasitic – consuming nutrients from the living

Zinnie scribbled the last line and groaned. She didn't have time to pursue these intriguing thoughts and how they might translate to better understanding. Scowling, Zinnie woke the computer, entered her password and waited.

When the icon for *Photos* came up, she clicked on it, and the computer began to whir. The rainbow circle on the screen began to rotate in a continuum, causing the skin on her arms to prickle in alarm. A banner erupted on the screen. *Files corrupted.*

Zinnie raged at the screen. All she needed was five minutes — five minutes! — with working files, and she could be on her way home. She visualized the photos of the lichens she needed to illustrate points in her project. She knew exactly which images she would use if she could just get to them. One favorite was a photo of a trumpet lichen showing lovely silver towers of reproductive podetia emerging like fairyland skyscrapers from a bright green lacy thallus base.

She noted the passing time at the corner of the computer screen. She hated every pixel of the corruption message.

Zinnie heard the door to the computer lab open. She sank down in the chair, trusting her short stature would be hidden behind the cubicle panel. She did not want to talk to anyone right now.

The door clicked shut. There was the sound of a shaking inhalation, followed by a deeper inhalation. Next came a ragged wail of sobbing that broke down into a trailing series of hiccups.

Zinnie rocked back in her chair and saw Laurel Baumgarten, leaning against the back of the computer lab door, tears streaming down her face.

"Laurel. What's wrong?"

Laurel instantly straightened up, and wiped her face. "I'm fine. I'm fine. Some allergies," she said. "Everything is fine."

"No, it's not." Zinnie stood up and walked to her young colleague. She put a hand out onto Laurel's shoulder. "You're not having an easy time at all. It's okay to be honest."

Laurel sniffed, then broke out in tears again. She launched herself at the older woman, putting her arms around Zinnie's shoulders. With shuddering gasps, she wept onto the top of Zinnie's head.

"It's all right, darling. It really is." Zinnie said.

Laurel stood up and swiped her face with the back of her hand. "God. This's so embarrassing." She sniffed again. "I can't lose this job. I truly can't lose this job."

"Don't worry. Bridget was teasing. Our Yousef is a great communicator and a decent man who will work hard to steer us to a good place. He's not about to do anything to anyone without lots of conversation. Nothing is going to happen overnight."

Laurel sniffed. "You don't understand."

"Worry and stress I do understand. Come on, I'll show you something." Zinnie took her colleague by the hand and led her to the back of the lab to an inconspicuous narrow door with a small keypad.

"Look, here's the code." Zinnie tapped on the keypad and pulled the door handle. The door swung open, revealing a storeroom over thirty feet in length.

"What's this?" Laurel stepped into the storage area, eyes wide at the rows of shelving. "How interesting. This is your anatomical collection?"

"*Our* collection. You're part of the team." Zinnie gave her colleague some credit, as Laurel was eyeball-to-eyeball with a two-headed frog floating in a jar of formalin and it didn't seem to rattle her at all. Larger jars sat underneath the row of floating amphibians.

One very large jar held a contorted Cyclops fetal lamb with its soft limbs mashed painfully to the bottom of the jar while the lamb's single eye gleamed out grotesquely from a prominent place against the glass. Above the jar rows, a rack held a collection of white skulls, ranging from a massive grizzly down to a baseball-sized rounded bobcat skull. Laurel surveyed the collection with a professional's eye. "You've got some rare stuff."

She knelt down to examine the Cyclops lamb, clearly unperturbed by the unnerving open eye. She said, "Is this from Idaho?"

"I don't know. There should be a specimen tag."

Laurel rotated the jar. "Ah. Yes. 1962. Idaho."

"What happened in Idaho?" Zinnie asked.

Laurel rotated the jar further, studying the bizarre lamb as she spoke. "I saw a TEDx video on this. There were years when maternal ewes were eating wild corn lilies which contained a six-ring molecule named 'Cyclopamine.' It's a compound that can turn off the Hedgehog gene. When it's turned off, the brain won't develop into two halves, and the body doesn't develop two eyes. Scientists followed the trail of on-and-off switching and came up with a chemical that halts some melanomas. We could use this in class as an example of how all things on the Earth connect biologically."

"You're a natural lecturer!"

Laurel stood up, with a wry smile. "The video had cartoon lambs instead of photos. Seeing this specimen explains why. It's rather macabre, isn't it?"

"Very. We keep quiet about this room in the fall. Otherwise Margaux starts fielding calls from people who want props for their Halloween parties. It's hard to say 'No' to a Dean."

"But Margaux is up to the job."

"Oh, yeah. She can be frosty."

"You know she's frosty with me? You heard how I screwed up?"

Zinnie smiled. "I heard you requested she call you Dr. Baumgarten."

Laurel had the grace to blush. "On the East Coast, it's an important title. I didn't know things are different here."

"We're reverse snobs here. The more educated you are, the more you insist you are just regular people."

"I didn't get the memo." Laurel sniffed again. "Now Margaux says, "Good morning, Dr. Baumgarten," and "Hello, Yousef," and I just die every time."

"Keep groveling. She'll forgive you." Zinnie looked closely at her colleague. "Laurel, how old are you?"

Laurel's eyes filled with tears. She said, "Twenty-four."

"You're twenty-four, and you've earned your Ph.D., and you are teaching at the university level?"

"I started college at fifteen. Academics aren't difficult. It's the social skill sets that are hard."

"You need to see this." Zinnie led the way to the back rack and pointed to the corner. "Welcome to the official 'away' spot."

A small armchair sat nestled in the gap between the end of the rack and the wall. An open-topped waste basket sat a few feet away, overflowing with crumpled tissues. A yoga mat paralleled the length of one set of shelves, and a rolled-up carpet rested at the end of the mat.

Zinnie turned to face Laurel. "I started coming back here several years ago when my son was in trouble, and my husband was diagnosed with cancer. One day Yousef found me back here, bawling my eyes out. He left and came back with the chair and the trash can. When Bridget said she needed a meditation spot, I brought her here. Then we both invited Mohan. His twin brother was killed a year ago, and he comes here every day for some private time."

"I had no idea."

"Most of the time people have struggles they don't talk about. We've all had our heartbreaks, so don't you be sad, and don't you be embarrassed just because it's your turn in the pits."

Laurel swallowed hard. "I get it. My life challenges aren't so bad."

"No. Your challenges are bad enough to be upsetting." Zinnie plucked a tissue out of the box and handed it to Laurel. "Please tell me what's worrying you."

"My parents are incredibly accomplished," Laurel said. "My mother is a trial attorney, and my dad's a judge. They wanted me to go into law or medicine."

"But you chose field biology."

"I had to! It spoke to me." Laurel sniffed back a new onslaught of tears. "Which would have been okay if I'd ended up teaching at a different college."

"Did your parents have one in mind?"

Laurel managed a watery laugh. "Princeton has been mentioned."

"Ah. Not teeny Summit College."

"I was lucky to find anything, but my parents don't understand. I know lots of people with Ph.D.'s who are still looking." Laurel's voice shook. "It turns out I love it here. I love the environment, and I love the students."

"And it's fine it's on the opposite coast from your parents?"

"There is that." Laurel dabbed at her nose. "I do love them. They are just a bit intense." She blew her nose, dropped the tissue into the wastebasket and reached for another. "They love me a lot. They think I'm marked for greatness. If they figure out just how small this department is and then learn I'm going to be let go, they'll think I'm some sort of failure. Or that they failed me."

Laurel hiccupped. "I haven't told them I am just a temporary hire while Dr. Anderson is away. I rushed out to start the term without telling my parents too much about the position. But now? Being home for a week? Trial attorneys and judges are experts at questioning. They just drill down. Question after question. And I'm a lousy poker player. I can't lie for squat."

The tears started to flow again. Laurel shook her head. "I can evade for a day or two, but not all week. I'm supposed to fly out tomorrow, and there's no way I'll make it all week without screwing up. I'll end up telling them the job is temporary and maybe not funded next year. That's when they'll be relentless with the questions and suggestions."

"What if you didn't go?"

"Didn't go for Thanksgiving?"

"Right."

"No way. They'd be so upset, they'd come here. They'd charter a jet if they had to." Laurel shivered. "I told them I have a great rental." She sniffed again. "It's a cabin in the woods, and I like it. It has ancient shag carpet and a musty sofa. They wouldn't be impressed." Laurel managed a smile. "There's an owl in the cedars. She's awesome."

"All right. Think tactically. What if you took a flight on Wednesday? Say you are helping an older colleague make a deadline."

"You?"

"My photo files are corrupted. I definitely need some help."

"Do you have a back-up?" Laurel wiped her eyes as she asked.

"I do, but how do I make sure I don't corrupt those files too?"

"Oh. I could help you. It shouldn't take long."

"Laurel," Zinnie said patiently. "If your parents are close to my age, do you think they have any idea of how long it takes to fix corrupted computer files?"

Laurel let out a laugh. "They haven't a clue." She sobered. "I like your idea, but I think I should have something more to report than fixing a photo file."

"You're all caught up with your students and your lecture plans?"

Laurel nodded. "Dr. Anderson left excellent outlines, and Yousef assigned me a teaching assistant." A small smile appeared as Laurel said, "Sometimes being a neurotic mess is a good thing. I don't fall behind on paperwork. Ever."

"That may change in time, but meanwhile check in with Bridget and do some brainstorming about her class. She definitely needs some help." Zinnie paused, then said, "How are you at finding a live-in roommate who could also be a part-time health aide?"

"For your husband?"

"No. He died last year. This is for help with my mother. She's declining into dementia, and she wanders."

"I heard. She's looking for a blue mushroom, right?" Laurel made it sound like a normal thing.

Zinnie found herself liking Laurel enough to relax and speak calmly about the horrible morning. She said, "Yes, she has been busy mushroom hunting — and the health aide we have is leaving. The agency is sending someone new on Monday, but I need additional help."

She sighed. "I haven't thought this through yet. My mother is getting worse, and I'm not ready. My brain goes haring off onto lichens as a defense mechanism against reality."

"Sounds reasonable," Laurel said. "How about listing the job on Craigslist? Or seeing if someone is offering services in an on-line eldercare forum?"

"Those are great ideas."

"You might post on a neighborhood forum, and there's usually a county Council of Aging with information and links."

"Laurel, those are excellent suggestions."

"Just make sure you check references." Laurel's gray eyes turned a darker shade of gray as she added, "People can lie on their resumes."

"Good point." Zinnie's stomach settled for the first time in hours. Of course, she'd check references — but there were people out there who wanted to work. Her mother was actually very cheerful, and her body was healthy. Advanced medical skills weren't needed. Yet.

Zinnie said, "I am going to get on those sites as soon as I get home. Are you going to reschedule your flight?"

"If I push back my flight to Wednesday, the airports will be crowded." Laurel spoke matter-of-factly, as if weighing the details academically.

"Righto. You'll be exhausted, won't you?" Zinnie smiled. "In need of multiple naps in the days you are there."

"You're rather cunning, aren't you?"

"Once in a while I manage," Zinnie said.

"Do not put your trust in princes."
Psalm 146:3

Chapter Four

The ad looked promising. *Hi! Do you need live-in help for your aging loved one? I have been a live-in caregiver for five years. I am certified, and I specialize in elderly/dementia care. I care for my clients as if they were my very own family. Seeking placement now. Sterling references provided.*

Zinnie sat on her bed with her cell phone, cherishing the solitude. Her mother liked watching old musicals. Tonight, Ursula was content to watch a cheery favorite in the family room. Zinnie's upstairs bedroom was well insulated. She sat in near silence. She didn't want to interrupt her moments of peace, but she had to stop procrastinating. Neena wasn't coming back.

Taking a breath, Zinnie tapped in the number on the ad. A woman picked up. "This is May Belle Pope. Can I help you?"

"Hi. I'm Dr. Zinnia Fazail. I'm calling about the caregiver?" Zinnie hated the desperate tension in her voice.

"That's me! It's May, like the month and Belle like the Beauty. Tell me what you need, dear."

"My mother is in the early stages of dementia," Zinnie said. "We have a health care agency providing an aide during the work week. My mother is declining, and I need to find additional assistance. I need some evening and weekend care. My mother likes to go out walking. I need someone who can keep up with her."

"Yes, I can provide care for her. No problem. I am looking for a live-in situation."

The sounds of dogs barking came through the cell phone. The dogs sounded like a cross between a dental drill and a jackhammer.

"Do you have a dog?" Zinnie asked.

"I'm visiting my brother's house tonight. My brother raises dogs professionally. He loves them. My sister-in-law too."

Zinnie glanced at the bedside clock, aware of the passing time. It didn't matter what May Belle's relations did. Surely "dog lovers" meant a family of caring people. She moved on. "Please tell me about your background."

"I've done a lot," May Belle said. "Eldercare, respite care, you name it. I've got excellent references. When do you need someone?"

"Right away," Zinnie admitted. "Monday."

"And you've got a room for a live-in? With its own bathroom?"

Zinnie paused. The only way for a live-in caregiver to have her own bathroom would be if the caregiver took the upstairs master suite — the room Zinnie had shared with her husband for two decades — up until his death.

"Hello?" said May Belle.

"Sorry. I'm a little lost in thought," Zinnie replied. "Yes, there is a room with an en suite bathroom." She tried not to groan. She'd have to move to Charlie's old bedroom downstairs. An exhaustion seeped to her core when she thought about the cleaning required to make his former space habitable.

May Belle's voice came booming through the cell phone. "Excellent! Why don't I give you my references now? You can call them this evening. I could come out tomorrow morning so we could meet."

Zinnie took down two names and numbers before May Belle said, "I have a third reference, but I know they are out of town. It might be a week or more before they're home."

"Two will be fine."

"Excellent! I'll see you tomorrow morning. About eleven."

Was everything going to be "Excellent!"? Zinnie tried to smother her sour mindset as she said good bye. Change was tiring. It was best just to get on with things. Zinnie tapped in the number for the first reference.

"Yeah?" The first reference sounded male and irritated.

"I'm Dr. Fazail, calling for 'Donnie' as a reference for May Belle Pope."

"Oh. She's a good gal. You'll like her." There was a clattering background noise that sounded like a bowling alley.

"What work did she do for your family?"

"Took care of my wife when she was ill." A voice in the background yelled, "Double!" Another voice shouted, "Donut! You're up!"

Donnie said, "I gotta go. Don't worry about May Belle. She's great." And he hung up.

Zinnie exhaled. *Give me data*, she thought sourly. *I don't know how to evaluate people.* She went downstairs and found her mother still immersed in the musical. Although she was doing her best to swear off procrastination, Zinnie rationalized a bout of fresh air would help before tackling the call to the second reference. She could fetch the mail.

She shrugged on a jacket and grabbed a headlamp for the short trek to the community mailbox. The November night breezes sent bronzed big-leaf maple leaves whipping by her ankles. The streetlights morphed the moving leaves into tumbling shadows.

Zinnie was on her way back when her neighbor's door opened. Marvin came out, hustling down his front steps with a wave. He met Zinnie at the end of her driveway, their bodies casting long shadows in the light of the streetlamp.

"Hey," he said. "How's your mother?"

"She's watching a musical and seems fine. I, however, am an agitated mess." She shook her head. "I'm trying to find a person to be a live-in assistant. I'm finding the phone interview and reference checking to be extremely stressful. How's your life going?"

"I stink at being a parent."

"Already? How's the daughter?"

"Not good. Not good at all. I'm not sure I can do this."

"Be a parent? Oh, come on. You're a lovely man."

"I'm not kidding. I'm an educator, but this is different." Marvin groaned. "I met her at the airport. She's scary looking. She has facial piercings. She's wearing about a gallon of eyeliner and black lipstick. She says her name isn't 'Allison.' It's 'Allie' like 'Alley Cat" only she uses an 'ie' to be 'original.' Then she stares at me like she's daring me to object. I managed to keep a straight face. Facial piercings I can ignore if I don't think about infections. I tried to be pleasant. I said something like, "We should go get your bag," and she rolls her eyes and says she was just planning to be naked in America."

Zinnie snorted. "She's fifteen?"

"Yes. She stares at me like I'm an insect."

"Get used to it."

"I have this urge to . . ." Marvin sighed. "I have an urge to slap her silly. I'm the sponsor of my school's Peace Club, for God's Sake!"

"Praise the good. Ignore the bad as much as you can."

"I know. Christ. I know. I work with middle-school kids, and I know this." He exhaled. "It really does help to know who she is now is not who she will always be. Your Charlie is a peach."

Zinnie said, "And I can tell you stories that will make your hair stand up. There was one month when he was ping-ponging between a white supremacist group and an anti-fa rage movement."

"Oh, my God. No one won his allegiance?"

"No. We were lucky. He discovered anger bores him. He's into action. His next passion was to become a spray-paint graffiti artist. He did say the Patriot barbeque ribs were better than the tofu vegan tacos."

Marvin managed a laugh. "Good points, all. We'll work at this and do our best. What's the next step for you?"

"I live moment to moment. I can't count on the next moment to have any sanity in it, but I may have found a live-in caregiver, which would be awesome."

Zinnie sighed and added, "The woman wants her own bathroom. I have to move out of the upstairs bedroom and into Charlie's — and that means moving a ton of Charlie's stuff to the garage. Tomorrow's going to be a long day."

"I wish I could give you a hand, but I don't think you want to meet this daughter of mine. She's a nightmare."

A slender dark figure detached from a nearby rhododendron bush and went sprinting down the road.

"Damn!" Marvin said. "That's her! Allie! Allie!" He went in pursuit of the runner, his ragged cardigan flapping as he ran.

Zinnie found she had a death grip on her mail. The daughter must have snuck up to eavesdrop and heard the unflattering words. How awful for Allie to hear her father's description. Zinnie stood in the light of the streetlamp for a moment, lamenting the challenge facing her neighbor with his difficult teen. The November air had a chill to it. Surely Allie would want to come inside eventually.

Then again, a defiant teen could get warm by building a bonfire. Charlie had done so on more than one occasion.

Zinnie trudged home, hoping her neighbor would find his daughter and engineer a relationship patch.

The musical was finishing as Zinnie stepped inside her home. It took an hour to help Ursula through going-to-bed preparations. Finally, Zinnie pulled the bedroom door closed on Ursula's room and stepped into the kitchen to check the wall clock. 9 p.m. She found her cell phone and tapped in the number for May Belle Pope's second reference.

"Hello?" The voice was female, high and sweet.

"This is Dr. Zinnie Fazail. I apologize for calling so late, but I'm checking a reference for May Belle Pope. May I speak to Sherry Knight?"

There was an inhalation and a pause. "This is Sherry. Give me a minute. I gotta put my cigarette out." There was a second inhalation and then the sweet voice said, "I know I shouldn't smoke. It's a nasty habit. So hard to quit."

Zinnie didn't know what to say as her brain darted off on the topic of nicotine. She couldn't remember the last time she'd spoken to a smoker. Some of her students vaped e-cigarettes, but rarely in front of faculty. Her brain raced on. Nicotine tested well as a self-medication for some mood disorders and could help some ADHD students with focus and anxiety relief. It was horribly addictive, acting on dopamine pathways and stimulating the formation of new blood vessels, a precursor to cancer. However, her recent reading on Alzheimer's disease indicated nicotine patches could improve some cognitive impairments associated with dementia.

"Hello? Are you still there?"

Zinnie's focus emerged from her wandering thoughts. She said, "I'm so sorry. My mind is easily distracted. Will you please tell me how do you know May Belle?"

"She was my caregiver when I was really sick. You could not find a nicer person."

"Does she have experience helping seniors?" Zinnie asked.

"Oh, yes. She's been doing this awhile now. Move over, please."

"Excuse me?" Zinnie said.

"Sorry. I was talking to the dogs. They hog my recliner. Hang on." There was the sound of a body shifting followed by a cacophony of yapping.

"How many dogs do you have?" Zinnie tipped the phone away from her ear. One of the barks had a particular staccato that sounded vaguely familiar.

"Too many. Today I'm pet-sitting some extras for my sister-in-law." There was a pause and the woman said, "You the live-in place?"

"Oh. You know about us?" Zinnie asked.

"May Belle called to say, ah, you might check references." Sherry spoke rapidly. "I hope you don't mind that we spoke."

Zinnie was distracted by a sharp stab under her armpit. She moved her arm and felt a long piece of metal curving over her left breast. It was the underwire of her bra. Lovely. Now her second-best bra was kaput. She had to go shopping and soon.

She shoved the thought aside and asked, "Can you tell me more about May Belle?"

"What?" Sherry coughed as the dogs in the background barked. "I'm sorry, I didn't hear you."

"What can you tell me about May Belle?" Zinnie raised her voice to a near shout.

"She's very efficient. Really works hard."
"You'd recommend her?"
"Absolutely. You'll be amazed at how much she can do."

35

"No man ever steps in the same river twice,
for it's not the same river and he's not the same man."
Heraclitus 535- 475 BCE

Chapter Five

The cell phone chirruped at the ungodly hour of six a.m. Zinnie rolled over and glared at the signaling rectangle on the nightstand. She grabbed it, scanned the caller ID line and then sat up, heart pounding. Why was her son calling so early?

"Good morning, Charlie!"

"Hi, Mom! How's it going?"

Zinnie flopped back onto the mattress, relieved at her son's normal tones. There was no stress in his voice, which meant no Charlie-centric disaster at hand. She said, "Yesterday was intense. Grandma disappeared on a mushroom hunt again. Today I'm interviewing a woman as a possible live-in person to give me some more help."

"Man, I am so sorry."

"Me too. She's eating well, and we're managing. How are you?"

"Great. I was thinking I'd like to come home for Thanksgiving. Can I put an air ticket on your credit card?"

"Of course!" Zinnie's mood soared. She had rarely seen her son since his research project had started. He was a graduate student at UC Santa Cruz investigating lichen and fungal responses to the state's work on reducing air pollution from motor vehicles.

Charlie's teasing voice came through the speaker. "Did you know California has an official state lichen?"

Zinnie mouth dropped open. "Really? How did I miss that?"

"Like I did. The bill was signed into law during Dad's hospice."

"Ah." Zinnie blinked back tears. She found a cheerful voice to ask, "What lichen did they choose?"

"A lace lichen. *Ramalina menziesii.*"

"What a marvelous choice. Very distinctive and beautiful."

"It's the only official state lichen. Washington needs one!"

Zinnie laughed. "I'll put it on the to-do list. Actually, some of my students might like suggesting some candidates. How's your work?"

"I'm almost through with my data collection. We're already seeing some interesting results. I can analyze anywhere. I could come home for a few weeks."

"That would be terrific."

"Good. I'll find a flight."

Words could not describe Zinnie's relief and joy at the thought of Charlie coming home, even if it was to a crowded house. She said, "If we have a live-in helper, things will look a little different. This lady wants her own bathroom, so I was going to move down to your bedroom today."

"I could sleep on the sofa, I guess."

"Oh, sweetie, we can make it work. Just come home."

"I will." There was a pause, and Charlie asked, "Are you moving stuff out of my old room?"

"Yes. I thought I'd box things up and put them in the garage. I was going to put my clothes in your closet."

"You might find a shoe box you don't want to open." Charlie laughed. "Heck, it's legal now in Washington State. Maybe you want to try some."

"I think I don't want to know what we're talking about," Zinnie said.

"Denial is an excellent parenting choice," Charlie agreed. "Hey. I gotta go. We're out collecting today. I'll look for tickets when I get back this evening."

"Be careful. Love you," Zinnie said.

"Love you too."

Zinnie clicked off the phone, energized by Charlie's call. She decided it was a day for a particularly happy shirt. She went to her bureau and pulled open a drawer to rummage through her collection of T's with lichen motifs and sayings. Lichens came in silver, brown, black, yellow, orange, white, red and many shades of green. She felt a professional responsibility to have a representative T-shirt for every lichen color.

She settled on a navy T-shirt with a very cheery depiction of a bright green *Peltigera venosa* on the front. The shirt caption said, "I'm lichen it!" Shirt decided, she raced through a shower and breakfast, all with the hopes of tackling Charlie's room before her mother got up.

It was not to be. As Zinnie bit into a slice of toast, there was a cry from Ursula. Zinnie set down the bread and ran to Ursula's bedroom.

Ursula's white hair swirled about her head as she cried, "*Mein Gott. Ach du liebe!*"

Zinnie could smell the urine from the doorway. Her mother had wet the bed. Zinnie rushed in and said, "No worries, Mom. It's just a little laundry."

It wasn't just a little laundry. The sheets, the blankets, the nightgown and even the floor were wet. Zinnie worked as fast and as smoothly as she could to get her mother rinsed off and dressed for the day. She escorted Ursula into the kitchen and settled her mother with a cup of tea and a bowl of cereal before dashing back to drag the bedding down the hall to the laundry room. Thank goodness Neena had installed a plastic barrier on the mattress.

Ursula was in better spirits after her breakfast. Zinnie was about to suggest watching a television show when there was a knock on the kitchen door. Marvin stood on the side porch, a slender girl in black at his side.

Zinnie opened the door and took in the girl's appearance. Allie wore an all-black outfit of skinny jeans and a leather jacket, augmented by a face of silver hooks, pins and piercings. Her heavily blacked eye sockets enhanced her bright green eyes.

She has Marvin's eyes, Zinnie thought.

The girl's shoulder-length hair showed a half inch of brown root growth at the base of an inexpert blue-black home dye job. The girl's scowl was consistent with her crossed arms and hunched shoulders.

"You must be Allie!" Zinnie smiled. "I am glad to meet you! I'm Zinnie."

Marvin's eyes radiated relief and appreciation. "We came over to see if you need extra hands to move things."

"Thank you! Some help would be fabulous." Zinnie opened the door wide, inviting them in, relieved Marvin had somehow reached a detente with his daughter. Zinnie ignored Allie's simmering air of distrust and said, "This is my mother, Ursula Fazail."

Ursula looked up, smiled, and said, *"Grüss Gott."*

Allie halted and bobbed her head in greeting. Her shoulders lowered and she mumbled back, *"Guten Morgen."*

"Mom," Zinnie said, "I need to move some things in Charlie's room, and Allie and Marvin are going to help me. Would you like to watch a cooking show?"

Ursula was agreeable, and Zinnie settled her mother on the couch before hustling her neighbors down the hall. "A potential live-in assistant will be stopping by at eleven," she said. "I'm really glad you're here. I can't get my stuff out of the closets upstairs until there's some space down here."

Allie unfolded her arms. She gave a curt nod. "Your mother is German, but you do not speak any German? Not any?" Allie's English was precise, well-enunciated and condemning.

Zinnie kept her tone light. "I'm old as dirt," she replied. "When I was a kid, immigrant parents were told to speak only English at home. We know better now."

She overrode the temptation to stare at Allie's facial piercings and concentrated on being welcoming. "You are about to see a time capsule. I've done very little in Charlie's room since he went off to college almost nine years ago. It's embarrassing. I haven't gotten anything done in here. Now he's off working on a Ph.D., and it still looks like a kid's room."

She pushed open the door to her son's tiny bedroom and was reminded why she had avoided this project. There was a narrow pathway to the bed and the rest of the room was a jumble of books, daypacks, gaming consoles and CD's, two skateboards, a trifold from a debate tournament, and a guitar. A bookcase along the far wall held reams of poorly stacked papers, threatening an imminent avalanche. The sliding closet door stood partially open as a jumble of clothes and boxes cascaded out.

"Behold the habitat of the young American male," Marvin intoned.

Zinnie laughed. "Let me go grab a couple laundry baskets. We can just ferry stacks of things to the garage."

Allie stepped into the room and gazed about in wonder. "You allowed your son to live like this?"

Zinnie snorted. "This represents the post-hoodlum period. I was actually quite delighted when we hit some sort of normalcy."

It didn't take long to get a system underway. Zinnie feverishly stacked and packed while Marvin and Allie streamed to and from the garage. Allie rolled her eyes frequently, but she moved briskly and said little.

After half an hour, they could see more of the floor. "We shouldn't store the guitar in the garage," Marvin said.

"Good point. It's a cheap guitar. I bribed Charlie with a beautiful Taylor one year, which he keeps with him, but he also likes this one. We should store it out of the damp."

"You *bribed* him?" Allie asked.

"You betcha. I saw value in his finishing high school. At the time he wanted to be a mercenary in the Congo. We compromised with two independent study classes, hand-to-hand combat classes, and a gorgeous guitar." Zinnie said this matter-of-factly. Allie's eyes went wide.

You're not as wild as you portray yourself. Zinnie smiled, but kept her thoughts to herself, keeping a smile buried as she moved past Allie.

Zinnie worked her way to the closet door where she saw the end of a small rectangular display case sitting on the shelf.

"This shadow box doesn't go outside either," she said, lifting down the wood-framed piece. "This photo is my mother as a girl on her twelfth birthday. She was keen to get 'grown-up' ice skates."

Allie stepped in to see. The shadow box frame had three divisions. In the middle, a very young and smiling Ursula wore a Bavarian dirndl with a white blouse and a dark green vest over a full-striped skirt and a lace-edged white apron. She cradled a pair of white-booted ice skates in her hands. The photo slot to the right of Ursula's picture held a tattered red patch and the space to the left held a yellowing sheet of mimeographed paper that ended "*die Weisse Rose lässt Euch keine Ruhe!*

Allie's chest rose as she rapidly inhaled. She suddenly looked like a very young fifteen-year-old. "Your mother was with The White Rose?"

"The White Rose?" Marvin asked.

"A student group at the University of Munich," Allie told her father. "They protested against the actions of Hitler, and most of them were executed. They were incredibly brave."

Zinnie said, "My mother was just a girl. Her father — my grandfather — was a bookseller and a devout Catholic. He helped distribute pamphlets. The Gestapo picked him up and he was eventually executed. My grandmother got word of the arrest and took my mother out of town to friends in the south. They evaded arrest for months, but finally were picked up and sent to Dachau."

Marvin whistled. "Wow."

"This was near the end of the war. There was typhus in the camp and my grandmother died. My mother got it, but recovered." She turned to Allie. "These childhood experiences are coming back to my mother now. Sometimes in the evening she is very anxious. She's sure someone is coming to get her."

Marvin pointed at the patch. "Did she wear this?"

"Yes. Red for a political prisoner. She wasn't even in high school."

"And this?" Marvin pointed at the faded phrase.

"It's about the White Rose group," Zinnie said.

"The White Rose will not let you alone," Allie translated.

Zinnie nodded. "The White Rose was the emblem because it represented purity. When my mom was put into a holding community after the war, she decided she wanted to be a botanist because of the White Rose. She wanted to become an expert in roses, but she had missed so much school she wasn't ready for college classes. She did learn to type. She learned English and got into a prisoner's resettlement program, which brought her to an agricultural extension office near Pullman, Washington. That's where she met my father. He was a botany student fleeing troubles in Kashmir."

Allie's green eyes radiated concern. "Kashmir. There are terrible troubles there."

"Yes. There have been for a long time. My father's family was killed in 1947." Zinnie ran a hand around the perimeter of the shadow box. "My father made this. He tracked down a pamphlet and put this together He was so proud of my mother for surviving. When he died, she threw this away, but Charlie rescued it from the garbage. I'm glad he did."

Allie's cynical sneer was gone. As Allie stood reverently looking down at the shadow box, Marvin caught Zinnie's eye and mouthed, "*Thank you.*"

She smiled back at him and snuck in a wink.

They heard the doorbell chime at the front of the house. Zinnie checked her watch. "If that's Mrs. Pope, she's an hour early!"

Chapter Six

May Belle Pope knew she was a sizeable woman. Any side-view mirror showed rounded buttocks cantilevered impressively in the air behind thick thighs, usually encased in black yoga pants.

Today she wore the pants paired with a green buffalo-check jacket. Orange-bronze leaf earrings matched bronzy streaks in her butterscotch curls. She had double chins and a wide smile. She knew her look. It had been hard in high school to be built like a wall. In the three decades since the miseries of those years, she had learned to use what she had. She didn't look threatening. She didn't look dangerous. She wore a heavy floral scent with strong undertones of sandalwood.

"What a lovely house!" she said. "Why I feel right at home already!" May Belle Pope made sure she kept the smile going. This gig could work out well. It was a nice neighborhood, and the home looked well maintained. There was some money here. Dr. Fazail read like a liberal do-gooder cream puff. May Belle ran an eye over the lichen T-shirt, knowing there was an insider's academic joke in the caption. The professor, with her tired eyes, looked stressed. As May Belle had planned, arriving early was unsettling.

Zinnie said, "I thought we said 'eleven.' We're a bit disorganized, I'm afraid."

"Oh. Did we? I thought it was ten! I am *so sorry* if I got it wrong!" May Belle could take a hit. The professor being discombobulated was the goal. It never hurt to start out sounding like someone who could admit a mistake. *Lovely,* May Belle gloated. She'd rack up a few more smooth moves shortly. It was important to gush over whatever ancient bag of a parent the professor cared about and to make a connection with any other household residents.

As May Belle stepped into the Fazail home, she noted the simple door lock and the professor's backpack bag and car keys resting on an entry-way table. These were good signs. Easy access to credit cards was always a good start.

The tiled entrance led to a hardwood-floored living room. May Belle preferred the silence of thick carpet. She did approve of the quality of the knickknacks on the mantel above a large fireplace. The amethyst geodes could be sold on-line, and the green stone fish might be jade. She didn't care for the floor-to-ceiling bookcases. Used books didn't convert to cash well.

She followed the professor into the kitchen and made sure she smiled at the white-haired lady watching television in the family room next to the dining nook. Granny looked thin and frail. Good. May Belle wanted someone she could handle.

"This is my mother, Ursula Fazail," Zinnie said. "Mom, this is May Belle Pope."

"*Grüss Gott!*" Ursula chirped.

"Well, *Grüss Gott* to you too," May Belle parroted back.

"Do you speak German?" Zinnie asked.

"Oh, good heavens, no. But I do work hard to make my people comfortable. There's nothing wrong with going the extra mile for our seniors." May Belle put some teeth into her smile.

May Belle saw a thin teenager with facial piercings and blackened eye sockets come down the hall, carrying a box. May Belle gave her a hard stare. It was fine to be sending out sunshine and rainbows when meeting with the grandmother, but she was not going to take any crap off a creepy-assed kid with a nose ring.

Allie eyed May Belle with a hard stare of her own before turning to Zinnie and saying, "This is the last box. We're going to the store later. Should we get you some more boxes?"

"Oh, Allie. Yes, please! I can't thank you enough." Zinnie turned to May Belle and said, "This is my neighbor, Allie. She came over with her father this morning to help me."

May Belle produced a smile. The kid wasn't a resident. This could work.

Zinnie introduced the man who followed the teen as "Marvin." May Belle beamed with an extra dimple as she scanned for any hints of sexual interest. She was open to a good time. Besides, a little smooch-and-tickle sometimes led to access to another home. She had one long-term stay where she'd ended up with keys to half a dozen homes on a cul-de-sac. That had been rich hunting.

Marvin didn't register her friendly signal. He nodded politely and focused on the professor, thanking her for an interesting history lesson.

"Mom and I may go for a walk this afternoon," Zinnie said. "We could show you and Allie some lichens, if want to join us."

Lichens? May Belle wrinkled her nose. Weren't lichens those slimy green things on trees? Like the drawing on the professor's T-shirt? Not edible and certainly not interesting. She couldn't imagine they had a cash value.

Researchers tended to have high-end electronics. She should look for expensive earphones and other accessories.

May Belle watched Marvin and Allie exchange looks. Marvin said, "Let us get back to you on the walk idea. We've got to do the grocery shopping first."

The neighbors went out the door with promises of checking in later. Zinnie closed the door behind them and turned to May Belle. "Shall I show you around?" Zinnie asked.

"Excellent! Please do!" May Belle kept up the stream of smiles. "Is it just you and your mother?"

"Yes. My husband passed away just over a year ago," Zinnie said. "Cancer."

"Oh, I'm so very sorry." May Belle thought, *Life insurance. I'll bet the old boy had life insurance.* She should keep an eye out for a computer password card or book.

The upstairs loft held more bookcases. The master bedroom and bath weren't her colors. She preferred pinks or mauve in a bedroom. This master suite had soft green walls and a bamboo floor. The teal blue bedspread was handsome enough.

Even better was the home computer set in a nook outside the bedroom.

She would have plenty of privacy up here. "I have a laptop I would bring," she said. "Do you have a secure router?"

Zinnie's eyes cut to a bookcase near the computer station as she answered. "Yes. If you are here, I can get you the password."

May Belle was ready to seal the deal. She could easily check every page in the bookcase for a cheat sheet or password book. This place was ripe for the picking.

She said, "May I show you a draft contract? Perhaps we can come to an agreement."

She watched closely and saw the tension lines on Zinnie's face smooth out. This was familiar turf for May Belle. People were always eager to look at a contract "draft." It sounded both nicely professional and open-ended.

They returned to the kitchen, and May Belle produced a document from her handbag. She said, "Why don't we try a seven-day trial? I can start dinner each afternoon at about five o'clock. We can sit down to a nice meal about six. I can help with clean up and the evening routines."

Zinnie's shoulders relaxed. May Belle watched and rejoiced. For most of her clients this dinner-making and evening help offer sealed the deal. Seniors with dementia were at their most difficult in the evening hours as confusion and anxiety set in. It could be exhausting to rush home from work, make dinner and get Grandmom settled in for the night.

May Belle added, "We can do meal clean up together or alternate as you like. Then I could also give you four hours of eldercare on each Saturday and two on Sundays, in return for room and board." She laid out the single page contract onto the kitchen counter, inking in a 'seven' in one line. "After a week we can revisit this and make adjustments. If either party isn't completely satisfied, then I'll find another placement." She signed her name and offered the pen to Zinnie.

It seemed so reasonable. A trial period. Help with dinner and a needed break on the weekends. Zinnie picked up the pen and dashed off a signature, feeling better than she had in days. "I'll finish moving downstairs today," Zinnie said.

"Excellent! If you don't mind," May Belle said, her voice calm and polite, "I'll move in this evening." She whisked the contract off the counter and folded it into her purse.

"I should get a copy," Zinnie said. "Let me run it upstairs to the printer."

"Of course!" May Belle turned her head to look at Ursula who was still sitting on the family room sofa, watching television. Zinnie's eyes followed. "Is your mother sagging a bit?" May Belle leaned in close to Zinnie as she spoke.

Zinnie coughed as May Belle's perfume rolled over her like an incoming wave. Half holding her breath, Zinnie walked quickly to her mother, who looked up, surprised

"*Grüss Gott!*" Ursula said.

"Hi, Mom." Zinnie searched her mother's face, finding no sign of injury. She turned back to the kitchen, disquieted that Ursula did not seem to know her, but feeling certain there had been no stroke.

May Belle was already at the kitchen door, hand on the door knob. "Look at the time!" May Belle said. "I'm supposed to meet my brother!" She fluttered a hand in a good-bye wave. "See you this evening!"

"I've lost my slippers," Ursula called — this in clear English.

Several minutes later Ursula's slippers were restored to her feet, and Zinnie realized May Belle had left without leaving a copy of the contract.

Zinnie checked the wall clock. There was time to bring down her clothes from the upstairs bedroom before making lunch. She was looking forward to an afternoon walk with her mother. Ursula, no doubt, would be ready for a nap after the walk. It might be possible to get to a few more tasks, including, perhaps, finding the shoebox of marijuana that Charlie had mentioned. She should get rid of it before Allie found it.

Surely, she could get a copy of the contract from May Belle this evening.

Chapter Seven

The Blue Heron Bakery

Allie blew gently on her coffee and sipped. A smile flashed on her face as she took a second sip. "This is good." A second smile appeared when a waiter placed a plate of pasta and salad next to her.

Marvin cherished the smiles as he attacked his own lunch of frittata and soup. "Thanks for helping Zinnie this morning."

Allie shrugged. She set her fork down and reached up to her face. She peeled off three of the rings hanging from her right eyebrow and laid the rings on the café table. She repeated this with the left eyebrow. She reached inside her lower lip and tugged, sending a labret ball in a tumble to her plate. Lastly, she unhooked a ring from her nasal septum.

Marvin stared at her.

"Eyelash adhesive and magnets," Allie explained. "The rest are real."

The rest was a comparatively sedate collection of a dozen ear piercings and one nose stud.

"Okay," Marvin said.

"You don't care?" Allie watched her father closely.

"I'm a librarian. We are all about the story inside."

Allie flashed another smile. "I wanted to scare you."

"Honey, you did that just by being a fifteen-year-old and existing."

Allie laughed. They ate quietly until each was scraping the plate. She said, "The woman who came in to Zinnie's?"

"May Belle?"

"She is cold. She is heartless and dangerous to Zinnie."

Marvin looked at her. "Okay."

"You believe me?"

"I am an educator. It's my job to believe young people."

Allie nodded. "Thank you."

"Tell me what you saw," Marvin said.

"Her eyes. They are hard. She challenged me with her eyes. Her eyes go around the room." Allie hesitated. "She is seeing what everything is worth, and how it can benefit her." Allie's eyes flashed with anger. "Zinnie is too trusting. That woman is very dangerous." She exhaled. "She is like my mother."

She had Marvin's complete attention. "I am sorry," he said.

"It's the truth. She told me she reached forty and decided she wanted a baby, so she used a needle to poke holes through a condom and then she seduced you."

"Ouch."

"Yes. But my mother does not share, so she did not share me with you." Allie glared out the windows of the café. "I have been looking for you for years. It wasn't until this year that I finally pieced together my mother's schedule the year before I was born." She laughed again, but this laugh had a grim edge. "We Germans are such good record keepers. I found her expense records for the conference, and it had a list of speakers."

"I spoke on award-winning chapter books that year," Marvin recalled.

"Yes. You were male and not too old. I traded something to my mother for her to admit the truth. She slept with you."

"Wow."

Allie waved a hand. "You see. I know this type of . . ." she searched for the word. "Sociopath?"

"A strong label. Let's go with 'manipulator,' Marvin said.

"Yes. Correct. Zinnie is no match for her."

"What do you think we should do?"

"I don't know." Allie smiled. "But I am glad you are asking my opinion. Thank you."

"I have an idea," Marvin said. "Let's call Zinnie and say we want to go on the lichen walk with her this afternoon."

Allie frowned.

"Hey. Zinnie is an expert. It could be interesting. Besides, don't think of it as a lecture. Think of it as reconnaissance. Our ally may soon be behind enemy lines."

That earned a quick nod of approval.

Marvin called Zinnie, who answered with a lilting hello.

"I'm glad you're coming," she said. "My colleague, Laurel, called and she'll join us. And guess what?" Zinnie bubbled.

"Let me put you on speaker phone so Allie can hear." Marvin leaned back in the café chair, smiling. He placed the cell phone on the table, and Allie leaned in.

"Laurel managed to uncorrupt my photo files," Zinnie said. "My picture of *Cladonia fimbriata* is intact and coming to me on her flash drive this afternoon." She added, "I'm relieved. It's a common trumpet lichen found throughout the Pacific Northwest, but this particular photo has great depth of field. It's difficult to photograph small things and keep everything in focus. This one has nice lighting, and it's perfect."

"Super," Marvin said. "We'll look forward to seeing it."

"Allie may like my photos of *Rusavskia elegans* more. That's a cructose lichen. It's the standard for lichenometry, and one of my photos is absolutely stunning. It's a lovely pumpkin orange."

"Ah, back up. "Cructose I know. That's the spray-paint-looking lichen. But 'lichenometry'?" Marvin arched an eyebrow at Allie, who responded with a confused shrug.

"Lichenometry is using lichen growth to determine how long a rock surface has been exposed. After a slow establishment period of ten-to-twenty years, called the 'ecesis,' we find *Rusavskia elegans* consistently grows at half a millimeter a year." Zinnie burbled on, adding, "We learned this by studying lichen growth on old gravestones. Those are exposed rock faces where we know the exact date of installation, which makes it easy to correlate lichen growth to a time line."

"Lichenologists do field trips to cemeteries?" Marvin asked. "I'm curious because this sounds like a good Halloween topic for my library. I have a constant battle against candy-focus among my students during the last two weeks of every October.

I'm not sure what I can do with this lichenometry, but if cemeteries are involved, it could be useful for an October display."

"I'd be glad to set you up with information and some specimens."

"Are you going to show us some of this graveyard lichen today?"

"I'm not sure we'll find it on this walk. Which is a pity, because it really is a beauty. Its common name is the 'elegant sunburst lichen,' which used to be the genus *Xanthoria* but then there's been DNA analysis telling us we were all wrong and . . ." Zinnie paused. "Sorry. I get into the topic. We'll see some nice things today for sure."

"Great. We'll go grab our groceries and get home."

"See you soon!"

Leaving the Blue Heron bakery, Marvin held open the exit door and spoke as Allie stepped by. "You said you promised your mother something she wanted. What was it?"

Allie's face went still. She walked silently to passenger side of Marvin's Prius. She looked over the top of the car at her father and said, "I don't want to talk about it."

"Okay," Marvin said. He didn't open the car. He stood looking at his daughter.

She looked away. Then she sighed and said, "She wanted a baby. I am no longer a baby, so she is done with me. I promised if she bought me a ticket to meet my father, I would leave to find you and never return." Allie scowled. "She started looking for tickets right away, and, finally, she started talking about you."

"What did she say about me?"

"You are good in bed."

Marvin felt his entire body blush.

Suddenly Allie's smile was back. Her eyes sparkled as she said, "It's a good thing to begin as a good time."

"Right. I'm ready to change the subject. Let's get some groceries and learn about lichens."

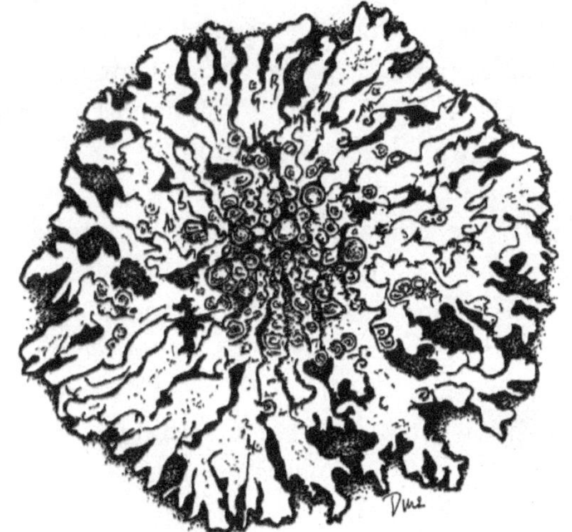

Rusavskia elegans

"The real voyage of discovery consists not in seeing new landscapes,
but in having new eyes."
Marcel Proust (1871-1922)

Chapter Eight

Allie shuffled along the dirt path, watching her neighbor carefully. Zinnie glowed in the fall sunshine as she peered at lichens through a small jeweler's loupe. Her happiness was contagious. Allie found her own mood lifting. The group moved slowly down a trail meandering between large cedars and Douglas firs. Laurel chatted with Marvin as Ursula tottered along with a pair of walking poles to help her balance.

"First stop," Zinnie called. "Everyone, look up!" The group gathered around her underneath the few remaining yellow leaves of a big-leaf maple. Allie found herself listening with careful attention as Zinnie lectured. "Tar spot fungus, *Rhystisma acerinum.* Grows only on the leaves of maples and sycamores. Deadly to horses."

"So, I should not ride my pony up the tree?" Ursula asked.

Allie raised an eyebrow as Ursula cracked a big grin. It was a pretty good joke for an old woman. Zinnie broke out with a laugh. "Right Mom. Okay. Poisonous if a horse eats the fallen leaves." She added, "Big-leaf maples are a great place to look for unusual lichens. Most of our ecosystem is acidic, but the cracks in maple bark often ooze an alkaline sap which can appeal to certain lichens."

"Huh." Marvin studied the maple trunk. "Any medicines from these?

"Nothing commercial at the moment, but there are hundreds of unique compounds produced by lichens — usually from the fungal partner. Penicillin is from a fungus, so such compounds are worthy of investigation."

Allie had to admit the walk hadn't been completely stupid. It was a nice afternoon.

Ursula smiled at Allie and spoke in English. "I love the woods. The evergreens, the birds, the maple leaves, the lichens.

So many things, and they are so beautiful. It is good to be together, but sometimes I like to be here alone."

"*Die Waldeninsamkeit?*"

"*Ja!*" Ursula beamed.

"What's walden . . . whatever?" Marvin asked.

"*Die Waldeninsamkeit,*" Allie said. "The first part is *Wald*, means 'forest.' The second part is to be solitary. It is the . . . feeling you get when you are alone in the woods. You are connecting with the nature." Allie swept an arm out, indicating the forest. "Away from people. We can connect with the earth."

"And there's a special word for it. Wow. Cool." Marvin stopped on the trail and looked around. "Is there a special name for this sort of woods?"

Zinnie grinned. "Lichenwald. Because there sure are a lot of lichens around here."

"I think most people would call it second-growth Douglas Fir forest," Laurel said.

"Spoken like an ecologist." Zinnie said.

"Ooh, look!" Zinnie pointed to the ground next to a moss-covered fir log. "A nice moist spot for *Peltigera membranacea*, also called the dog lichen."

Allie looked down at the soggy brown mass and said, "It has warts."

"Apothecia. The spores form from the fungal part of the lichen. The spores can shoot out like shells from artillery cannons — but the lichen will have better success in reproduction when a part of the thallus, or 'body of the lichen' breaks off. Animals or the wind can carry along a chunk with the fungus or *mycobiont* with a bit of the *photobiont*, which is either a green alga or a cyanobacteria."

"I know this species," Laurel said. "It has a cyanobacteria that fixes nitrogen."

"Right!" Zinnie squatted next to the dingy heap. "Anytime it is a dark lichen, we expect a cyanobacteria in the layer under the cortex, either by itself or in combination with a green alga.

There's always at least one fungus and one photobiont in every lichen, and now we know there can be yeasts as well."

She picked up a twig and prodded the lichen. "It's like a lasagna. There is a top layer, which can be a bit tough. It's called the *cortex,* and it's made of fungal fibers. The next layer is the green algae, or the blue-green cyanobacteria, or sometimes both. The third layer down is more loosely structured fungal fibers we call '*the medulla*', and then there may be a bottom cortex layer with little root-like things called '*rhizines.*'

"Ugh," Allie groaned. "Too many vocabulary words. It's like school."

Zinnie laughed. "I've heard that before. We're only scratching the surface because lichens live many different ways, and there are specific names for every structure of every variation. This is incredibly complex stuff because this combination of fungus and algae didn't evolve once. It has evolved many times, in many variations. It's even more complex than cell phone plans."

Allie laughed. She had to admit Zinnie knew a lot and knew how to make it interesting. She liked Laurel too.

In the pattern of a professor, Zinnie didn't stop. She said, "There's even a few genera that don't seem to reproduce sexually at all, but are still evolving into multiple new species. How that happens is a real mystery."

Marvin knelt down to study the lichen. "Is it reproducing right now?"

"It's daylight so the photobiont layer should be taking in sunlight and making carbohydrate. But, yes, the reproductive structures are doing their thing too." She smiled and added a wink. "It's multi-tasking."

"It's gross," Allie said. She scowled. "They look like zombie leaves."

"The lobes of this lichen are thick," Zinnie admitted. "At first they do look like leaves. Most of the structure is the fungus. Usually, there is only a thin layer of the algae."

"Can you separate the fungus from the algae?" Marvin asked.

"In a laboratory, yes. And each can grow — but neither will grow in this shape. If you separate the fungus from the photobiont and then try to combine them together again, they don't turn back into a lichen. Getting the partnership to kick off is hard to do. The initiation of 'lichenization' is still very mysterious." Her eyes sparkled as she added, "I'm confident understanding lichenization will help us better understand the origins of life on our planet."

Allie looked down at the small sprawling mat and tried to care the way Zinnie did. Allie kicked part of the mass with the toe of her boot and was surprised to see the underside was a bright cottony-white with long strands that reached for the ground, which was almost as gross as seeing the blue-white belly of a fish.

Zinnie stood up and said, "There's a storm moving in this evening which should bring down branches. Tomorrow the lichen hunting will be even better because of the windfall, which is also good for the forest. Lichens that fall eventually decompose and enrich the soil. Tomorrow we'll see the things that have been growing high in the trees."

"November brings our worst storms," Marvin said. "Do you think the power will go out?"

"Maybe. We've got some warm days coming, so more opportunities to hunt lichens and fungi. I love this time of year." Zinnie smiled and moved down the trail

As Marvin followed, Laurel motioned Allie to stop. Laurel whispered, "Have you met Zinnie's new roommate? The live-in help?"

"I don't think 'help' is the right word," Allie said. "We met her this morning. I don't like her. I think she's shopping for things to take."

"An eldercare thief?" Laurel asked.

"I do not know for sure, but maybe."

"Oh, man. That sucks. I'm the one who told Zinnie where to find on-line ads. I was wondering if Zinnie knew the right kind of questions to ask. Is this woman already moved in?"

"I think she's moving in tonight."

Laurel said, "Let's trade phone numbers. I'm not flying out until Wednesday. Will you let me know if you see something worrisome?"

"Ja." Allie typed in Laurel's number and yelled, "Coming" to her father's call. As Allie walked down the trail, she reviewed her resources. Her father was a smart man and surely would take action to help Zinnie if he saw something illegal. But he struck Allie as being sheltered. She knew how fast and smart a manipulator could be. Allie's mother often needed just seconds to take advantage of a situation. She'd seen her mother steal and lie convincingly, her thievery doubted because of a professional librarian's nametag and big-eyed protests of misunderstandings.

If Zinnie and Ursula were to be protected, it might take more than proper channels. Allie thought about the box of marijuana she had smuggled home from Zinnie's. Was old marijuana still potent? Could she use it to put May Belle to sleep? If May Belle was doped up, then maybe she wouldn't be a problem. Some people put marijuana into brownies. Did the recipe need to change? She was already thinking of Ursula as 'Oma' or 'Grandmother.' Would it hurt Oma Ursula if she ate such a brownie? It might be difficult to give to only May Belle.

Allie followed Laurel down the trail, pausing to kick a stick off the path. There was also the barbaric nature of Americans to consider. They had the death penalty. If she really screwed up, would they shoot her like the victims of Dachau?

She embraced a moment of rich mental theater. Perhaps she would face the guillotine like the students of the White Rose. She could not recall any American news stories about guillotining death-row inmates. These days it was poison, wasn't it? That seemed fair. If she killed someone with a poisoned brownie then, perhaps, she deserved to die by poison.

She could go to her death with honor if her actions defeated the wicked. Allie kicked another branch aside. It would be better to defeat the wicked and not get caught.

It would be really smart not to do something resulting in the police being called. American police scared her, and her sarcasm was at its worst when she was frightened.

Clearly, it was time to do some research. If May Belle was moving in this evening, then it might not be long before manipulations began. Zinnie was too sweet. She did not know the signs. Allie frowned. She knew the signs too well.

Allie pushed past gold bracken and green sword ferns swaying in the dappled light of the forest. It was pretty here. Allie stopped and inhaled the fir-scented air.

She should think this through. Maybe she was transferring her rage at her mother onto this May Belle. Perhaps May Belle wasn't such a bad person. Maybe it was teen hormones that were making up this danger. *Too many movies*, Allie thought. Maybe May Belle was just an ugly woman who didn't like teenagers.

A raven swooped into the woods and landed high up in a cedar. The black bird croaked an echoing call followed by a second call which sounded exactly like a dripping water faucet, leading Laurel to smile and point.

The raven's mimicry pushed Allie's wavering mind back to dark certainty. It was a bird, not a dripping faucet. She should trust her instincts on May Belle — at least until there was abundant evidence that all was well.

She found Zinnie, Laurel and her father with their faces close to the bark of a massive Douglas fir. Ursula stood to the side, turning her face to the sun.

"See the tiny red spots?" Zinnie said.

Allie moved close, and her father moved aside. "Looks like shaggy green pipe-stem cleaners with red lips," Marvin said.

"Huh." Allie squinted a bit and decided the odd tubes had a funky charm. "What is it?"

Zinnie said, "*Cladonia bellidiflora*. The lipstick lichen."

Zinnie proffered her hand lens to Laurel who peered through the glass and said, "rough stem."

"Right. Stems are important to identify lichens and mosses."

Ursula leaned forward to look. The tip of her walking pole slipped, and she went down to her knees in a slow-motion crash. She looked dazed as Zinnie and Marvin helped her to her feet.

"Are you all right, Mom?" Zinnie asked.

"*Ja. Ja.*" Ursula exhaled and looked around, stress creasing her face. "*Schwammerl?*"

Allie stepped forward and said, "She's asking for mushrooms." Allie gently said, "*Keine Pilze hier.*"

The wind picked up, chilling the air. "We should get Mom home," Zinnie said. She took one of Ursula's poles and tucked Ursula's arm under her own to better stabilize her mother. They slowly walked down the trail to return to the subdivision.

Marvin fell in step with Allie and Laurel. "I didn't quite hear you. What is Ursula wanting?"

"Mushrooms," Allie replied. "Oma Ursula, which means "Grandmother Ursula," is Bavarian. She uses, '*Schwammerl,*' which is a word for mushrooms in the south. In my area we say, '*Die Pilze.*' I told her there were no mushrooms here, which is not true. I saw some little brown ones just a minute ago."

Laurel said, "I'm glad you didn't point them out. Some of the little brown mushrooms around here are psychoactive. We don't want Ursula picking them."

Allie filed the information away as they followed Zinnie and Ursula. "Psychoactive" was a new word for her, and it bore exploring. Another thing to research.

Clouds rolled in, and the early twilight of November was upon them as they reached the subdivision. Ursula stopped every few feet to look around with confusion on her face.

They finally reached Zinnie's driveway where an old silver van sat parked next to Laurel's teal blue Nissan Leaf. The side door to Zinnie's house was propped open with a large duffel bag.

"Looks like Mrs. Pope is here," Zinnie sighed. "Early again."

"You already gave her a key?" Marvin asked.

"The lock on the kitchen door doesn't catch right. One good shove, and it pops open. I'm not keen that she's making herself at home, but I guess I'd better get used to it." She patted her mother's arm and said, "We have a new roommate."

Ursula studied Zinnie with frightened eyes.

"It's all right, Mom. It'll be fine."

A shrill stream of barking came from inside the house, quickly joined by a second yipping voice. A tan Chihuahua-mix and a brown-and-white Jack Russell terrier emerged from the open door, playing tug-of-war with a long pink rag. They came bouncing forward like miniature kangaroos. The Chihuahua hung onto the pink cloth as it galloped. The terrier dropped the tugging game and began an intense barrage of barking.

May Belle Pope came to the door and shouted, "Get back here!" — a direction both dogs ignored.

The dogs raced down the long driveway. Marvin put his arm out, signaling to Allie and Laurel to stop.

As the Chihuahua-mix arrived, growling around its stuffed mouth, it became clear the dog's cloth treasure was torn pink lingerie.

"My bra!" Zinnie cried. Her one bra still retaining some color and support was now a three-foot rag.

Ursula stopped, bringing Zinnie to a standstill too. The small dogs skittered to a halt, then broke into another round of furious barking. Ursula turned to Zinnie and said, "Neoteny!" After that Ursula refused to take another step.

Chapter Nine

Laurel watched helplessly as Zinnie tried a tug on her mother's arm. Ursula descended into a bout of rage and tears. She anchored her feet and shook her head.

Allie screamed "Shut up!" at the barking dogs. They took this as an attack. The two ratty canines circled the group, dashing in with a growl and then barking with an intensity that astonished, even as the tan dog held onto the bra and barked around the mouthful.

Zinnie leapt forward and managed to put a boot on the bra being hoisted as a doggie treasure. The little tan yapper went into overdrive, pulling and growling until the bra ripped, snapping the dog with four inches of elastic.

Zinnie scooped up the bra remains and wadded them into her pocket, a sour fury on her face.

May Belle Pope was no help. Laurel found she agreed with Allie. Zinnie was way out of her league with this woman. May Belle carried a suitcase inside, ignoring the chaos in the driveway. A few minutes later May Belle emerged on the porch, acting as if nothing was amiss until Allie kicked at one of the dogs. May Belle rushed down the steps, managing a rapid hustle, yelling, "Leave them alone!"

Marvin took action. He stepped onto the front lawn, knelt down and made the high-pitched wail of a dying rabbit. The shrill little dogs bounded over and leapt into his arms. He tucked a barking dog under each arm and marched up the driveway, calling to Allie to open the driver's door to May Belle's van. As soon as Allie got the door open, Marvin pitched each dog across to the passenger side seat and closed the door.

The dogs immediately resumed their jackhammer barking, but one could think with the dogs behind window glass.

Laurel sighed with relief, but the ugliness wasn't finished. May Belle shouted, "Don't you manhandle my dogs! You don't touch them! They are service animals!"

Marvin ignored May Belle. He put a hand on Allie's shoulder just as Allie tensed to leap into a physical attack.

"Let's go," he said firmly. He shifted to put his arm around his daughter's shoulders and pulled her along. Laurel watched him speak quietly into Allie's ear as the two walked to the house next door.

Laurel stood frozen, hating her gob-smacked uselessness. She finally rallied to help, stepping close to Ursula who responded with a look of fear. Laurel halted, and said, "Neoteny means the animal has retained juvenile features. The dogs look that way, don't they? Big eyes. Small feet."

The small interchange helped for a moment. Ursula's eyes cleared, and she nodded at Laurel. Then Ursula turned to her daughter and said, "I want to go home."

"We are home," Zinnie said, her face severe with frustration.

"*Nein. Nein.*" Ursula shifted her weight, rocking back and forth. "I want to go home."

May Belle Pope turned her back on the group. She stood next to her van and cooed at her dogs through the glass. The dogs kept barking.

Laurel wished the earth would open up and swallow the mini-van whole. It wasn't a particularly helpful thought. There was nothing in her brain pan that was better. Her mental gears were not engaging, a rarity for her that she struggled to acknowledge.

She watched as Zinnie inhaled and said, "All right, Mom. It is time to go home. I just need to pick up something from this house. It will only take a minute."

Ursula let herself be led up the driveway with Zinnie on one side and Laurel on the other.

"How can I help?" Laurel whispered.

"I'm not sure," Zinnie said, voice shaking. "I'm making this up as I go." She scowled. "One thing I know, those dogs are leaving." Zinnie inhaled and steadied her voice. "Laurel, I may have screwed up. I signed a contract with May Belle, and I didn't read it carefully, and I didn't get a copy."

"Oh, no," Laurel said.

"No kidding. I am only now realizing I don't know my rights or responsibilities here. I only skimmed the document. I don't recall anything about having a pet. I do know we said we'd have a seven-day trial period, but I sure as hell don't want those dogs around for a week."

They stopped at the base of the steps. Zinnie said, "Come on, Mom. Up we go. We're invited to tea."

Laurel finally felt she could help. She put on a bright smile and said, "What a lovely house. I'll bet the inside is charming."

Ursula put her hand on the handrail.

"It *is* charming," Zinnie chirped like a realtor showing a home. "I am excited to show you both. I'm really ready for a cup of tea. A hot drink would be fabulous."

Ursula nodded and put a foot on the first step.

With constant cheerleading, Ursula made it up the stairs and into the house.

Zinnie helped Ursula settle on the sofa before putting on a teakettle. "Do you want a cup of chamomile?" she asked Laurel. "Or a slug of whiskey?"

"I'm fine — I'll go home and research," Laurel said. "I'd be glad to find some background material and landlord guidelines for you. I could call my parents too."

Zinnie's mouth pressed into a firm line. Laurel thought perhaps she had intruded too far with her suggestion. Zinnie finally nodded. It was, Laurel thought, no time for pride.

As Laurel left the house and clattered down the steps, she saw May Belle sitting in her van in the near dark of the late November afternoon, cuddling the dogs.

Soon Laurel was driving home with a flurry of thoughts swirling in her head. May Belle called the unruly little dogs "service animals." What did that mean? Was it a special category that landlords were required to accept?

Her worn rental cabin felt like a paradise after the intensity of Zinnie's driveway. She fixed a cup of tea and called her parents.

Her father answered. "How is the computer repair?"

"It went well. All the files are recovered," Laurel said with a twinge of guilt. "Now my colleague has a situation with legal aspects, and I'm calling for some advice."

"Let me get your mother on board."

Laurel heard him yell, "Sweetheart! Laurel needs a lawyer!"

"Dad!" Laurel complained. "That sounds awful."

"It'll get her to the phone," her father said cheerfully.

Her mother picked up on an extension. "Laurel?"

"Dad overstated, Mom. I'm fine. I've got a colleague with some challenges, and I was hoping I could get some legal insights from you." Laurel described what she had observed, finishing with, "I told Zinnie I'd research landlord responsibilities."

"It's going to boil down to what is in the contract," her mother said. "If it really is a contract. Was it notarized?"

"I don't know. Let me make some notes." Laurel flipped open her laptop and opened a new file. "What do we need to know?"

"What the document says. Are there any penalties described for early termination? Also, how are the parties and terms described, what are the rental and deposit terms, the requirements for notification of changes . . ." Laurel's mother began.

"Hang on. Typing here," Laurel said.

"It might be easier if you searched for a sample contract for Washington State," her father said. "She's going to want to be in compliance with local ordinances."

"Okay. Local ordinances."

"This does sound problematic," her father said. "The landlord is exchanging housing for eldercare. Your friend may have responsibilities to pay into Social Security as an employer."

"Wow. I bet Zinnie hasn't thought of that." Laurel swallowed hard. "This sounds complex."

"She should insist on having a copy of what she signed," her mother added. "Once she has it, scan it and send it to me. I'll take a look."

"Thanks!"

"This could get ugly," her father warned. "In my court, I mostly see slum landlords skating around the law, but every now and then I've seen a crafty tenant make a landlord crazy — which can work when the landlord is naïve. Make sure your friend knows the "Thou shalt not" list."

"The what?"

"There are things a landlord is not permitted to do. In most jurisdictions she can't, for instance, change the locks on the door or create a hostile living environment."

"No strangulating horrible little dogs?"

"Definitely not, on several levels." Her father's laugh came as a low rumble. "And no putting the tenant's belongings on the street. A tenant has a right to privacy, so no pawing through her things. And absolutely no threatening gestures. A landlord can go to jail for years for threats."

"How does a landlord get rid of an awful tenant?"

"It's not easy," her mother said. "These days many landlords ask for big deposits as a way to screen, which doesn't help struggling families. You said there is a seven-day trial period?"

"Yes. That's what Zinnie said."

"Her best approach may be to bear it for a week. Don't give the tenant any ammunition."

"I'll tell her."

"We'll still see you on Wednesday night?"

Laurel heard the tone of worry in the question. She felt a wave of love for her intense and accomplished parents.

"You bet," she said. "I can hardly wait to give you both a hug."

"We know you like to be a rescuer," her father said. "Don't let this woman's life challenges torpedo your own career. These landlord-tenant disputes can be messy."

"Oh, honey," her mother said. "Laurel's too smart to get sucked into her friend's staffing troubles."

"All right, then," her father said. "Just remember to wear gloves. Don't leave fingerprints."

Peltigera
membranacea

Chapter Ten

Zinnie said a silent word of thanks for the family's old DVD player. Ursula's descent into sun-downing dementia eased when she watched a favorite musical. Ursula sang with the show, smiling and tapping her foot during each dance scene. Zinnie sent good karma thoughts out to Neena, their friend and aide who had known familiar music could shift elderly moods from combative to pleasant.

Every tool was welcome. Neena had suggested a pet at one point, saying it could be calming to watch a canary or a parakeet. Zinnie wasn't keen on having a caged bird, nor was she excited about a cat, who would surely come with a litter box. When she had asked, "Is there a Rent-a-pet?" Neena had laughed. They'd settled on musicals and daily walks until Ursula's fever for blue mushrooms made the walks more than Neena could manage.

The musicals worked with the exception of the second half of *The Sound of Music* with its imposing S.S. officers threatening the children at the climax of the story. The storyline evoked horrible memories for Ursula. The one night that Zinnie had worked upstairs well past the happy wedding scene became a night filled with tears and nightmares.

Tonight's *My Fair Lady* was a safe choice.

Zinnie sat in the kitchen and sipped the last of a rum toddy, a vast improvement over her earlier idea of chamomile tea. She slipped off her fleece sweater and pulled the ruined bra out of the pocket. It was beyond repair, the tag faded to an indistinguishable smear. Zinnie tried to remember what brand and what size she wore. This lack of basic information had contributed to her on-line ordering disaster.

She didn't have the data to succeed, and she'd need to find a cloth measuring tape to proceed. Did she have a measuring tape? Where did one get a tailor's tape these days? The craft store she visited had forty-five colors of markers, but no measuring tapes. Zinnie stared at the ruined bra and hated her bra-buying incompetence.

May Belle passed through the kitchen.

Zinnie knew she had to get out of the chair and address May Belle. The dogs were a disaster. This roommate business wasn't going to work out. Zinnie took a last swallow of the rum toddy, preparing for a confrontation.

Out of the corner of her eye, Zinnie saw May Belle carrying a plastic gate of the sort used to keep toddlers off steps. The gate and the woman disappeared up the staircase. A few minutes later, May Belle descended.

Zinnie met her in the hallway and said, "This isn't going to work."

May Belle's eyes grew large and sad. She said, "Please. Let me get my puppies out of the cold, and then we can talk."

Zinnie hesitated. May Belle sounded so sincere. Zinnie had to admit Ursula had been in a very difficult stage in the driveway. Her mother had been tired and rattled from her fall on the trail.

"Please, let's talk," May Belle pleaded. "I'll be right back."

Zinnie lost her momentum as May Belle swept by and made a second trip to her vehicle, returning with the two little dogs in her arms. The dogs were, for the moment, blessedly silent. May Belle took them up the stairs and deposited them behind the toddler gate.

Moments later May Belle came into the kitchen, her buffalo-check jacket radiating cold. The waft of cool air and heavy perfume had Zinnie twinge with guilt. May Belle had been outside a long time, sitting in the van with the two dogs.

May Belle said, "I am so sorry my little dogs were a problem this afternoon." The sullen and defiant woman of the driveway was gone. This May Belle was gentle and apologetic.

Zinnie motioned May Belle to follow her into the kitchen where Zinnie rinsed out her mug at the sink. Setting the cup on the counter, she said, "I know you love your dogs, but this is not going to work. I can't have two barky dogs here."

May Belle inhaled and burst out with a quavering wail. "They're my babies! Ever since my son died, they've been my family."

Zinnie winced, thinking of her own son, Charlie.

"Just let's give this a try for a few days," May Belle begged. "I think JoJo and Toad are extra barky because of the move. I know they'll settle down and be quiet. I promise they will."

"I can't have them destroying my property," Zinnie insisted. She said this through an open mouth, trying not to inhale May Belle's abundant fragrance.

"I know. I am so sorry. JoJo must have smelled something a bit ripe in the laundry basket, and before I knew it, he had that thing in his mouth."

Zinnie was not going to admit the "bit ripe" might have been correct or the "thing" had been one of her two functional bras.

"I can make dinner," May Belle said. "Is there something you had in mind?"

Zinnie stammered. She had not thought about May Belle being present for this evening's meal. So much for the idea of a bowl of cereal and a piece of fruit for her mother and a microwaved pizza for herself.

Sensing uncertainty, May Belle pressed. "I'm a good cook. It's the least I can do."

Zinnie caved. She said, "There're some cod steaks in the freezer. Could you defrost them and put them in to bake? We could have the fish and some brown rice, and there's a bag of salad."

"I'll take care of it," May Belle said. "Why don't you go enjoy the show with your Momma?"

"Actually, I have some work to do," Zinnie said. "Mom should be okay for a little while. If you'll put dinner together, then I'd have some time for my manuscript."

"Of course. Don't worry. Dinner will be ready in about an hour."

* * *

May Belle began the dinner prep with precision. An important aspect of professional gas lighting was to deliver moments of sweetness and caring interspersed with mind-bending cruelties. She was very good at her trade. Tonight, the fish and the brown rice would be seasoned and cooked to perfection. She put water on to boil and started the oven before defrosting the fish.

She needed to prioritize. The smell of urine wafting from the family room told her Ursula had wet herself. The old girl needed adult diapers and perhaps an antibiotic to fend off a urinary tract infection. This was an area where some sweetness and understanding this evening would go far to establish a supposedly good heart.

May Belle slid the fish into the oven and thought through her objectives. Her first priority was access to the home desktop computer, and it was best if she had abundant time with it. Zinnie's desk and main computer were upstairs, behind the toddler gate where the dogs were sleeping. May Belle watched Zinnie disappear into the small bedroom downstairs with a laptop. That worked. The simple installation of the toddler gate had adequately designated the upstairs as May Belle's dog turf. The more Zinnie stayed downstairs, the better.

May Belle rummaged through the pantry and turned up some slivered almonds and the ingredients for a vinaigrette. She added these flourishes to the salad and continued to plan. Once she was at the home computer, she had her routine to follow. It was easiest if the desktop was not password protected, but if it was, her first task would be to look for a password book in the desk drawer or on a nearby bookshelf. She'd also look for paper scraps taped in somewhat hidden spaces. As she searched, she'd keep an eye out for opportunities to act as a system administrator. If all her steps failed, she could always bring in her own laptop and use a Windows Password Key program.

Mac computers could be harder to access, but May Belle was ready to navigate the challenge. It looked like there was an Apple TV unit next to the ancient DVD player in the family room. It would be relatively easy to mess with settings on the screen until the machinery called for the Apple ID to be inserted. There was a very good chance she could ask Zinnie for help and be specifically told the password.

There was other hunting to plan. Zinnie did not look like the sort of woman who had much in the way of jewelry, but it wouldn't hurt to look around for a lock box. Passports were lucrative. So were guns.

May Belle studied the photographs on the refrigerator. Most were of a dark-haired boy through the many phases of childhood. These photos had inspired her to tell Zinnie about a lost son, and, since the tale had garnered sympathy, it should be embroidered and used again.

She would collect details on this dark-haired boy in the photos.

May Belle checked the wall clock. The fish would take another twenty minutes. She stepped out of the kitchen, onto the cold porch and called her sister-in-law. The wind was rising, carrying yellow maple leaves down the street. She turned her back to the driveway to block the breeze. "I'm in," she said.

"Good. Much there?" Sherry's anxious voice came through the phone, augmented by staccato barking.

"I just moved in! Don't worry. I'll know more later tonight. Right now, I've got to be sweetness and light. I'll help get Grandma out of wet pants and then dish up some dinner."

"I'm nervous. I always am." Sherry added, "The wind bothers me. The storm will be here soon. Donnie's out with his buddies again. I wish he'd come home."

"Sherry, he's just bowling. He loves you. I'll bet he's home by nine."

"You're right. I should get some crocheting done. I hope the power doesn't go out."

"Got a flashlight handy?"

"Yeah. Of course."

"You'll be fine."

"I know I shouldn't be complaining. You and Donnie have the hard jobs. Please be careful."

"This place has 'easy' written all over it. If it all goes well, they'll go to bed early, and I'll get started. I'll send you pictures. If the power's still on you can go ahead and start drafting the ebay and Etsy ads."

"I'll be up — but this little spaniel is underfoot. I did get one doll jacket finished, but it was sure hard to do with Biscuit sitting on my feet. She doesn't like the wind either."

May Belle smiled. "Don't forget — Biscuit is worth two grand to us. If Biscuit stays a problem, I think I can get these people to take her until Crybaby comes up with the cash. I'll call as soon as I've got it set up."

"This new house wants a blind, old dog?"

May Belle snorted. "Honey, when I'm done with them, they'll do whatever I say."

"What the eyes see and the ears hear, the mind believes."
Harry Houdini (1874-1926)

Chapter Eleven

Zinnie shifted and punched the pillow. She'd had a restless night in Charlie's narrow twin bed. She should have washed the sheets. The leftover smell of a sweaty young man permeated the bedding. Her sleep was disrupted by the heavy patter of rain, and the cracks of branches breaking as the storm passed. She had one vivid dream sequence featuring small barking dogs — or perhaps it had been a reality—before a wave of quiet finally allowed deep sleep.

The deep sleep didn't last near long enough. By seven, Zinnie was rousing and tossing with discomfort and irritation in the unfamiliar bed. Drowsy but awake, she heard a car start and back down the driveway. When the car headlights danced over the curtains in Charlie's room, a wave of alarm jolted through her frazzled system. The car moving down the driveway was *her* car.

Zinnie threw back the covers and ran to the window, peering out into the still dark November morning, to see her mother competently shifting the Subaru Forester into drive. "No!" she shouted, as her mother drove off into the gloomy morning.

Zinnie shucked her pajama bottoms and yanked on a pair of jeans. She fled to the kitchen, where she stuffed her feet into garden boots before grabbing a fleece jacket. She was aware her pajama top didn't disguise her sixty-year-old breasts sagging halfway to her waist. There was no solution to that now. Her one remaining functional bra was still dripping dry in the bathroom after a late-night rinse.

She threw a look up the staircase. There was no sign of May Belle or the dogs. She did hear prodigious snoring. No help to be had there. Zinnie plunged out the kitchen door and ran through a light rain to Marvin's house. To her surprise, Allie immediately answered her frantic door rapping.

"You're up?" Zinnie blinked.

"Jet lag," Allie answered as Marvin appeared at her shoulder.

Zinnie said, "My mother just took off in my car. She should not be driving. Marvin, can I use your vehicle to go after her?"

For a terrible moment Zinnie thought he might refuse. Instead he said, "You may need some help. Any idea where she went?"

"Yes. My family often goes to a nature trail just north of campus after a fall storm. We go kick through the down leaves and look for lichen fall and new mushroom growth. I'll bet she's going there."

"You'll need an extra driver to bring your car home," Marvin replied. "Why don't you give me a second to get dressed for the weather, and I'll come."

"Me too," Allie said. "I can help look." She picked up her cell phone and began typing. "What is the location?"

"Just north of campus, off Driftwood Lane, toward Snyder Cove." Zinnie inhaled. "Thank you." She checked her watch. "I should bring some dry clothes for my mom."

"All right. We'll be ready in a few minutes."

"You'll want wet weather gear. The woods will be sopping after the storm last night," Zinnie told them.

Zinnie raced home to collect extra clothes, granola bars, a water bottle, her wallet and a daypack. She dashed into the downstairs bathroom to don a still damp bra and a gray British Lichen Society T-shirt before adding a fleece pullover.

Chest heaving, she scribbled a note for May Belle, shoved her feet into hiking boots and ran out the door to climb into the front seat of Marvin's Prius.

"Thank you," she said again as Marvin backed the car down his drive. Allie smiled from the back seat and handed Zinnie a travel mug filled with coffee.

"God bless you!" Zinnie said. "And I really do appreciate you coming out with me."

"No problem."

"It's embarrassing to keep losing my mother."

"Don't go there. Let's talk about something else. How is the roommate this morning?" Marvin asked.

"Sound asleep." Zinnie added, "She was incredibly nice last night."

Zinnie watched as Marvin's eyes flicked to the rearview mirror. He frowned and shook his head. Zinnie turned her head and saw Allie looking thunderous. It didn't matter. Allie's moods would have to wait. Zinnie's thoughts flew back to her mother. What on earth had possessed Ursula to drive? She hadn't been at the wheel of the car in over a year.

Zinnie said, "I think the storm inspired my mother to go out this morning. She enjoys finding lichens on the trail that have been blown down by the wind."

"Could she be hunting a rare species of lichen?" Marvin asked.

"No. With lichens you usually have to do a workup in the lab to know if you've got something new, which is my thing, not my mother's." Zinnie sighed. "God only knows what is going on in her brain."

"Any chance your mother is going to find a blue mushroom today?" Marvin said as he turned the car onto Evergreen Parkway.

Zinnie stared at him a moment before realizing he was trying to distract her agitated mind. What a nice man. She inhaled and went along, despite the nervous sweat prickling down her back.

She struggled to focus and came up with, "Not likely, although it would be fun to come across a blue chanterelle. They are very handsome. It's in a genus called *Polyozellus*." Her lecturer's mind was filling in the needed words even as her fingers tapped nervously on her jeans leg.

"What?" asked Allie.

"*Polyozellus*. The Latin genus name. The blue chanterelle contains a compound called polozellin, which is under research.

It seems to halt the creation of the amyloid precursor proteins that are part of plaque build-up in Alzheimer's disease."

Zinnie made herself take a sip of coffee. An alert brain might be useful, particularly if her mother wasn't at their usual trailhead. Where would she be if she wasn't north of campus? Zinnie's mind raced through a long list of possibilities. It was exhausting to try and think the way her mother might be thinking. There was always a logic of some sort. If Ursula wasn't lichen hunting, where might she be?

"Could Oma Ursula be cured if she ate the blue mushroom?" Allie asked.

"No. It's not straightforward." Zinnie twisted in the car seat to look at Allie. "There are lots of components to dementia. Diet, exercise, education, stress and genetics are all part of the puzzle. It's complicated. There's reasons why no one has found a magic pill."

Noting Allie's distressed face, Zinnie worked to calmly add, "I doubt we'll see a blue chanterelle. They usually grow at higher elevations. We're almost at sea level near campus. The coolest thing we're likely to see is yard-long strands of a lichen called "Methuselah's Beard.""

"Fruticose?" The question came from Marvin as he changed lanes.

"Huh?" Zinnie looked at him. She blinked, realizing that her heart was thudding away in high agitation, despite the effort to be comforting with Allie. She had better calm down, or she'd have a heart attack. Zinnie tried a deep, calming breath. It didn't do much.

"Fruticose lichen?" Marvin repeated, gently. "You mentioned the lichen types. Spray-paint, salad or twiggy ropes." He projected his voice to Allie. "Remember what Zinnie told us yesterday? Cructose lichens look like they've been spray-painted on the rocks or trees. The foliose lichens are bushy and bi-colored, and the long, rope-like lichen are called fruticose, right? I'm associating the 'r' in the word with the rope look."

Zinnie nodded. "Fruticose." She inhaled a second calming breath and focused on lecture as a replacement for her agitation. "Fruticose lichens are the same color all around. Methuselah's Beard looks like long strands of gray twine."

She added, "For decades it was called *Usnea longissima* and then it was renamed as *Dolichousnea longissma* about 2004, but hardly anyone is using the new name. It's the longest lichen in the world. We're lucky. It's very susceptible to air pollution, and it's become an endangered species in much of Europe, but we have it in lots of places in Thurston County."

Zinnie felt her mind seize up and her voice trailed off. Normally she could talk about lichens for hours. Right now, she found her nervous system whizzing with stress hormones. Cortisol. She must be experiencing a cortisol flush. That's why her brain wasn't coming up with more lichen details. Stress triggered cortisol production, and high cortisol levels increased appetite. She would soon be the size of an elephant at this rate. Her mother had no business driving — and what if she had gone somewhere new?

Marvin turned the car onto Driftwood Road. They saw a blue car parked by the side. He said, "Look! There's Laurel!" The young ecologist stood next to her car, ready for the trail in hiking boots, rain pants and a bright purple jacket. Laurel waved as Marvin piloted the Prius closer.

"I sent her a text," Allie said. "We can use more eyes."

"Thanks. And there's my car," Zinnie said. Laurel's blue Nissan was parked behind an old green station wagon, partially pulled into a flattened patch of salal. Ursula's parking had been aggressive.

"We got here fast," Marvin said as he parked behind Laurel's car. "Your mother can't have gone far."

It was a nice thing to say, although Zinnie still felt sweaty and slightly nauseous. She knew this section of woods. The ferns of the underbrush reached nearly waist height, and the trail leading from the cars would split frequently in the yards ahead.

As she climbed out of the car, she spoke to Laurel. "Thanks for coming. Any signs of my mother?"

Laurel shook her head. She said, "The key is in the ignition. And Zinnie?" she said with her forehead creased in concern, "There's a jacket on the seat and boots in the passenger foot well."

"Oh, God." Zinnie turned to Marvin. "Mom normally changes into boots when we arrive. I think she forgot."

"What do you think she has on?" he asked.

"A pair of bunny slippers."

Chapter Twelve

Allie studied Zinnie, waiting for instruction. It didn't seem like Ursula could have gone far, but Zinnie stopped at the forest's edge.

"Let's do a huddle," Zinnie said. "And get our thoughts aligned."

Allie wasn't sure what a huddle was. Her father curled his fingers, signaling she should step in close to Zinnie, who took another deep breath and said, "We have one elderly walker who will not be moving fast, and we have evidence from the presence of my vehicle that we are in the right area. As Marvin pointed out, we are not far behind her."

Zinnie turned to Laurel and said, "I think we should instigate the same protocols we use when a student does not return with a group. We'll split into pairs, explore the most likely trails for no more than fifteen minutes, and then decide if we need to call in Search and Rescue."

To Allie and Marvin, she said, "We never want to turn one lost person into multiple lost people. Please stay together and keep your cell phones on."

"I think it is most likely my mother took the right-hand trail, so Laurel and I will go right, and you two please go left. Please, please don't go more than fifteen minutes out. We'll either find Mom quickly, or we'll need the professionals. We don't want to waste time looking for each other if we get to that point."

Allie was impressed by Zinnie's logic in a time of stress. Allie followed her father down the left-hand trail, waving as Laurel and Zinnie moved down the right branch. Allie looked down at a stretch of unmarked mud and said, "I don't think anyone has come this way."

"I agree, but let's follow Zinnie's instructions. We also don't want to miss any off-trail signs." Marvin said.

"I don't get how Oma's brain is working," Allie said. "Oma Ursula can drive, but she forgets to put on her boots and jacket?"

"Dementia is strange," her father replied. "Sometimes old memories and skills are still there even as a person can forget to do something basic, like remembering how to use a spoon."

They hiked through the wet woods, stepping over fallen branches from the recent storm. They stopped to call and listen before moving on. A light breeze ruffled over the tops of the knee-high salal, adding to the November chill.

They walked until they reached the top of a steep ravine. The path dropped off into darkness with a wet zigzag.

Marvin looked over the edge. "I can't imagine Ursula went down this."

Allie's phone chimed, and she opened a text message. "They found her! They're on their way back to the car."

"Great." Marvin threw an arm around his daughter's shoulder. "Thanks for being here."

Allie slipped an arm around her dad's waist and hugged him in a quick tug and release. "I'm glad to help." To her surprise, she found she meant it.

Marvin started back down the trail. He stopped by a stump speckled with pinky-beige blobs. "Here's one lichen your old man knows. It's the 'Fairy barf' lichen."

"Barf?"

"Vomit," Marvin said. "Barf is another word for vomit."

Allie looked at the dots on the stump. "A very cool name. It fits." She reached down and picked up a short stick covered with wide silver leafing. "This has to be a lichen. Do you know it?"

"No. But we could take it back to Zinnie."

Allie stuck the stick in her jacket pocket.

Marvin said, "Hey, thanks for keeping quiet when Zinnie talked about the new roommate. I know you don't like May Belle."

Allie shook her head. "Dad." It was the first time she had called him this, and they both hesitated. She began again. "I know you don't really know my mother. You don't get it. Zinnie doesn't get it." She fumbled for the words. "Living with my mother is crazy. She always has meanness in her." Allie screwed up her face and concentrated. "There can be some tranquility. For a few days it can be sweet, and you start to hope maybe, just maybe, this time you will live together in happiness, but it will not last. There is always some sort of nastiness that is right there, so it is living . . ." her eyes filled with tears, "it is living near a knife point. It is a roller coaster ride of up and down, but the meanness is always there."

Marvin gave his daughter a second quick hug and said, "Sounds like an abusive relationship."

Allie nodded. "Yes! There doesn't have to be hitting. It is mind games. I think May Belle may be doing this. She looks like she is sweet, but I do not think she is sweet at all. The kindness last night was just to keep herself in Zinnie's house."

"We'll keep checking in on Zinnie. Let's get back, and we'll see what Zinnie needs next."

They moved down the trail at a fast pace. Allie continued talking. "I am lucky. My mother farmed me out all the time. I spent time with normal families. I saw there are people who don't live with scheming in their hearts all day, every day."

"Why do you think your mother is that way?"

"Getting some excitement in manipulating people? Power, maybe? Making things happen like a puppet master can be fun, I think. Her life isn't bad. She has a nice apartment."

Marvin noted it was "she has" and not "we have."

"You know, your English is amazing."

His daughter snorted. "My mother likes to spend August in Italy. Alone. So, every August I went to English immersion camp. Even when I was very small." She viciously kicked a stick off the trail. "I wanted to ride horses, but horse camp is only one week. English is four weeks."

She kicked another stick, revealing an orange blob. "What is this?"

"Ah, another thing I do know. It's a lobster mushroom — which is a mushroom that has been infected by another fungus." Marvin squatted down. "A prize edible." He broke off one edge and turned it over, revealing a mass of small worms wiggling in the gills of the mushroom cap. "Well, sometimes."

"Ugh. I would not eat such a thing!" Allie declared.

"I'm not too keen on worms myself."

* * *

The bunny slippers were a soggy mess, and Ursula angrily swung her walking poles as she shuffled down the wet trail. "It is my business when I go out!" she insisted. "You are not the boss of me!"

Many bitter retorts swirled in Zinnie's brain. She thrust them all down, knowing her mother of today was not her mother of six decades. She chose a reasonable tone and said, "You didn't leave me a note telling me where you were going. The family rule is we always say where we're going hiking and when we plan to return."

Zinnie navigated a muddy stretch of the path back to the cars, trying to stay calm. Laurel had disappeared, offering to run back to the cars for dry socks and Ursula's boots, leaving Zinnie to walk back slowly with her furious mother.

"I couldn't find any paper to leave a note," Ursula complained. She stopped in the middle of the trail and added, "The house is a mess. Boxes going everywhere!"

Zinnie closed her eyes, willing away a flash of rage. The house was in disarray because they needed help for Ursula, which was blisteringly obvious to everyone but her mother — but standing on a muddy path on a cold November morning was perhaps not the time for truth owning. Not that Ursula would give an inch against all the logic in the universe. Zinnie felt her stomach swoop and grumble.

"I'm hungry," Zinnie said. "I haven't had breakfast yet. Have you eaten?"

Ursula looked confused and then said, "I don't know." She stared at Zinnie and added, "My feet are cold."

Zinnie felt her anger drain away. Her mother simply wanted more of the things she had always loved. Walks in the woods. A house that was neat and snug. Music. How horrible to have a brain making these things difficult to access. Zinnie thought of an offering which might turn the morning around. She said, "Laurel will be back soon with your boots. We can get your feet warm. Marvin and Allie have been out in the woods too. I don't think they've had breakfast yet either. What if we get your feet into boots, and I take us all out to the Shipwreck Café for pancakes?"

"*Sehr Gut!*" Ursula smiled and she started down the trail, passing Zinnie. "Finally, you say something smart."

A spasm tightened across Zinnie's chest. She knew this belittling, infuriating woman in her mother's body wasn't the loving woman who raised her. Unfortunately, Ursula's unkind comments held the sting of a disappointed parent. Zinnie made a face at her mother's back and tried to console herself with thoughts of coffee and bacon.

* * *

May Belle re-read the note from Zinnie. The old lady had driven off! Interesting. May Belle checked the kitchen clock. It was hard to know just how long it would take for Zinnie to find her mother.

She called Zinnie's cell phone and learned Ursula had been found and the group was headed to a restaurant for breakfast.

"How nice," May Belle said into the phone. "You have a good time." She tapped off the phone with a smirk.

The breakfast and driving home should take at least an hour. The uninterrupted hour would be enough time to dig into drawers and closets for treasure. She should give Ursula's room a good going over.

It was Sunday and that meant she would have old lady care for a couple of hours later in the day. It'd be best if she could convince Zinnie to leave to do some errands. May Belle's smile broadened. Two opportunities to search on her first day in the home was an outstanding start to the gig.

JoJo, the brown Chihuahua-mix, barked. Toad joined in. May Belle smiled down at her little dogs. "We're going to have a full day today."

The little dogs ran to the family room and jumped up onto the sofa, barking all the way.

Ursula had not taken to her sweet little dogs, a detail to be navigated. May Belle made a point to acquire medications every time she had a client. Her collection of "granny pills" had depth. She liked to start her charges with a combination of an antihistamine and a sleep aid. If the duo of over-the-counter pills wasn't sufficient to induce a compliant zombie state, then she had some prescription goodies to move things along. She had three different benzodiazepines and four antipsychotics. These drugs had counter-indications for the elderly, but who expected grandmothers to live forever?

Ursula would not be a problem.

Chapter Thirteen

Breakfast helped. The comfortable brown vinyl booth seats and worn wooden floors turned the Shipwreck Café into a cozy harbor from the cold of a late November morning. Zinnie watched her mother's color improve as she demolished a plate of pancakes and an order of bacon. There might be a day when Ursula no longer recalled how to use a knife and fork, but that day was not today.

Their cheerful waitress returned frequently to top off coffee cups. Allie and Laurel had a lively debate on the merits of vegetarianism while Marvin cheerfully refused to take sides. It was a happy discussion. The day was definitely improving.

When Marvin left for the men's room, Zinnie leaned over to Laurel and whispered, "I'm at a crisis point. I'm down to one bra, and I need to get some backups, fast. Have you ever successfully ordered bras on-line?"

Laurel nodded. "It works if you know exactly what size, cup, brand and model number to order. I've been successful with replacement shopping when I have those details. It's harder if you don't know what you want. It can take multiple orders and returns."

"Damn." Zinnie leaned back in her chair, scowling. "My one remaining bra is ancient. The tag is completely illegible."

"If the bra is more than a couple years old, the current shape might not resemble the original," Laurel said. "And the manufacturer may have changed the design."

"There's no hope for it. I'll have to go to the mall." Zinnie sighed.

"I can help. I'm well trained as a gopher."

"A gopher?"

"Yep. I 'Go-fer' the next item needed. My mother is a trial attorney. Everything she wears has to be absolutely perfect, including foundations. She's trained me as a shopping assistant.

She stays in the try-on room, and I go fetch according to her instructions. It saves her bags of time. Let me come with you. I'm good at this."

"Oh, I couldn't," Zinnie protested. "You have more important things to do."

"Not really. I'm going to dinner with Bridget and Chloe tonight to talk about the beginning biology class. I've got some ideas there — but I'm around this afternoon if you want to shop."

Zinnie saw Marvin wending his way back to the booth, and she found herself keen to change topics. She shouldn't care if Marvin heard about her needs, but she found she wasn't ready to say "bra" in front of her neighbor. Instead, she pointed to the lichen mass on a stick Allie had laid next to her plate and said, "Nice shield lichen."

"Shield lichen?" Allie frowned.

"I'm not sure why it's called a shield. Maybe because of the silvery color?" Zinnie said. "And see the way the lobes of the lichen hug the bark? This is genus *Parmelia*. They are always a foliose, or leaf-like lichen. Anytime we see a silvery or blue-gray ruffle-edged tree lichen, we think "shield lichen.' I'd say this one is the Hammered Shield lichen, *Parmelia sulcata*. It's common, but also wonderfully handsome."

"Is it edible?" Marvin slid into the booth, looking at the lacy lichen with doubt on his face.

"Most lichens are if you soak out the acids. They don't have a reputation for being delicious. I don't recommend it," Zinnie said. "This species can be used to make a lovely red-brown dye."

"It's cool," Allie said. "I like the silver — and no warts."

Zinnie said, "I'm glad you like it." She added, "We used to think a lichen was just a fungus living with an alga, but recently we've learned the cortex of lichens also contain yeasts. I was telling Neena about this yesterday. The yeast affects the look of the lichen. Changing the yeast changes the color and shape of the whole structure. Who the team members are matters."

"Cool."

"We're also learning that the algae feeding the fungus turns on some special chemical making properties in the fungus. There are biochemical compounds which occur only inside lichens. Some of the chemicals provide protection from UV light, so lichens might be a future source of a natural sunscreen."

Marvin laughed. "I could see a business selling lichen-based sunscreen. Very West Coast."

Zinnie smiled back at him. "Some of the interior lichen compounds also prevent desiccation, so we could be selling face cream as well. Our woods are wonderfully rich and complex. I wish everyone could have a class in lichenology."

"Right." Marvin's eyes twinkled with humor. "I'd love to see you convince a legislative committee of the need for funding."

Zinnie laughed. "Good point. I'll get down from my ivory tower." She leaned forward and swept her eyes around the table, "Marvin, Allie, Laurel — Thank you for helping me today. I would have been stuck without you all."

"Glad to help," Laurel said.

"Yes. Of course," Allie nodded strongly. "No problem."

"We're here if you need us," Marvin said. "Along that line, let's get my number and Allie's into your cell phone. You can call us if Ursula has another adventure."

"I want in," Laurel said, pulling out her own phone. "I'm here for another two days. I might as well be useful."

Zinnie pulled out her phone and opened the contacts page. "Ready."

She smiled as Marvin recited his number. She said, "It's only one digit different than Charlie's. His ends in a two."

Marvin thumbed Zinnie and Charlie's numbers into his phone. "Good. We can all keep in touch."

"You are very strange people," Ursula announced. "You have a shield lichen on the breakfast table."

* * *

May Belle studied the contents of Ursula's jewelry box. The dozen brooches and assorted trinkets looked like costume jewelry with the exception of one small gold locket. May Belle opened the locket and stared, uncaring, at the tiny photos held inside by a delicate perimeter band of gold. One headshot showed a dark-haired man in a mid-century suit. The other side of the locket showed a woman in a funny pillbox hat with a draped veil.

She sensed these were the parents of Zinnie's father. Where was the father was from? Cashmere? Or was it spelled with a K? Kashmir? How typical. Her targets were always people with some sort of known family history. Zinnie's dad had been from some God-forsaken corner of the world and yet had the money for photographs of his parents — and the money for a locket.

She had no family photos. A lump rose in her throat and she swallowed. No time for tears now. She was past tears. It was time to get on with things. May Belle photographed the rhinestone brooches with her cell phone. She'd send the pictures to Sherry. The mushroom pins were cute. They might be worth something.

May Belle sat down on Ursula's bed. May Belle liked to imagine she was Goldilocks, trying out the beds and chairs and treasures of others. She didn't feel like that game today. Ursula's bed linens smelled of bleach.

Bleach was a better smell than urine.

May Belle had to admit bleach was a better smell than most things she had known. Bleach was a better smell than mold. The RV she'd grown up in had always stunk of mold. It was a wonder she and her brother Donnie hadn't died of mold poisoning. Or pneumonia. Winters in the RV had been so cold.

Jojo, her sweet fur baby, leapt onto the bed and settled into her lap. Toad followed. May Belle stroked the dogs and told them, "We're not finding much. We have to keep looking."

She noted the collection of silver frames on the nightstand next to Ursula's bed. In one, a black-haired boy in a high school graduation cap and gown laughed as he faced the camera with one arm draped around a grinning tall man. This must be Zinnie's son and husband — the same kid was in the photos decorating the face of the refrigerator. Damn, he was a handsome kid. The husband was good-looking too. She'd do either one.

The kitchen photos of the kid had inspired her lie. She'd have to remember she'd told Zinnie she had a dead son. She could milk that line for sure.

Behind the boy's graduation picture was another framed photo. This was of Zinnie in a graduation gown with a colorful wide ribbon added to the ensemble. College, May Belle guessed.

College. The gateway to professional jobs where a person could earn a living wage and have a retirement fund. There had never been a hope of college for May Belle. It was unfair. She would have been a good student.

Her threadbare path to a high school diploma coupled with a round face and a big body meant no open doors. She was too soft for the military and too fat for customer service. No one would hire and train her to drive a truck. Donnie got to, but the trucking companies of twenty years ago hadn't welcomed women.

Funny, that left bookkeeping, childcare and eldercare.

People who wouldn't hire her to sell lipstick or blusher trusted her with their most valuable assets and family members. That, May Belle mused, was their mistake.

Being financially and socially vulnerable didn't put a person into a generous or kind frame of mind. She'd grown up angry. Now it was fun to see how vicious she could be and get away with it.

May Belle fingered the picture frame. She hated college graduates. She hated their confidence, their healthy bodies, their quick verbal comebacks, and even their pragmatic but expensive Volvos and Subarus.

Frowning sourly, she picked up the picture. She flipped the frame over and switched open the backing brackets. She lifted the back of the frame and used a red-lacquered nail tip to loosen the photograph. Then she smiled.

May Belle stood up, spilling the dogs to the floor. She carried the silver frame out to the living room where she slid the frame into her large tote bag. Then she went to the kitchen and fed Zinnie's graduation photograph into the garbage disposal.

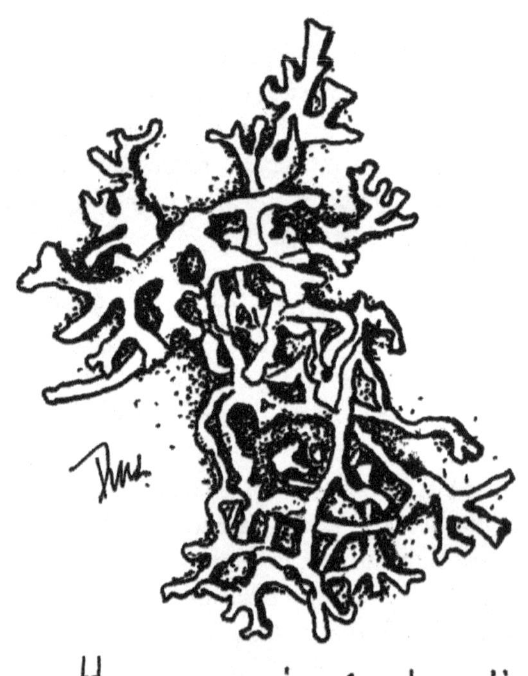

Hypogymnia imshaugii

"The lichen on the rocks is a rude and simple shield
which beginning and imperfect Nature suspended there."
Henry David Thoreau

Chapter Fourteen

"I need a nap," Ursula said when she and Zinnie arrived home. They had greeted May Belle and had been barked at before May Belle called the dogs upstairs.

"Sounds great." Zinnie said as she guided her mother to the bathroom.

If Ursula slept, then she could have an hour or so to work on her proposal, *Connecting Ecological Aspects of Biological Soil Crusts to the Vertical Lichen Communities of Forests of the Pacific Northwest.* As Zinnie followed her mother down the hall, she began crafting the opening section in her mind. She would have to explain that a Biological Soil Crust was a community of lichens, mosses, algae and fungi which existed in many arid regions.

She recalled a birding trip to southeastern Oregon where she and her husband had driven dirt roads at dawn to hear sage grouse strutting and calling with remarkably odd clicks and burps. The biological soil crust communities played an important role in the sagebrush ecosystem by slowing down rain and protecting the soil from wind and water erosion.

The lichens with cyanobacteria also fixed nitrogen into the soil, which was critical for the growth of grasses. Heavy livestock grazing destroyed the biological soil crusts and threatened sage grouse survival.

Ursula disappeared into the bathroom, and Zinnie used the moment to think about the connections she wanted to explore. She knew tree lichens better than the arid land lichens. The desert biologists were ahead in their understanding of the inter-weavings of species in an ecosystem. Dry climate lichens could be both fragile and resilient — susceptible to disruption from livestock grazing while also able to withstand long droughts. The biologists in Australia and the high plains of the U.S. had really looked at biocrust ecosystems.

Comparatively, the forest lichens she so often saw living in communities on branches were functioning as micro-ecosystems that were not completely understood.

She was seeing abundant new research on the communications between trees and fungi. Mature trees shared carbohydrates with younger ones, and the mycelium networks of fungi were capable of sending signals long distances. There was so much more in the woods than lumber and mushrooms growing. Lichens were part of the pageant, especially when cyanobacteria were in the lichen thallus, fixing nitrogen.

"Lichen fall" after a storm was essential in bring nitrogen to the forest floor, just as the arid land lichens were important to building soil in the desert.

The sound of the toilet flushing pulled Zinnie's mind to the present, although when Ursula opened the door and the hall light reflected off the bathroom mirror, Zinnie immediately realized she should be sure to include "albedo" or light reflection measurements in her proposal. The bright whites and grays of arid plants in deserts reflected light and warmed the air near the surface, creating specialized microhabitats.

The forests also had light gray and bright green lichens. Millions of them. Perhaps the albedo score varied. As light gray lichen coverage diminished in areas of air pollution, would the woodland albedo score change? What would be the effect on global climates over time?

Ursula stepped into her bedroom and sat down on the bed. Zinnie followed her and knelt to unlace her mother's boots, her mind staying on the proposal and all the details she would like to know.

The boots took some tugging to come off.

"Do you want your socks off?"

Ursula sat for a moment before nodding. The socks came off. Ursula stood so Zinnie could pull back the covers on the bed. Her mother sat down again and inhaled before swinging her legs up onto the bed.

Zinnie pulled the covers to her mother's chin, thinking how the biological soil crusts kept a huge amount of carbon tucked away, like a body under blankets. As temperatures increased, algae tended to photosynthesize at a higher rate, sequestering more carbon, but this only happened if there was sufficient water for the algae to function. How would lichen communities and forests change as the earth's climate warmed?

Ursula adjusted her pillow and said, "I behaved badly this morning, didn't I?"

"A bit," Zinnie agreed. "I was frightened that I might have lost you."

"No. Not yet." Ursula smiled. "I will live to be older than a map lichen."

Zinnie snorted. Her remarkable mother had just named a lichen known for its thousand-year longevity.

Ursula's eyes were fluttering closed only to pop open when May Belle's dogs began barking again. She focused on Zinnie and said, "While I may live to be old, I may also soon be in jail for murdering small dogs."

"I'll close the door," Zinnie said. As she turned away from the bed, she noticed the bedside stand. There was the picture of Charlie and a water glass. Where was her graduation picture?

Ursula had already turned her face to the wall. Zinnie left the bedroom, frowning.

She walked down the hall to join May Belle, who was fixing a cup of tea in the kitchen. May Belle hummed and swayed with earbud cords dangling down to a pocket on her jacket. Her small dogs were in the front living room where they stood on the back of the sofa at the picture window and barked at a neighbor walking by.

"May Belle," Zinnie said. There was no response. "May Belle!" Zinnie shouted.

May Belle turned, ear buds in, and smiled. "Hi."

"Can we talk?"

"Huh?"

"CAN WE TALK?"

May Belle thumbed off her music and removed the ear buds. "Hi," she said, sweetly.

JoJo and Toad's shrill barks built into a new crescendo.

"My mother is trying to sleep. The dogs need to be quiet."

May Belle sighed. She marched to the living room and yelled, "Shut up!"

The dogs kept barking. May Belle picked up a dog under each arm and brought her darlings into the kitchen. "Everything is so new to them," she said. "Everyone passing by is a stranger."

"I can't have this level of noise. My mother is resting, and I have some writing to do."

"I'll take them upstairs and give them a chew toy," May Belle said. "I know they'll settle down in a day or two." Her voice smoothed to a tone that sounded sincere.

"Thank you." Zinnie hesitated and then asked, "Have you seen a silver-framed photo of me? There's normally one in my mother's room, and it's gone."

"Good Heavens!" May Belle turned the force of her full bosom to confront Zinnie. "Do you think I took it?"

"No. No. I'm just wondering if it was moved."

"Perhaps your former assistant took it? As a memento?"

Zinnie could not imagine Neena doing such a thing. "Maybe it slid behind the nightstand," she said. "I'll check when Mom wakes up."

"I'll be glad to help." May Belle smiled. "Don't forget, I'm glad to watch your mom a few hours today if you need to do some errands."

"I'll think about it. Let me see how my writing goes."

* * *

The writing did not go well. It did not go well at all. Zinnie sat at the student desk in Charlie's bedroom and found she couldn't concentrate. She managed a paragraph on the ability of lichens to take up water. Lichens were wonderful storage units, contracting when dry, and expanding with moisture. They were astonishingly effective in mitigating rain runoff.

Desert soil crust lichens definitely kept soil erosion at bay during heavy rains. In contrast, in the forest many arboreal lichens were on Douglas fir with swooping, downward limbs that shed water through three seasons of significant rainfall. How did the difference in structure affect the function of lichen communities in the forest?

Zinnie groaned. This aspect of project development was the worst. She'd been here before, with the rocket ride of early visions giving way to a tedious slog through an impenetrable mental swamp of muddled thoughts.

She should keep going. She could prune things into shape once she knew the shape she wanted. In general, she wanted to compare and contrast lichens and their functions in the landscape, comparing those from flat, arid lands to the lichens growing on tree trunks in the wet Northwest.

Knowing what to do and doing it were two different things. Right now, the branching paths of her thoughts were leading her into mazes with no outlets.

What were the important aspects of northwest forest communities? Abundant rainfall.

"Okay, rainfall," Zinnie muttered, leaning back in her chair. "Let's start at the beginning — the early days when lichen lives began."

Lichens had a messy family tree. The cyanobacteria *Nostoc* was an ancient thing, forming colonies of long filaments, which could take in nitrogen from the air, and then fix that nitrogen into a solid form, which could be consumed by plants and animals — all absolutely critical for the building of cellular DNA.

With *Nostoc* super-handy nitrogen supply talents, it made sense that various fungi had formed partnerships with it. However, being alluring with special talents also made *Nostoc* the third party in many more developed lichen relationships. Small dots of *Nostoc* showed up in the outer cortex of some lichens which already had a green algae photobiont.

Mobster-tough fungi managed to have two relationships going at the same time. And did *Nostoc* have something going with the newly discovered yeasts in lichens? Another side gig?

If a person understood all the things that could happen to *Nostoc* in the desert and in the woods, then perhaps one could understand better the interlocking relationships making the ecosystems work.

Maybe she should title this paper, "*The many lives of Nostoc: a precursor to the damsels in distress and adaptable ladies so often found in literature and film.*"

This reasonably solid joke whirled away to nothing as she struggled to pin down her concepts in words.

The dogs were quiet, which didn't help. They were twin time bombs. She was on edge, expecting another round of barking to erupt at any moment.

Zinnie gave up. She called Laurel, and said, "I'm thinking of running over to the mall on an emergency bra run. If you're still available, I'd appreciate your help."

"I'll meet you there in fifteen minutes!" Laurel said.

Zinnie stepped out of Charlie's bedroom, looking for May Belle. She wasn't downstairs. "May Belle?" she called up the stairs.

Jojo and Toad raced to the toddler gate at the head of the stairs and began to bark.

"Shut up!" May Belle barked at the dogs and they barked back as she called down, "What?"

Zinnie chose to ignore the belligerent tone. "I'm going to run over to the mall. If my mother wakes up, could you offer her a sandwich?"

"Sure, honey. I'll take care of her."

Zinnie collected her backpack bag from the sideboard and picked up her car keys. "I need to find another place for these," she grumbled as she put on a rain jacket. "Or we'll be out after Mom again."

She left the house thinking about her mother and her neighbors. She should do something nice to thank Marvin and Allie. Cookies perhaps.

As Zinnie backed the Subaru down the driveway, she saw the little dogs resume their spot on the back of the living room sofa. May Belle must have removed the gate on the staircase already.

Zinnie saw the dogs follow the car as it rolled backward down the driveway. The pair began jumping on the sofa back like a pair of pop-up toys. The sound of their barking pierced through the insulating layers of the triple-paned picture window and the rolled-up windows of the Subaru.

Not my worry, Zinnie thought. *If Mom wakes up, May Belle will have to deal.*

Zinnie drove away with her thoughts shifting to bras. She did not see Allie leave Marvin's house and make her way to May Belle's van.

* * *

Allie used the shadows of a row of rhododendrons to hide her reconnaissance. The November sunshine was weak and at a low angle, casting early long shadows. It would be dark by five.

She eased through the bushes and sidled up to May Belle's silver van. The driver's side door was locked. Allie studied the locking button. There might be a YouTube video showing her how to get inside. She dropped to a crouch and peered under the van. Nothing there.

Straightening, her eyes caught a motion through the window in the kitchen door at Zinnie's house. Allie froze. She realized she was seeing the backside of May Belle.

Allie hunched over and scurried around the front of the van to take shelter at the edge of the narrow porch. She stretched to sneak a second quick look. May Belle was still standing with her back to the kitchen door, talking on a cell phone.

Allie slid across the porch like an eel, and laid an ear onto the kitchen door. She could hear May Belle speaking, but the words were unintelligible.

Inside, the little dogs began a barrage of barking. Allie mashed herself against the kitchen door as two boys rode bicycles by the front of the house.

Allie pressed her lips together, thinking furiously. The dogs had a good field of view from their perch on the sofa back at the picture window. As long as she stayed on the side porch, she should be out of sight. She had to be careful. She might be seen if she moved behind the van.

It was time to go home, before her father came looking for her. The thought surprised her. Marvin's beige house with its stacks of books and poor housekeeping was now her home.

It would do, she decided.

Allie lowered her body to the deck and crawled forward to the edge. She slid off the porch and ran across the driveway, headed for home. She'd be back.

Chapter Fifteen

"I'm here all afternoon," May Belle told her brother. "Bring the dog over anytime."

She ended the call and picked up a large tote bag that held the items she'd collected. She had a nice digital camera, an e-reader tablet, and a video projector. She ferried the bag to her van and retrieved another large tote and a worn towel from the back of the van. She'd pack up the two tall amethyst geodes next and it would be best if they were cushioned. She didn't want a geode to crack.

JoJo and Toad barked at a delivery truck lumbering down the street. May Belle returned to the kitchen with the empty tote and scowled.

Ursula stood in the hallway.

May Belle set down the tote bag and spoke to Ursula. "Would you like a sandwich, dearie?"

"Who are you?" Ursula asked, peering at May Belle's face.

"Your new health care aide. Come have a seat."

Ursula let herself be guided to the kitchen table. May Belle studied her. Ursula seemed a bit groggy. Perhaps she could be nudged back to bed. "What you need," May Belle said, "Is a little something to help you sleep."

* * *

Zinnie waved as Laurel entered the main mall entrance. "Thanks for coming," Zinnie said.

"Glad to help!" Laurel said. "I called my mom for specific instructions on how to do this fast and right."

"I'll listen. I need all the help I can get."

"No problem. Mom said we were to go to the nicest department store and find the oldest saleswoman in lingerie. She also said not to be cheap."

"That sounds ominous."

Minutes later they were speaking with a formidable matron with a gentle cloud of dark gray hair and exotic Slavic-edged English. She took in Zinnie's sagging front and said, "After age fifty, structural support is required. Is expensive."

"Fine," Zinnie said. "I've only got an hour, so let's get this done."

The saleswoman led the women to a plush private try-on room and said, "Shirt off. Bra too."

Zinnie stood half-nude as the saleswoman whipped out a measuring tape and repeatedly measured Zinnie's chest under her breasts, saying, "Breathe in, Breath out. Breathe deep. Breath again." She adjusted the tape measure over Zinnie's breasts and ran through the exercise again. Finally, the saleswoman nodded in satisfaction, saying to Laurel, "We go."

Within minutes Zinnie received an education in bra diversity. There were smooth bras, lacy bras, X-backed bras, front-hooking bras, halter bras, plunge bras and sports bras. There were bras with wide straps, narrow straps, double straps and no straps. Some straps were set wide, others close and a few were convertible. There were underwire bras, pushup bras and bandeau bras. Soon the dressing room bench was a jungle of colors and patterns as Laurel delivered bras in pinks, tans, spots, stripes and florals.

As Zinnie worked through the stack of try-ons, Laurel paused and looked at the heap of discarded bras and said, "In evolution, form follows function. There has to be a body and situation that matches with every single one of these." Laurel smiled, inviting the saleswoman into the conversation.

"Yes. Bodies of all types. And many are in-between types." The woman's eyes twinkled. "Transitory forms."

"Are you a biologist?" Laurel gasped, delighted.

"I studied one year in Warsaw. Long ago. I am salesperson now."

Zinnie laughed. "I was just thinking of *ecesis*."

"This word I do not know."

"It's how something becomes successfully established. I'm a lichenologist, and a lichen can attach to a spot and take a decade or more to start growing." She waved her finger in a circle. "I think it'd take me at least a decade to get used to shopping here. This is a difficult habitat for me."

"You come back. Ask for me. I will take care of you," the saleswoman said. As she scooped up a pile of bras for restocking, she said, "Ecesis. My grandson has this. Fifteen-years-old and he is in video games all the time. How can he grow his mind with his face in the screen?"

Zinnie snorted. "He's in a safe place. I would have adored for my son to be home with video games. At fifteen, my son took himself to a church Christmas pageant. He dropped his pants and mooned the congregation in front of a choir of kindergarten angels."

"No!" The saleswoman's hand flew to her chest to touch a small cross dangling on a dainty gold chain.

Laurel rocked with laughter.

"Oh, it's funny now," Zinnie admitted. "The only reason he didn't end up in juvenile detention was because the responding officers were heathens with a sense of humor."

"I am liking this ecesis more," the saleswoman said. "I will be patient with my grandson. Now, I think there is a new bra in the stockroom you should try. I will bring."

"Your Charlie sounds like he has a great sense of humor," Laurel said.

"He does. It took a while for him to understand others often paid a price for his fun," Zinnie said. "I had to change where I went grocery shopping. I couldn't look those angel mothers in the eye. Who knew Episcopalians could hold a grudge?"

Laurel snorted.

Zinnie ditched a plunge bra and picked up an underwire bra with lace trim. She thought of the dust lichen genus, *Lepraria*, which continued to speciate into new types despite having no discernible sexual reproduction. Bra diversification was clearly in response to need, but what were the needs of *Lepraria*? Could reduced gene flow from extreme isolation result in new phenotypes? Isolated cave salamanders evolving to be white and blind were a classic example of parapatric speciation.

Zinnie had salamanders on her mind as she tried on a burgundy bra with a gray lace inset. Who chose these color combinations? What were they thinking? Was there a developmental reason for colors in fashion?

Before she could share these questions with Laurel, the saleswoman returned with another style. When Zinnie tried it on, the saleswoman scowled. "Too big. Smaller cup for you. I will bring."

I can do this, Zinnie thought. *I'm not going to let a cup size adjustment ding my ego.* She watched as a tidal wave of bras went out the door, and a new collection swept in.

"This one," the saleswoman said as she held out a midnight-blue bra.

Laurel read the tag. "No Sag Bra."

"That sounds right," Zinnie said.

Any reserves of modesty Zinnie ever had were gone. She peeled out of a poor-fitting pushup bra and donned the midnight-blue, no-sag bra.

"Good!" The saleswoman beamed a wide smile.

"Marvin would approve," Laurel said.

"Marvin? Thanks, but he's a little young."

"Ah, he's, what, fifty-three?" Laurel countered. "Not exactly robbing the cradle there."

"I'm sixty!"

"Next year you are sixty-one" said the saleswoman firmly. "Buy this bra. You will be ready for sixty-one." She waited a beat and added, "And ready for Mr. Fifty-three also." She smiled and stepped out of the cubicle with an armload of bras to restock.

"How did you know Marvin's age?"

"I looked him up online." Laurel grinned. "Clean driving record." She added, "I tried to find May Belle Pope, and I couldn't."

"You found nothing?"

"Nada. Not Facebook, not Twitter, not even online Yellow Pages. And that's really unusual."

"It's a little scary, actually." Zinnie said as she checked the time. "I should get home."

"Do you want that bra in some other colors?"

"Yes, please."

"I'll go grab some. I think it comes in beige, lime-green and tangerine," Laurel said.

"Tangerine. A color first for me. Although, if I have any future as a neighborhood cougar, I have to be bold."

Laurel burst out laughing. "Checking out Marvin doesn't make you a cougar."

"It makes my brain explode, which may not be entirely a bad thing."

A few minutes and an eye-popping bill later, Zinnie walked out of the mall with Laurel. "I can't thank you enough," Zinnie said. "Your help was terrific."

"That was fun."

"Habitat specificity contributes most to rarity. Because lichenologists practically never overlap with shopping malls, it's no wonder I'm not successful here. You helped bridge me to a microhabitat of expensive bras with shopping support where I could succeed."

Laurel's eyes danced with humor. "I'm not sure I'm going to put it on my resume, but you're welcome."

Zinnie's cell phone pinged. When she saw her home landline number, she quickly swiped at the screen to answer.

"Mom?" she said.

"Zinnie?" Ursula's voice was frail and wavering.

"Are you okay?"

"I don't feel so good."

"Talk to me. What exactly are you feeling?"

"I'm hot. The nurse gave me some pink capsules. Are they my pills? I don't think so. I think you should be here."

"I'm on my way

Cladonia fimbriata

Chapter Sixteen

"I'm going for a walk," Allie called to her father. Marvin didn't look up from the computer. He raised one hand in a wave and grunted. Communication duty fulfilled, Allie stepped out of the house, toilet plunger in hand. Dusk had arrived along with intermittent sprinkles of rain.

She had reviewed half a dozen approaches to entering a locked car, courtesy of YouTube. May Belle's old van didn't have the old-fashioned mushroom-top locking buttons. Lassoing the button with dental floss was not going to work. The van door locks were grooved plastic rectangles, impossible to yank upward with string of any sort.

She didn't have a pry bar or a locksmith's slim-jim, and a quick check of Marvin's closets revealed only plastic coat hangers. According to YouTube, the push and pull of a toilet plunger on the outside of the car door could pop open some locks.

Allie slid through the rhododendron border and bent down as low as she could while working her way to the driver's side door of May Belle's van. To her surprise, the locking button was up. May Belle must have made a trip out to the van recently.

The van door opened with a small creak. Allie set the toilet plunger down on the driveway and climbed into the van, gently shutting the door behind her. It was dark inside the van. She inhaled, coughed and tried breathing through her mouth. The interior stank of dog, perfume and cigarettes.

As her eyes adjusted to the dim light, Allie began to examine the contents of the van from her place in the driver's seat. The box between the front seats held a pile of clutter, including tissues, loose change, and sunglasses in a monogrammed case. Allie leaned over in a long stretch and opened the glove box. The hinged door slid up, and a stack of paper cascaded out.

"Sheisse!" Allie flattened and stretched to collect papers, trying to keep them in order.

A blast of light pierced the night above her as a vehicle pulled up behind the van. Allie froze with a handful of papers halfway returned to the glove box.

There was the slam of a vehicle door and a bellow, "May Belle!"

Allie carefully kept her face looking down at the floor of the van. She knew light could bounce off a pale face, and, no doubt, hers was now as white as it could be. She did tilt her head slightly as a giant shadow passed. Someone was moving by the van.

She heard the kitchen door open and the sound of feet clattering down the porch steps.

"Thanks, Donnie," May Belle said.

"No problem. Sherry is glad to be rid of this one. Too needy."

"Poor thing's blind."

"Life stinks sometimes."

May Belle laughed. "I'm asking two thousand for her. Hopefully by the end of the week."

"Okay. Phone bill is a monster. Sherry's meds need refilling too."

Allie did her best not to breathe. Her heart was pounding. If they came to the van, her best bet would be to run. Could she get a head start from such an awkward position?

A large shadow traveled past the van window. Allie heard a door slam and the lights faded as the vehicle pulled away.

Allie had a brief moment of hope that May Belle would return to the kitchen. The small hope died when she heard May Belle say, "Let's get you out on the lawn so you can go potty."

Damn. It sounded like another dog had arrived. Allie rolled her eyes even as her side hurt from the prolonged stretch across the van seats. She would just have to wait until the dog was done.

* * *

Zinnie sped down the road, slowing only for the speed bump in front of the Chens' house. She was surprised to see a maroon pickup leaving her driveway. She slowed as the vehicle came her way. Its lights were blazing with some aftermarket upgrade that lit the road like a night game at a football stadium. She flicked her own lights to high and back. The truck kept coming with bright lights blazing, ignoring her signal.

She averted her eyes as the truck came closer, saving her pupils from pinpricking completely. As the truck roared past, she swung her eyes up. The driver was big. There was a faded business logo on the truck door. *Good Knight Kennels. Old Olympic Highway.*

Zinnie turned the station wagon into her driveway, parking behind May Belle's van. She had a glimpse of May Belle as the station wagon's headlights swept the front lawn on the turn.

May Belle was out on the lawn with a pale dog on a leash. May Belle's two dogs were inside, standing on the back of the sofa in the living room, barking like banshees as they jumped at the picture window.

The dog on the lawn was a new dog.

Zinnie's mind had been on her mother, but now her focus was on verifying this was yet another dog.

The lamps in the living room cast soft light on the yard. The dog in the yard was a blonde Cocker Spaniel with a sweet face. The dog's head rotated in the direction of the driveway, tail tentatively wagging, casting an odd, moving shadow.

Zinnie emerged from the station wagon, snatching up her leather daypack and her shopping bag. She stalked over to May Belle, bags swinging and said, "And who does this dog belong to?"

"Oh, it's terrible," May Belle said earnestly. "Her owner died, and I'm just keeping her a few days until the family can pick her up. This is Biscuit. She's twelve years old."

"I'm sorry about the tragedy, but this is not a dog kennel. Whoever just dropped her off has to come back and pick her up."

"She's a blind old dog!" May Belle protested.

"Speaking of old, how is my mother?"

"She's asleep!" May Belle managed to look shocked, injured and outraged all at once. "I'm just out here a second for the dog. I've been inside all afternoon!"

Zinnie felt her indignation falter. It was hard to stay with Ursula for hours. She knew that. The little Cocker Spaniel looked up with a hopeful and confused face. "I can't have a house of dogs," Zinnie said, trying to sound firm.

Toad and JoJo bounced on the sofa, yapping. A piercing whistle sounded from deeper inside the house. The dogs stopped their incessant barking and left the picture window.

The kitchen door opened. Ursula walked out into the cold November dusk wearing a pair of purple wool socks and nothing else. She carried a pork chop.

May Belle's two dogs scampered out the door, each leaping for the raw meat. Ursula tossed the pork chop onto the driveway and turned toward the house, her slender naked form surprisingly elegant in the shadows of the evening. Ursula opened the kitchen door and stepped inside. The door slammed shut, and Zinnie heard the door lock click.

JoJo and Toad raced to seize the meat. They enjoyed a brief tug-of-war before the pork chop split. It was demolished in seconds, bone included.

Zinnie knew of one pink pill her mother could not tolerate. It made her so warm that she might shed clothes. "Did you give my mother an antihistamine?" Zinnie all but shouted.

May Belle stammered, and finally said, "Her nose was stuffy!"

"She is agitated and hot with an antihistamine," Zinnie said. "You are to never, ever give her anything!"

"Okay! I'm sorry!" May Belle's apologies were buried under the barrage of barking streaming from JoJo and Toad as they circled the little Cocker Spaniel.

"Now we're locked out," Zinnie said. She knew the door lock would give with a strong shove, but she wanted to make an impression on May Belle. Belatedly, Zinnie remembered May Belle had already discovered the weakness of the locks during her move in. Zinnie's stomach bubbled with acid as she tried to look stern.

May Belle said, "I'll put the dogs in the van, and then we can get the door open." She picked up Biscuit and strode to the van. She pulled open the passenger side door and shrieked when Allie sat up, a fist full of papers in her hand.

"No great discovery was ever made without a bold guess."
Isaac Newton (1642-1726)

Chapter Seventeen

"What are you doing in my van?" May Belle shouted. JoJo and Toad took up a supportive position at May Belle's feet and barked incessantly as Allie sat up, her face clouded with embarrassment.

Zinnie, no stranger to teens doing the inexplicable, said, "Let's calm down and discuss this."

"Calm down? Calm down? This hoodlum is stealing! I should call the police." May Belle quivered with a rage that seemed a bit convenient.

"There's quite a few things to talk about," Zinnie countered. She was relieved to see Marvin's porch light flicker on. His door opened, and she saw his head silhouetted behind the screen door. "Marvin!" she called. "Please come over now."

Her tense tone registered. He came down the steps and across the lawn in a rapid jog, slowing only to ease between the rhododendrons.

"Allie?" Marvin said as he rounded the front of the van. The two small dogs surged forward, yapping at Marvin's ankles.

Zinnie's hopes for de-escalation vanished when May Belle reached into the van and seized Allie's arm. May Belle pulled while Allie held onto the steering wheel to resist. May Belle pulled harder. The little Cocker Spaniel yelped in fright as the leash yanked her into the middle of the conflict.

"Hey!" Marvin rounded the van door. He stepped in, elbowing May Belle in the chest and using his body as a wedge between woman and daughter. "Keep your hands off her!"

Allie surged out of the van with fists wind-milling. Marvin hugged her tight and carried her to the lawn. Allie fell to the ground, taking Marvin with her.

"Stop it!" he yelled as his daughter continued to wiggle and swear.

"I'm calling the police," May Belle said as she loomed over the pair on the grass. The little spaniel quivered at her feet.

"You go right ahead," Zinnie said. "I'll report you medicating my mother without my permission."

Allie stilled on the lawn. "Is Oma okay?"

"I need to find out," Zinnie said. "Right now, she's naked as a jaybird, and she just locked the door."

"Let's go home," Marvin said to Allie, his tone ominous. "Let's get you settled, and then I can help Zinnie with Ursula."

Allie surrendered to being guided by the elbow back across the driveway, although she turned to stick her tongue out at May Belle before passing through the rhododendrons.

JoJo and Toad swirled about May Belle's ankles, barking in a hyper-delirium of excitement. Little Biscuit sat, hunched, silent and shaking.

"The girl is a thief!" May Belle said. "She should be in jail."

"If I don't get in to check on my mother in about three seconds, I'm going to be calling the authorities myself."

"Here." May Belle thrust Biscuit's leash at Zinnie. "Take this thing, and I'll load Toad and JoJo."

Zinnie didn't care for the instruction even as it made sense. Biscuit came along easily, clearly ready to be out of the driveway battleground.

JoJo and Toad did not cooperate. They fixed beady dark eyes on a man fifty yards down the road, walking to the community mailbox. After a moment of frozen study, the dogs were away, barking a challenge as they raced to meet him. May Belle went after her dogs, shouting for their return.

Zinnie started up the stairs to the porch, gently tugging on the leash. Biscuit halted at the first step. Biscuit sniffed the stair riser and raised a woebegone whiskered face in Zinnie's direction.

"You poor thing. You can't see, and I'll bet you can't climb." Zinnie picked up the dog and carried her to the kitchen door.

Opening the door was easy. Zinnie stood sideways to the door and bumped the mid-panel with her hip. The door popped open. Neena was right. The locks were garbage.

She stepped into the kitchen and saw her mother sitting on the couch in the family room, television on. Zinnie closed the door and carried little Biscuit over to her mother.

Ursula looked up, bare-chested and rosy-cheeked. "*Hündchen!*" she cried, reaching for the dog.

"This is Biscuit." Zinnie carefully lowered the dog into Ursula's lap. At least Biscuit covered Ursula's lower nudity. "Can you hold her? I'll get you some clothes."

Ursula crooned at the little dog and gently stroked her head. Biscuit sighed and lay down in Ursula's lap.

It took three trips to Ursula's room to find a clothing combination she agreed to wear. Zinnie used all her coaxing skills to get Ursula to set Biscuit aside long enough to slip on baggy drawstring shorts and a clashing Hawaiian shirt.

The kitchen door opened. May Belle came in, a dog under each arm. She sailed past Zinnie and Ursula without speaking, and ascended the stairs to her lair. A puff of cold autumn air followed her, flavored with May Belle's perfume.

Zinnie saw the kitchen door standing open. Was May Belle passive-aggressive, or was it simply her hands had been full?

Passive-aggressive, Zinnie decided. Very, very passive-aggressive. It behooved her to ignore such behavior, but at what cost to her heating bill? It was all too ridiculous. This roommate wasn't working out.

Zinnie stood up to close the kitchen door. She was ready to take on May Belle. It was important to hold on to this resolve. She should not waver now. Zinnie firmed her lips and strode to the open door.

Reaching the entry, she saw a rectangle of light across the drive as Marvin's front door opened. She stepped onto her porch, closing the door behind her and waited as Marvin pulled on a jacket, crossed his lawn and passed through the rhododendrons. It was now fully dark, and a light rain showered down.

"Zinnie?"

"Yes!"

Marvin came up the steps and opened his arms. She stepped into his embrace, and they hugged fiercely. Zinnie stepped back, shaken by both the actions of the evening and the sudden comfort of his touch.

"Are you okay?" they asked simultaneously.

"I'm surviving," Zinnie said. "I got Mom into a pair of shorts and a shirt, and now she has the new little dog in her lap. They seem to be getting along. May Belle just blew by and went upstairs. How is Allie?"

"Righteous. She is certain your roomie is up to no good. I told her, in no uncertain terms, to stay out of May Belle's vehicle. I do have to say I can see why Allie is concerned. May Belle is not a likeable woman."

"I know. I was an idiot to have someone move in who I didn't check carefully. Laurel did some research on tenants for me — her parents are attorneys. They said I should let the trial week run out. I can't lock May Belle out. I can't do things to make her uncomfortable. I just have to make it to next weekend, and then the agreement is done."

"Wow. It'll be a long week. So, you were out, and May Belle was here with your mother?"

"Right. I made a fast trip to the mall. Oh, my God! I left my bags on the lawn!"

"Let me. I'm already wet." Marvin descended the stairs and darted into the rain. He returned with Zinnie's backpack purse and a sodden shopping bag.

"You're a knight in the shining mist."

"More like a sap in soaked fleece, but thanks all the same."

There was a rasping sound from overhead. An upstairs window was opening. Zinnie and Marvin froze.

May Belle's voice floated out into the night. "Hang on. I'm dying for a cigarette."

"She's smoking!" Zinnie whispered. "I didn't say anything about not smoking."

Marvin put his hand on her arm, signaling for silence.

"Yeah." May Belle's voice came from the window. "The dog's downstairs. You're going out when? All right. I'm gonna call her now. Bye." There was a short silence before May Belle's voice came out, rough and strong. "It's me. I need my money."

A pause and then, "Your baby and your hospital bill are not my problem. Your granny's dog is going blind, and she's been in specialty boarding care for three weeks now. I want two thousand by Friday, or I will have her put down."

Zinnie held her breath as a second pause unfolded. May Belle finished the call by saying "Yeah. I am sorry your grandmother died. But deaths are expensive. Sell some of her stuff, get into her life insurance, or hock something, but pay up."

A moment later the window crashed down.

Zinnie turned to Marvin. "She's extorting money for the little dog? It that what this means?"

Marvin's voice was measured but firm as he said, "This means War."

Chapter Eighteen

Zinnie woke with a start, feeling like a badger had died in her mouth. Rain pinged against the window as she rolled over and looked at the clock. The digital face read 9:16. She sat up, gasping in surprise. How could it be so late? Where was her mother?

She tossed back the coverlet and swung her legs to the floor, still disoriented from sleep and being in Charlie's old bed. She heard voices coming from the kitchen.

Zinnie poked her head out of the bedroom and looked down the hall. Her mother sat at the kitchen table, and a lanky woman in pink-patterned nursing scrubs stood at the sink. This must be the new aide sent by Neena's former agency.

Ursula seemed safe at the moment. Zinnie allowed herself a rushed shower before pulling on a new bra and a mossy green 'I'm lichen hikin' T–shirt. The handsome graphic featured silver foliose lichens on branches surrounding the outline of a backpacker. She squeezed into a pair of jeans and added slippers before joining her mother and the new aide in the kitchen.

"Good morning. I'm Zinnie, and I'm afraid I overslept."

"I'm Darla," said the woman in pink. Her limp blonde hair had four inches of dark roots, and her teeth were long and yellow. She was somewhere between forty and sixty. Life had been hard on Darla.

"I apologize for not being up to welcome you this morning," Zinnie said.

"No problem. May Belle let me in. Your mother is just finishing her breakfast."

"Good morning, Mom!"

Ursula looked up from her cereal, one hand on a spoon, and the other fondling Biscuit's ears as the dog lay curled in her lap. Ursula looked at Zinnie and said, "My daughter has that shirt."

Zinnie nodded slowly. "Yes. I know she does." She found a cereal bowl and sat down next to her mother, who was eating slowly. Biscuit sat up, a look of worry on her small furry face.

"You okay, Biscuit?" Zinnie asked.

Biscuit licked Ursula's spoon hand and lay back down.

"Where's May Belle?" Zinnie had a mission this morning. She and Marvin had agreed she would research the origins of Biscuit. A bright cheerful morning conversation with May Belle was on the agenda.

Darla turned from wiping down the counter. "She's upstairs on her computer, I think. Do you have a routine you want me to follow?"

"I'm not sure what will work best today," Zinnie said. "Mom had some antihistamine last night, and it kept her up until after midnight. We're not on our usual schedule. Normally Mom is up until lunch, has her shower, and then takes a nap."

Ursula's spoon clattered on the table.

"Mom?"

Ursula looked at Zinnie and said, "*Ich muss schlafen.*"

"You want to go to sleep?" Zinnie asked.

"*Ja.*"

Zinnie helped her lower Biscuit to the floor. Darla came to one side and steadied Ursula as she stood. With a helper on each side, Ursula made her way to the bedroom and lay down on the bed.

Ursula looked at her daughter in confusion as Zinnie pulled the coverlet up to her mother's chin. Ursula sank under the duvet, closed her eyelids and turned her face to the wall. Biscuit curled up on the rag rug next to the bed.

"This is new," Zinnie said as she and Darla left the room and pulled the door shut. "Mom hasn't been taking morning naps."

"Sometimes the aging process leaps forward quickly," Darla said. "I can do some quiet dusting in the living room, and I'll check on her in an hour."

"Thank you." Zinnie decided to postpone chatting with May Belle. "I have some writing to do. I'll be in the front bedroom if you need me."

* * *

Darla found dusting rags and furniture polish in the broom closet and went to work in the living room. She had recognized May Belle's type. When you grew up poor, you hustled to keep afloat — and a certain flexibility about "shoulds" and "morals" were a part of survival. May Belle was a survivor.

As a home health care aide, Darla had seen a lot. Every day she got a close-up eyeful of humanity.

She moved around the living room, picking up knick-knacks and photos and dusting underneath before carefully repositioning each piece. May Belle had invited her to be a spiritual sister. Why else had she tucked forty dollars into Darla's front pocket? Forty dollars was enough for her to pay the power bill on time for a change.

It wasn't "Nice to meet you" money. It was "Don't say anything about what you see" money. She wasn't stupid.

May Belle was fast, she'd give her that. When the woman had said, "I'll just add a little brown sugar" as Ursula started her cereal, it took just a heartbeat for something to fall from May Belle's hand with the sugar. Whatever it was, it was fast-acting.

The stuff disappeared down Ursula's throat right away.

Then May Belle brought out the money and tucked it into Darla's pocket.

It happened so fast. Darla hadn't said anything. Her brain didn't think that fast. Not when she suddenly had money in her pocket..

Maybe the powder was "Vitamin K," which Darla had heard of recently. Ketamine. That was its real name. Or, maybe May Belle had ground up a roofie pill. Darla paused, dust cloth in hand. Someone like May Belle economized. The powder might be some homemade GHB, which was called "Easy Lay"

119

for a reason. Ten bucks on the right street corner got you GHB. It wasn't just "Easy Lay," it was also "Easy Find."

Funny how much she knew about pharmaceuticals. Every client she helped had them. So did spouses, grown children and teens. People these days had prescriptions the way her grandpa had a tacklebox — every slot was filled with goodies. It was so easy to add a little something into the mix to keep the old ones compliant. She'd seen it before. Often.

Darla finished the center of the room and moved to the perimeter. Whose side was she on? Did she team up with May Belle and see what she could take out of this house to sell? If the professor was at work and the old woman was stoned, what was possible?

Darla dusted a stack of books on a side table. This house was full of books. She knew about people who had books. Snotty or nice, they tended to make connections.

She needed more info. How good was May Belle? She needed to know if the gig was worth the risk.

It'd take a day or two, but she'd figure it out.

*　*　*

Some fifty miles away on a rocky slope of Mount Rainier, a thousand-year old cructose lichen secreted a depsidone acid. The acid combined with the minerals of the rock face, making the rock more soluble.

As the November rain pelted down, droplets of water ran down a crevice to halt at the lichen foothold. The drops of moisture would overwinter in this spot, first in liquid form, and then would crystalize into ice as the rock face froze.

As the water droplets changed into ice, the bonds between water molecules formed in an open structure some nine percent larger than the liquid form. This significant increase in the size of the water droplets caused the rock to slowly split from the mountain. One day the rock would fall, but not yet. Not yet.

Chapter Nineteen

Zinnie slipped into the bedroom to check on her mother. Ursula's breathing was steady as she slept, curled sideways, mouth open, drool seeping down to make a wet circle on the pillow. Zinnie tried to convince herself the aftereffects of yesterday's antihistamine were in play, but a tickle of unease remained.

She should read some more about the transitions through the stages of dementia. It made sense there should be a combination of slow changes with more sudden deterioration.

Biscuit lay curled up on the rag rug on the floor next to Ursula. She raised her head, and her short tail wagged slowly.

Zinnie gave Biscuit a pat, and the dog put her head down, signaling *Visitor identified and friendly, more napping needed.*

Darla was in the kitchen, having a cup of coffee. "I thought I shouldn't run the vacuum," she said. "Anything else you want me to do?"

"Would you be willing to chop some vegetables for our dinner tonight? I have ingredients for a stew."

"Sure."

There was a tap on the window of the kitchen door. Zinnie saw Allie with Marvin at her shoulder. This was part of Marvin's war plan. Allie was to apologize nicely to May Belle, setting the stage for further reconnaissance. Together they would learn more about Biscuit and May Belle's history. "Better late than never," Marvin had said.

Allie was ready for her mission. She had removed all but two of her piercings, and she wore only a slight arc of eyeliner. The black skinny jeans and the black leather jacket remained. At the moment her natural intensity was buried under a veneer of smiles.

Zinnie opened the door and said, "You have a future as an actress." Allie pursed her lips and produced a more characteristic smirk in response. Zinnie introduced her neighbors to Darla, and then called up the stairs, "May Belle, Allie is here with an apology."

JoJo and Toad raced to the toddler gate at the head of the stairs and barked. May Belle called down, "I'm in the middle of something. It will take me ten minutes to finish."

It was a harsh take-it-or-leave-it tone. Zinnie raised an eyebrow, and Allie shrugged. They would win this skirmish by being sweet.

"Let's have some hot chocolate," Zinnie said. "We can sit in the family room."

Marvin and Allie followed her into the kitchen to help with the cups. "Where's Oma?" Allie asked.

"She's asleep. I'm a bit concerned about her. She started drooping in the middle of breakfast, and said she was sleepy."

"Any chance of a stroke?" Marvin said.

"Her body motions were fine as I helped her into bed. It was more like . . . she was drugged."

Darla stood chopping vegetables at the kitchen counter. She hunched her shoulders and kept her eyes down.

Marvin eyed Darla's stance as he took a cup of cocoa from Zinnie. When they sat down on the sofa in the family room he leaned over and whispered, "Any chance Darla or May Belle gave her something?"

Zinnie clutched her cocoa mug as a wave of rage engulfed her. Who had given what to Ursula? Was May Belle at it again with something stronger than an antihistamine?

Marvin reached a hand out and put pressure on her knee. "We don't know enough," he said quietly. "Let's collect data."

Allie chose to sit cross-legged in the large recliner. She looked at her father and Zinnie, sensing trouble.

Marvin's next words were louder and light in tone. "Allie and I were talking about blue mushrooms last night, and we have some questions for you." He jerked his head toward the kitchen where Darla could be seen, back turned to the family room as she stood at the counter, hands stilled over the chopping board.

"Right," said Zinnie. She struggled to stay calm and conversational. "What would you like to know?"

"Why are they rare?

"A good question. I lecture about this in week two of my summer program. Ready?"

Allie refrained from an eye-roll, which Zinnie took as a sign of interest. She said, "There are three things that contribute to a species rarity; its geographic range, the number of habitats where it can live within that range and, lastly, how dense the population is in a suitable habitat."

She sipped her cocoa before continuing. "For example, humans aren't rare. We live all over the earth, from Siberia to Timbuktu. We have a broad geographic range and within that range we adapt to lots of habitats, like high mountains or tropical islands. And we can live in abundance even in very close quarters wherever we set up."

"Like cockroaches," Allie said.

"Even more so," Zinnie said. "But other species can be instructive. There's a cute mushroom with a white stipe or stem and a red cap covered with white dots."

"Of course," Marvin said. "You see it in picture books all the time —especially in fairy tales."

"It's *Amanita muscaria*," Zinnie said. "It's found in Russia, Europe, and North America, and it has spread to Central America and northern Africa and Australia. It lives in partnership with trees, but it's not very picky about which trees. So, *Amanita muscaria* is not rare. It has a wide geographic range."

In the kitchen, Darla went back to chopping.

"We have geographic range, and then we look at how much of that range is successful habitat for the species. Raccoons and coyotes are generalists. They can live in the woods, or in the suburbs, or in the cities because they can eat birds or berries or tossed-out pizza. In contrast, a panda has to have bamboo. A koala has to have eucalyptus leaves."

"Raccoons are common, pandas are not," Marvin said. "Being a specialist is a harder deal."

"It can be. When there are abundant resources, like lots of bamboo or eucalyptus, it's great to be a specialist. The challenges come when specialized habitat is diminished. There are a number of blue mushroom species, but I suspect most of them have a narrow geographic range and specific habitat requirements."

Zinnie set down her cup, and said, "And the last thing is population density. Wolverines, for instance, are solitary. They don't live in big herds like caribou."

"There's a scary mental picture," Marvin said. "A herd of wolverines."

"What's more frightening to a biologist is an invasive species — when something new and robust is introduced to an ecosystem. The new thing becomes the opposite of 'rare.' It takes over."

"Invasive species," Allie muttered as May Belle came down the stairs.

May Belle wore a deep plum jacket, and long navy and plum earrings dangled from her thick earlobes. She had a navy leather handbag slung over her shoulder as she cradled JoJo and Toad in her arms.

"I have an appointment," she said. She looked at Allie and said, "And I think you're a delinquent who belongs in jail."

Allie began to apologize. She had only spoken a few words when Zinnie's phone chirped. Looking down, Zinnie saw her son's number in the ID line. He rarely called in the middle of the day.

She stood up and stepped into the living room, her arms prickling with unease. "Charlie?"

"Hey Mom. We've got a problem. I went to get a plane ticket, and the credit card number was declined."

"The card was refused?" Zinnie's voice rose as she tried to process what Charlie was saying.

Allie's voice stopped.

Zinnie stepped into the doorway of the family room. Her eyes met May Belle's as she said, "Are you sure you gave the right card number?" She knew the answer. Charlie would have checked and double-checked before calling her. May Belle stared back, twisting her face slightly as if to hear the phone conversation.

"Mom, our card's been compromised," Charlie said. "Maxed out."

Zinnie turned back to the living room. She paced its length, her eyes sweeping left and right. Something wasn't right.

"Let me think," she said. "I'll call the credit union." She looked up at the mantelpiece and said, "The geodes are gone."

"The amethyst geodes?" Charlie said.

"Yes. They are both gone."

She heard the kitchen door shut. Zinnie whirled and said, "I'll call you right back." She sprinted for the kitchen.

It was too late. May Belle started her van, her two little dogs bouncing and barking on the passenger seat. May Belle pulled the van forward, then reversed around Zinnie's Subaru, crashing thorough the rhododendron border as she went.

Allie and Marvin stood in the family room, looking shaken. "She just turned and went for the door, fast," Allie said.

"You said 'the geodes are gone'," Marvin said. "And she booked."

"I think I'd better call the police." Zinnie looked back at the mantelpiece, angry and bereft.

* * *

"Thank you, detective." Zinnie tapped off her cell phone and groaned.

Marvin reached over and patted her knee. "No luck?"

"Not much. The detective said this happens all the time. Not just eldercare help, but also just plain roommates. Credit cards max out, something disappears, and fingers are pointed every which way."

"I could have taken these things." Allie hunched over her drawn up legs, still in the large recliner.

Zinnie snorted. "I rather doubt that."

"How do you know?" Allie said. "I am a teenager. Maybe I took the geodes. Maybe I drugged Oma." Her voice shook. "You don't know me." Tears streamed down Allie's face. "Maybe I am the bad guy."

Zinnie stood up and went to kneel in front of Allie. Zinnie said, "Teens are capable of stealing, and teens are capable of doing injury, but remember — I classify things for a living. I think you are a Drama Queen, not a thief." Zinnie reached out to touch Allie's bare knee which protruded through a rip in her black jeans. "I also think you are rather rotten at sneaking around. You've only been here a day or so, and you've already been busted sneaking into May Belle's van."

Allie hiccupped.

Marvin cleared his throat. "I think I'm supposed to say something, but I don't know what." He coughed and tried again. "Allie, you were with me all morning. How could you have gotten Zinnie's geodes and credit card?"

"In the night, maybe!"

"Nope. You snore."

"I do not!" Allie sat up, tears halting.

"Do too." Marvin smiled at his daughter. "Don't get us sidetracked. Help me help Zinnie. That's why we came over this morning, remember."

Allie wiped her eyes, smearing black eyeliner to her hairline. "I didn't even get to apologize. We have learned nothing about Biscuit!"

"The day's not over yet," Marvin said.

"I think May Belle is the bad guy." Allie said. "I know she is. How do you get her out of your house?"

"Working on it," Zinnie said. "The detective said I should consult an attorney about the document I signed." She returned to the couch and plopped down next to Marvin. "But the first task is to call my credit union and get a new card ordered. Plus figure out what is a legitimate charge on the stolen card. Then the detective suggested I do a home inventory. He said he might be able to stop by this afternoon if his time in court went well, but he didn't make it sound likely."

"We can help," Marvin said.

"Of course," Allie said. She wiped her face with the back of her hand. "Sorry about the Drama Queen part."

"It's my week for them," Zinnie said. "It's going to be my turn to meltdown next."

* * *

Darla stood at the kitchen counter, frozen, knife in hand over a pair of carrots. She needed to think this through.

She had been a home health aide for two decades now, and knew one thing for sure. Drama over belongings was never a short story.

Darla started in on the carrots. She'd check on Ursula soon and ask Zinnie what to do next. If the cops were going to stop by, she wanted to be done for the day.

Thinking about it further, Darla realized she didn't want to answer questions at all. Not today. Not with forty dollars in her pocket.

She looked out the window at the row of flattened rhododendrons. Even if the police didn't come to take a report, her instincts told her to be gone as soon as possible.

She knew eldercare thieves. Denial, gas-lighting, and excuses were part of the package. Convictions were rare. Extended battles were common.

Chapter Twenty

Zinnie spent ninety minutes on the phone with the credit union, coming to the realization that her expensive bra shopping was not expensive when compared to the four laptops recently ordered from her home computer and delivered at express speed to a drop box locker nearby.

She tapped off the phone and flopped down on the family room sofa, furious and exhausted.

Marvin set a plate down on the coffee table. It held a grilled cheese sandwich and a pickle. Zinnie felt tears well up as she acknowledged her hunger for food and kindness.

"I should check on Mom," she said.

"Darla's with her, and I think they are talking about a shower."

"Thank God. She seems okay?"

"I think so. Why don't you tank up on some fuel here, and then see for yourself? You'll be a better judge than me."

"Right." Zinnie bit into the melted cheese and felt her salivary glands rejoice.

"How bad is it?" Marvin asked. "The card charges, not the sandwich."

"The sandwich is divine," Zinnie said around a mouthful of cheese and toast. She swallowed and said, "The thief ordered four laptops. The credit union said they sent an email to ask about the charges because they were outside my usual shopping habits. They also said I responded with an approval from a recognized computer." She swallowed again, this time tamping down a wave of rage.

Allie was sitting, cross-legged, in the big recliner with a sandwich in her hands. She said, "Is there a home computer May Belle could access?"

"Upstairs," Zinnie said. "Are we absolutely certain it was May Belle?"

Allie rolled her eyes.

"I'm serious," Zinnie said. "Whoever was responding to my credit union had to have my password. I haven't told it to anyone. Maybe this is an online hacker."

"Got a password book on a shelf upstairs?" Marvin asked.

Zinnie closed her eyes, feeling stupid. She opened her eyes, exhaled and said, "Yes." She finished the sandwich and said, "I am having a hard time accepting I invited this disaster into my life."

Marvin shook his head. "You are not responsible for May Belle's choices."

"I am responsible for procrastinating on getting help until I had to move fast," Zinnie countered. "I should have done in-person reference checks."

"Which can be hard to set up," Marvin said. "And you can still get misled."

"I think I would have at least learned about the dogs."

"Biscuit's nice," Allie said.

"She is. Speaking of whom, Biscuit may need a trip outside."

"I'll do it." Allie stood up and extended a hand to take Zinnie's plate, earning a smile from her father.

Allie stopped in the doorway, frowning. "Her name is May Belle Pope?"

"Yes," Zinnie said.

"Then why does her eyeglass case have a 'K' on it?"

"You saw a monogram?"

Allie hesitated. "I'm not sure of the word. The initials of her name in stitching. The big middle letter was 'K' and the others were 'M' and 'A'."

"Sounds like a monogram," Zinnie said. "Laurel told me she couldn't find May Belle Pope online. Maybe 'Pope' isn't her real last name."

"After I take Biscuit out, I can text Laurel," Allie said. "Maybe she knows another way to find a person with a name beginning with 'K'."

"Thank you."

"I'll add a suggestion," Marvin said. "See if Laurel can come over. If Ursula is up to it, perhaps she can answer some questions about how she felt this morning, and we can make a research plan. We need to find out about Biscuit, and we need to know what else is missing. The more minds, the better."

"Good idea," Zinnie said. "My brains are swimming in an ocean of lava. Laurel might get me thinking like an analytical academic."

* * *

The painted sign said *Good Knight Kennels* in white script on a green background. May Belle turned off the Old Olympic Highway onto a rutted dirt road, passing a second sign advertising *Puppies for sale.*

Donnie and Sherry had a good site for their kennel. The dirt drive descended gradually into a small valley surrounded by Douglas fir and hemlocks. A large barn with an outside kennel run stood at the edge of the road, providing a wind block to the house and its large graveled parking area. The secondary growth woodlots with large swaths of blackberry tangles on each side of the low ground kept walkers and curious drivers at a distance. Even when the kennel had been full, they'd never had a noise complaint.

They sold two hundred puppies in their best year. The apple-head Chihuahuas sold for $900 apiece. The bulldog pups brought $2000. Sherry left her job at the bank to manage the sales. Her artistic touches in creating certificates and her skill in finding names of long-ago dog show champions meant the pups left the kennel with impressive looking paperwork that suggested fine bloodlines.

May Belle bought the van that year, and Donnie bought his vintage truck. Sherry insisted the three of them take a weeklong cruise in the Caribbean. They had loved it. Clean sheets. Blue ocean. And the food!

They should have replaced the roof on the farmhouse and graded the drive. May Belle gripped the steering wheel firmly as she inched the van over the deep ripples in the road. She knew to hold her mouth closed so a sudden bump didn't clack her teeth together. She'd cracked a molar once and it had been five hundred dollars to fix.

Five years building the business. One really good year. Only one. The following year had been a disaster. Donnie's back and hip went bad. He couldn't sit for long. He lost his trucking job. Then parvovirus swept through the barn, killing entire litters of pups. Donnie cried as he buried the puppies. Sherry cried with him.

May Belle would never forget that spring.

The three of them had fought to keep the puppy mill going, disinfecting the barn and rebreeding the bitches.

In November, an investigative report in a Seattle newspaper soured Craigslist buyers on puppy mills. The idea of puppies-for-Christmas fell out of favor with the educated elite who could afford a thousand-dollar dog. Sales cratered.

Then Sherry had a lump in her breast, and the surgical deductible had been staggering.

Donnie got depressed. Who wouldn't?

He'd had a hip replacement in January of the next year. His hip still hurt. His back hurt too. He was in constant pain. Sherry had it worse, with her fibromyalgia.

And in April that year, May Belle recalled bitterly, just when they were aching with the cold rainy weather, the management changed at her bookkeeping job.

She lost her position. The supervisor who fired her said she should join a gym. She'd feel better, he'd said.

Join a gym. She was getting groceries from the Thurston County Food Bank, for Christ's sake. You don't feed three sick people on a bookkeeping salary. You damn sure don't join a gym.

She knew no one would hire her for customer service. Not with her looks. Not in a slow economy.

She'd kept the three of them afloat by returning to freelance eldercare work. It didn't pay enough, but a little creative shoplifting, and Sherry putting things on eBay got them through the summer.

An offer of live-in eldercare in the autumn of the horrible year changed things. That's when she got good at creating opportunities.

May Belle braked carefully before rolling the van through a particularly deep puddle. She'd raced to the parcel delivery box and rejoiced when she saw all four laptops were in the bin. She didn't want the boxes to slide around now. The laptops had to stay pristine. She also had a chainsaw from Zinnie's garage.

They wouldn't get full retail on the laptops. Not selling them for cash.

She'd talk to Donnie and Sherry about the week ahead. There was more money in the Fazail household. She had some ideas on how to get to it.

She shouldn't have taken the purple geodes. It was a stupid move. Next time she'd play it better. Investments first, credit cards second, trinkets third.

May Belle shook her head and spoke to her little dogs. "I shouldn't lie to myself. I took the rocks because they were pretty. They'll make Sherry smile. She needs some smiles."

JoJo barked, and Toad joined in.

The Cocker Spaniel needed to pay off soon. May Belle firmed her lips as she navigated the van down the last incline to the house. Property taxes on the farm were past due.

They needed big money. They needed breathing room. The big money was in Ursula's savings at a credit union. Thirty-three thousand dollars.

May Belle reached the farmhouse and parked the van in the rutted square of gravel partially shadowed by the barn. A large yellow-green cypress tree drooped just beyond the gravel, a remnant of a long-ago effort to landscape the yard. Sometime in the '70's the farmhouse had been home to hippies up from California. There was a surf scene painted in the bathroom and a mosaic walkway out back that led to what might have been a grow box for marijuana.

The Monterey cypress in the front partially hid a slowly disintegrating gazebo. Both tree and gazebo needed to go, but Donnie didn't have the strength, and there was no money to hire a crew. The cypress sent foot-tripping roots into the gravel. Worse, it dripped a sticky sap during the spring and summer.

She hated the tree.

May Belle put the van into park and sat, thinking. She could take Ursula on a road trip up Hood Canal to a bank in a small town. They could open an account together and transfer the money. Have a nice lunch and be home by dark.

She'd have to think of something to tell Zinnie about why she'd rushed out. Some emergency, said with indignation and misery should explain things away. Politicians did it all the time. Discarding the conscience was such a smart move. It so helped with survival.

JoJo and Toad jumped around the passenger seat and barked.

"It's good to be home," May Belle said. "We'll take a break, but tonight we have to go back."

Chapter Twenty-One

Laurel surveyed the row of battered rhododendrons bordering Zinnie's driveway. The bushes should survive after the splintered branches were trimmed away. Meanwhile, the formerly handsome rhododendrons had the crushed look of a post-wildebeest-migration.

She mourned the bushes as she parked behind Zinnie's station wagon and strode up the driveway. Allie's text indicated there were bigger problems than smashed shrubbery. Laurel jogged up the steps and walked into the kitchen without knocking, feeling instinctively at home. She felt a wave of protectiveness as she saw Zinnie at the kitchen table with Allie and Marvin.

"How bad is it?" Laurel asked, stooping to give Biscuit a pat. The little Cocker Spaniel peered up at her and responded with a happy wiggle.

"My credit card is maxed out. The card's been canceled, and the purchases ruled as fraud," Zinnie said. "The thief bought four upscale laptops and had them delivered to a drop box. I called the police, and they said it wasn't worth their time to surveil the drop box because, almost certainly, the pickup has happened."

"We're having coffee and planning a response." Marvin said. "Want some java?"

"I can get it." Laurel poured a cup and helped herself to milk from the refrigerator, again surprising herself at her comfort in moving about Zinnie's house. How odd that self-service made her feel this way. Laurel tucked the thought away as she sat down at the table, next to Allie.

"There's more," Zinnie wearily rubbed her eyes. "A pair of large amethyst geodes are missing from the mantelpiece."

"That was a stupid move for her," Allie said. "You noticed them missing right away."

"We're not absolutely sure it's May Belle," Zinnie countered. "My door locks don't really lock. Maybe it's a stranger."

"It's May Belle," Allie's eyebrows came together in an angry chevron.

"You've made your point," Marvin set his coffee cup down. "Let's bring Laurel up to date."

"May Belle has an eyeglass case in her van," Allie said. "The monogram is a 'K'."

"You were in her car?" Laurel sat back in the kitchen chair. "Did you look at the registration papers?"

"No. She caught me. There were papers in the . . ." Allie pantomimed opening a drawer."

"The glovebox."

"Yes. There were papers, but I did not get a chance to read them. Can you look up someone with the last name starting with 'K' who drives a silver van?"

Laurel shook her head. "It's not enough to go on."

"We can get back into the car," Allie began.

Her father cut her off. "No way. That's a vehicle prowl, and it's illegal. Let's try to keep ourselves on the right side of the law here." Marvin turned to Zinnie. "You could still replace your door locks. I can help. It may not stop this thief, but it might stop the next one."

"Don't give May Belle a new key!" Allie said.

"Can't do it," Laurel said. "A landlord can't lock a tenant out." She told Allie about her father's advice. "The landlord can't do anything to create a hostile environment."

Zinnie held up a hand. "One thing at a time. Lock replacement is still a good idea. Let me grab a notepad and start making some notes."

"You don't use a laptop?" Allie said.

"Old school here. I think better with a sheet of paper."

"You should check your garage," Marvin said. "See if any tools are missing."

"Right."

A door down the hall opened and Ursula stepped out, guided by Darla. Ursula looked dazed. She was dressed for the day, her hair freshly combed, her gait unsteady. She looked at the group with a face reserved and uncertain. Laurel felt her heart twist as Ursula shuffled forward, looking much frailer than she had just the day before on the woodland trail.

"This way," Darla said. "Let's get you to the sofa."

Zinnie went to her mother. "How are you feeling, Mom?"

Ursula studied Zinnie's face. "*Wer sind Sie?*"

Laurel felt her heart ache with a deeper pinch. She knew a smattering of German — enough to know Ursula was addressing her daughter with the formal 'you' of German, as if they were strangers.

"Let's sit down," Zinnie said.

Biscuit raised her head, squinting in the direction of the family room. She stood and trotted to Ursula's feet, tail wagging enthusiastically.

"*Hündchen!*" Ursula smiled as Zinnie lifted Biscuit up into Ursula's lap. She began stroking Biscuit's long ears and crooning to the old dog.

Darla turned on the television and asked, "How about a garden show?"

Ursula nodded and leaned back into the sofa, hands caressing Biscuit.

Marvin told Laurel about the conversation he and Zinnie had overheard the night before, concluding with, "We haven't figured out her target yet."

Laurel felt her mouth drop open. "May Belle is a *dog-napper?*"

"Boggles the mind," Zinnie agreed. "I keep wanting to disbelieve, but I'm starting to get a clue."

"What's on Biscuit's dog tag?" Marvin asked. "Can some young eyes take a look?"

"Come on, Allie, let's do it." Laurel said. They went into the family room. Allie spoke to Ursula in German, saying they wanted to read the tags on Biscuit. Ursula agreed. Allie rotated the dog's collar, and Laurel knelt to read the tags. She fished her cell phone out of her jeans pocket and took a picture of the tags as well. Biscuit peered up into Allie's face, with cloudy eyes.

"I can help research," Allie said. "I can look up eye problems."

"Go for it." Laurel led the way back to the kitchen table, rapidly tapping on her smart phone. "Biscuit's tag says she belongs to Avery Tallman," she said. "But the voice mail says this number is not in service. I'll look for her on Facebook."

"Not a common name," Marvin said.

"A good thing. I'm seeing six on Facebook," Laurel replied. "There's also an obituary for a woman from Oakville who was 86."

"That could be the grandmother who May Belle mentioned," Zinnie said. "Would her granddaughter have a different last name?"

"Oakville is a small town," Marvin countered. "Let me call the librarian."

A few minutes later they had their answer. Avery Tallman had been a long-time resident of Oakville who owned a blonde Cocker Spaniel. Avery's daughter was Anne Clark who was currently in hospice care. Anne's husband was deceased. Anne's daughter, Jennifer, lived in Montesano, and had a new baby.

"I should make a donation to the library," Zinnie said. "Librarians are amazing."

"Glad you think so," Marvin said, his green eyes lit with humor. "But she didn't know Jennifer's married name."

"It's horrible." Allie looked up from her cell phone. "Cocker Spaniels have all these illnesses — eyes, the knees, the hips, heart, thyroid, cancer. They are high-risk dogs."

"Let's try the local veterinarians," Zinnie said. "If Biscuit is a high-mileage patient, somebody has to have records on her."

"I can look up vet clinics," Laurel spoke while tapping at her cell phone. "But is any veterinarian going to talk to me about a client?"

"We can give out my number and say we've got Biscuit. Most vet offices will pass along the number of a person finding a dog." Zinnie said. "If we do get a call, I can say I'm ready to give Biscuit a good home."

"You're offering to adopt Biscuit?" Marvin asked carefully. "That's a big door to walk through."

Zinnie reached out and patted his hand. "You are a sweet man to worry. I'm trying to find some silver linings here. Mom likes the dog. Neena said a pet can help with dementia, and I'm not a cat or bird person. I'm not a dog person either, but Biscuit I like. If she needs a home, I'm offering."

She smiled and said, "To me, this isn't such a big door. Deciding to let Charlie spend a weekend in jail was a was far more unnerving. Decisions are all relative." Her eyes danced. "And when one of your relatives is Charlie, there are a lot of decisions."

"Why was he in jail?" Laurel set down her phone. She was finding Charlie stories to be an insight to teen years spent very differently than her path of academic pursuits.

Allie looked up from her phone, still and clearly listening.

Zinnie looked at the two young women. "Let's not have any Fear of Missing Out. A dramatic life is interesting, but has costs. Everything Charlie did wasn't for drama. It made sense to him at the time — he's actually quite logical."

She continued. "A man who lives a few blocks from here left a lawn tractor running when he went into his house for his hat. The phone rang, and he took the call. During the five minutes of the phone call, Charlie breezed past a No Trespassing sign, found the running tractor and used two planks from a pile of lumber to make a ramp to the bed of a pickup sitting next to the house. From there he made another ramp to the top of a carport. Then he managed to park the tractor on the guy's roof."

"At that point a board dropped. It cracked the windshield of the truck and bounced onto a gas meter, knocking a regulator off a connecting line. Thank goodness the homeowner knew how to turn off the gas."

"But with Charlie sitting on the tractor on the roof, the fellow knew exactly who was responsible for thousands of dollars of damage and the creation of a potentially deadly situation. It was a colossal mess that began with the question of 'where could a running lawn tractor end up if left unattended?' Charlie still insists it was a valid line of inquiry."

"We were lucky," Zinnie said. "A weekend of teen incarceration can be disastrous, even life-destroying. However, for Charlie, it gave him time to think, which did instill an introduction to visualizing consequences prior to taking action. It was the first time he'd dealt with truly significant consequences."

She shook her head. "I cried all weekend and my husband made sure Charlie knew it. It was beyond ghastly."

Zinnie pointed at Biscuit who was asleep in Ursula's lap. "So, following, gingerly, in Charlie's footsteps, let's work to be logical — only let's be productive instead of destructive. Biscuit's clearly used to being a lap dog, and she's helping Mom be calm. I think keeping Biscuit would not be disastrous. Biscuit could be our blessing from all of this."

"Okay," Marvin said. "If we can get the granddaughter's approval, we keep the dog." Marvin rubbed his eyes. "So, the next step is to make a list of vet clinics and start calling?"

Laurel suppressed a smile. A few moments ago, Zinnie had reached out and patted Marvin's hand and now Marvin was saying, "we." This was exciting and interesting to observe — a lot slower than college hookups, but not completely glacial.

She had to hand it to her colleague. In Zinnie's shoes, she would be a weeping mess over the identity theft, but Zinnie was moving forward, taking in a dog, connecting with Marvin, mentoring Allie.

"I can't believe you're so calm," Laurel said.

"Truthfully, I am so angry, I'm scaring myself." Zinnie looked over to her mother, still sitting on the family room sofa, cuddling with Biscuit. "If anyone hurt my mother, I think I could commit murder. It helps to have you all here because focusing on Biscuit is a healthier alternative."

Darla stepped into the kitchen. "I've finished tidying in the bedroom and the bathroom. Your mom seems happy with the dog and the gardening show. Is there anything else you'd like me to do today?"

"I think we're good," Zinnie rubbed her eyes and exhaled. "Thank you so very much. I'm hoping tomorrow we can get back to Mom's usual routine."

Laurel watched as the aide nodded, collected her coat and said good-bye. Laurel used the pretext of refilling her coffee cup to go to the kitchen window. She watched Darla walk down the driveway and turn right, the direction to the neighborhood bus stop.

"How well do you know Darla?" she asked, returning to the kitchen table.

"She comes from the same eldercare agency our friend Neena came from," Zinnie said. "Why do you ask?

"Just getting a feel for everyone who has access to your house."

"This was her first day. She couldn't have ordered the laptops."

"I know." Laurel sat down with her coffee. "She kept putting her right hand into her pocket. It was odd."

"Like a student who isn't sure yet if she's in trouble," Marvin said.

"Yes," Laurel nodded.

"I slept in," Zinnie admitted. "Darla met May Belle at breakfast before I got up. I don't know what they talked about."

"Is this another one of those lichen things?" Allie complained.

The adults at the table looked at her.

"Two independent life forms working in a partnership," Allie recited. "I think May Belle is evil, but do you really think she's already partners with the new helper?"

Laurel shrugged. "I think we should keep an eye on her." She looked at Zinnie. "Unfortunately, there can be paranoia in situations like this."

"Tell me about it!" Zinnie leaned back in the kitchen chair and brought her hands up to pull on her hair. "I'd be really nuts without you guys."

"I think we need a group name," Allie said.

"Do we have time for that?" Marvin asked. "We have a full list of things to do already. Locks and inventory are on the list. So is calling vet clinics." He lowered his eyebrows and said, "Car prowls are off the list."

Zinnie smiled and said, "Thank you, everyone. I'm grateful for your help." She turned to Allie and said, "I'm okay with a group name. What did you have in mind?"

"I like the lichen I found in the woods," Allie said. "The shield lichen." She looked at her father and said, "I think we should be the Order of the Silver Shield."

"We'll be a shield for Zinnie? That was quick and I like it!" Marvin said.

Laurel thought about it. If having a comic book name helped Allie help Zinnie, Ursula and Biscuit, then she'd be in the Silver whatever. She took a sip of coffee and said, "I'm all for mission clarity. Research, locks, inventory are all good steps, but if we really want to help Zinnie, we need to move to anticipating, so we're not just reacting."

Marvin whistled. "Laurel, your thinking is impressive. You are so right. We're in reaction mode."

"Zinnie got my brain there," Laurel said.

"I did?"

Laurel nodded. "Today you taught me the word 'ecesis' and ecesis worries me more than locks or inventory tasks."

Marvin and Allie waited as Laurel took a second sip of coffee and finished, "Ecesis is the period of time spent waiting before major action begins."

Chapter Twenty-Two

Good Knight Kennels, Old Olympic Highway

Sherry had a hoarding problem. Hoarding came from anxiety. May Belle knew that. Sherry had experienced many heartbreaks and cruelties in her past, and memories of any one of the multitudes could trigger present-day anxieties.

Even understanding the roots of hoarding and loving her sister-in-law, it was hard for May Belle to step into the farmhouse and see, once again, the belongings stacked ceiling high. Boxes, clothes, giant plastic bins, Christmas decorations, a spinning wheel, and a twelve-pack of oversized paper towels were crammed into the front mudroom.

The house stank. The entryway stank of wet boots and mold. The living room stank of poorly maintained carpet, cigarette smoke and dog. The kitchen stank of sour milk and composting onions.

May Belle carried JoJo and Toad in her arms with her big handbag slung over her shoulder. She made her way past a laundry rack and a waist-high pile of ancient magazines to the den at the back of the house. Sherry was asleep in an oversized recliner, cigarette butts overflowing an ashtray on the table to her right. She, as usual, wore a faded floral sundress and a man's navy cardigan. Sherry had a hard time finding clothes that fit. Her once long blonde hair was now mousy-gray and held in place by a black velvet headband. Her dog was asleep on her lap. Sweetie was a dirty mop of a dog, now stone-deaf at age eleven.

"Shh," May Belle told her dogs. She backed out of the den and went upstairs to her bedroom, closing the door with her hip before setting her dogs down on a narrow strip of mauve shag carpeting.

She sat down on the edge of the twin bed. It was a well-worn room. The light was good. She liked the view to the back of the property, where towering Douglas firs mixed with hemlocks. The window glass was dirty.

May Belle sighed and looked around the room. The floral wallpaper she so happily installed years ago now bubbled up in half a dozen places. The whole room needed cleaning. She didn't have the energy.

She stretched out on the bed and stared at a water stain on the ceiling. They really had to fix the roof. Six thousand dollars to take off two layers of roofing and lay down new shingles. More if there was underlayment repair. Judging by the size of the water stain, there would be underlayment repair.

Dogs barked out in the barn. They only had two bitches with puppies left, but Donnie wasn't keeping up with them. The runs Donnie so proudly washed twice a day when they moved in, now got a rinse every week or so. He didn't feel like doing much.

The barking surged. Donnie must be home. She heard Sherry move across the den, her weight making the floorboards creak.

May Belle made herself roll out of bed. She opened her large purse and pulled out a small framed picture. She went downstairs and followed her brother into the kitchen, setting the picture down on the counter.

"Hey there," he said. Donnie stood at the sink, six feet tall and thick through the middle. A large jiggly belly made him "Jelly Donut" to his bowling buddies.

Donnie fished a large tomato out of a sack of groceries. "Making sandwiches," he said. "Tomato and cheese. Want one?"

"Sure." May Belle nodded at Sherry, who was feeding slices of white bread into a toaster.

Sherry smiled and made her usual joke, "Time for Hillbilly High Tea."

They sat in comfortable silence at the kitchen table, eating sandwiches and sipping diet soda. It was nice to see Sherry having a good day. Her doctor had cut her oxycodone, leaving Sherry in misery until Donnie found a dealer — another stream of money out the door. May Belle concentrated on the taste of Kraft singles and tomato. She tried not to think about money.

"Got anything for us?" Donnie said.

"Four laptops, new," May Belle said. "And a chainsaw." She retrieved the picture from the counter and handed it to Sherry. "Baby hummingbirds."

"Oh! How adorable!"

"The grayish-green stuff in the nest is lichen. It's what the professor studies. Lichens. Grows on trees."

"I'll be."

Donnie smiled at his wife. "We could put it here in the kitchen."

"That'd be nice," Sherry said. "They're pretty."

"I also have some big purple rocks," May Belle said. "You'll like them too."

"Any troubles?" Donnie looked at May Belle over his sandwich.

"Some," May Belle admitted. "When I take decorative pieces and do the credit card buying after, it narrows my working time. I got out of there fast today when I heard the professor notice her big rocks were gone. I can get back in again, but maybe not for long."

"Anything else we can sell?"

"There's a Goretex jacket that could get us forty bucks on eBay. I didn't find guns or a gun safe. I'll bet there's passports. Most of what the professor has is books."

"Not much money in books," Sherry said. "Any first editions?

"I looked a bit. There was one book on Egyptian mummies. Lichens again. The mummy makers stuffed bodies with lichens."

"I'll be." Sherry shook her head in amazement.

"Should we just call it good?" Donnie said.

May Belle smiled at her brother. He was always looking after her. "Thanks, but I think I should go back. The grandma has thirty-three thousand in a credit union savings account."

"Damn!" Donnie leaned back in his chair. "That's a pile."

"I was thinking I could take her on a road trip up Hood Canal, and we could stop at a small bank and get things transferred."

"Too risky," Sherry said. "How many customers come into a country bank and transfer that kind of money? You'd be better off in Seattle."

"She's right," Donnie said. "They'll remember you if you go into a small-town bank. There'll be security footage too."

"On-line," Sherry said. "Get into her account with her saved password and transfer the money to one of our accounts. The credit union will send a confirmation email to the home computer. You've got to be there to approve it. You should do it all from the home computer because she's probably got her security questions auto-saved. That's the way to go."

"It might be hard to pull off." May Belle thought for a moment. "The college is on break this week, and the professor will be at the house."

"Anybody else around?" Donnie asked.

"A homecare aide. She's downstairs with Granny the whole time." May Belle frowned and said, "The one who really worries me is the teenager who lives next door. About fifteen. Ugly, skinny, Goth-looking thing. I caught her snooping in my van. She's sharp, and she doesn't back down."

"Kids these days," Donnie said. "No respect."

"She could be a problem."

"When does she go back to school?" Sherry asked.

"She just got here. I don't think she's even enrolled." May Belle's fingers tapped the kitchen table with a staccato frustration. "I've got to do this soon. Tomorrow would be good."

"How about tonight?" Donnie asked.

"Tonight?"

"Yeah. I could drive over to this neighbor kid with some dogs in the back of the truck. The little Lab puppies are cute. When the girl comes over to take a look, I can sack her up and toss her in the back of the truck. Then everybody will be looking for her, and you've got a shot at getting the transfer done."

"Honey, you wouldn't hurt her?" Sherry said.

"Nah. I'd just drive her out of town and dump her. A walk back to town won't hurt her. You just gotta say I was here with you the whole time."

"Okay." Sherry nodded. She looked at her husband. "You're sure the girl will be okay?"

"As long as she behaves, she'll be fine."

Parmelia sulcata

"Oh, what a tangled web we weave when we first practice to deceive."
Walter Scott (1771-1832)

Chapter Twenty-Three

Laurel remembered the key code to the storage area. Of course, she did. She had near total recall of numbers and facts on almost all occasions. Understanding concepts and making connections were also not a problem.

Anxiety was a problem. She pulled the door open and stepped into the storage area, fumbling for the light switch as she eased the door closed.

She did not want to explain her presence to the department head, although Dr. Berbera was Zinnie's friend. Even more so, she did not want to explain herself to Margaux, Dr. Berbera's formidable administrative assistant.

Laurel leaned against the closed door, gathering her thoughts. Anxiety, she knew, originated either in the brain's amygdala or cortex and knowing the place of origin could lead to success in managing the symptoms.

She inhaled and concentrated on reducing her heart rate. If she could intellectualize her feelings, perhaps she could gain control of her current reactions.

Hah. It wasn't a reaction. She was suffering from *over*-reactions. This was silly. She was on staff. She had been given the security code to the storeroom by a colleague. It was a break week with no students on campus, but it was entirely reasonable for her to be here to . . . review the available materials in preparation for her next semester's coursework.

Right.

She was here to help Zinnie.

Zinnie was too trusting. Allie had said so. Laurel agreed. Zinnie was still hoping an on-line hacker had stolen her identity.

Yes, Zinnie's plan was for May Belle to leave — after the seven-day trial period was finished. That wasn't good enough. Some people were just too law-abiding. Laurel managed to find a moment of irony in the thought. No one exemplified Ms. Goody-Two-Shoes better than herself.

She was here to grow beyond her anxieties by helping Zinnie. Take that, inner mess!

Zinnie couldn't do things to harass May Belle, but, as Allie had quietly pointed out, she and Laurel could.

Marvin and Zinnie had inventoried the house and garage while Allie and Laurel sat near Ursula and compiled a list of veterinary clinics. As Ursula stroked Biscuit, Allie had suggested an aggressive Get-Out-the-May Belle campaign.

Allie had some vicious ideas. Laurel nixed them. But when Laurel mentioned bringing out the grotesque Cyclops lamb pickled in formaldehyde, the idea of it as living room décor was approved by both young women.

"It will just be a knick-knack to Zinnie," Allie said. "It sounds totally gross."

And somehow Laurel found herself offering to fetch the specimen *tout de suite.*

Of course, she spoke French. As a product of East Coast private schools, of course she spoke French.

So did Margaux. Flawless, beautiful French.

Laurel swallowed hard. How could she have so many credentials and be such a weenie? She could justify her presence and be an academic who did not need to explain this particular activity.

She knelt by the giant jar that held the contorted lamb. It was so heavy she should be very careful with the lift — one more thing to worry about.

She thought about the paired amygdala, the root of her current anxiety. Each amygdala was an almond-shaped mass located deep inside the mid-brain. People usually had two amygdalae — one located just left of skull center, and one located to the right. The right amygdala was well known for its connections with feelings of sadness or fear. The left amygdala was more versatile, also registering feelings of happiness.

Fear conditioning occurred in the right hemisphere upon the presentation of an unpleasant experience, which could include simply the *fear* of an injury.

In her case, she had said, "I'm *Doctor* Baumgarten," when Margaux had addressed her as "Laurel."

It had been a colossal social *faux pas*. Margaux had silently arched a silver eyebrow, and Laurel had instantly understood; she had assumed a social standing existed in the department that Margaux was choosing not to follow. In truth, Margaux was a senior member of the team who knew the department better. The department had an informal social air, not a lackadaisical assistant, and Laurel misread the situation.

Laurel recalled her cheeks flushing with humiliation as her right amygdala recorded the lesson thoroughly. In fact, she was blushing again just with the memory of that most horrible moment.

Now Margaux terrified her. It was silly to take the back stairs to avoid walking by Margaux's desk, but in the fantastical reaches of the amygdala, Margaux had transformed into a silver dragon, guarding access to Dr. Berbera with a cold laser eye-beam of disdain.

Stimulating the amygdala could hijack the rational brain. The thinking part that had the ability to say, "Oh, that's ridiculous" went on a rapid vacation as the amygdala commandeered attention, sweat glands and the heart.

Laurel exhaled. Mental ruminations tended to heighten anxiety.

It was time to get on with things.

She needed to get the Cyclops lamb jar out of the storage room, across the lab and then down to the car.

Laurel lifted the heavy jar with cupped hands under the flat bottom. Her arm muscles sent out instant protests as she rose to stand. She duck-waddled across the storage room and managed to pull open the door with a stretched pinkie that also complained.

She crossed the computer lab with a mini-marathon of muscular effort. She reached the entrance to the lab and set the jar down, upper body aching. It was silly to carry such a heavy item in her arms, but she didn't want to bother with fetching the cart from the downstairs botany lab. She'd have to take more time to fetch and return the cart. Besides, the cart rattled like an empty train car.

'Stealth and silence," she murmured. Although the students had the week off, it was completely possible to run into someone completing a project or hiding from a family gathering. For many academics the Biology Department was a twenty-four-hour refuge from the stresses of 'real' life.

Laurel pulled the door open and glanced down the hallway. No one there. No one on the staircase to the left either. She pushed the lamb jar through the doorway, pulled the door shut and squatted to repeat her grip and lift of the heavy jar.

The door to the woman's restroom opened and an elegant voice said, "Why, Dr. Baumgarten. Whatever are you doing?"

* * *

Intellectually Laurel knew she was too young to have a heart attack — and yet her sympathetic nervous system was not functioning according to reason. Her galloping heart sent blood pounding through her system and her armpits squirted sweat as she gasped for air.

She sat down heavily, knees askew, and put a hand over her heart.

"Breathe deeply," Margaux said.

It wasn't a kind tone of voice. It was the voice of the playground monitor who was about to march a child to the principal's office just as soon as the pain of a fistfight ebbed a bit.

Laurel closed her eyes and tried to inhale. *Distract*, she thought. *Think of something else.* She tried to think of a beach in Hawaii. Her brain took a leap to a running lawn tractor on top of a garage. This was followed by the thought of a teen boy mooning a Christmas concert. Thinking of Zinnie's Charlie helped her focus. Charlie had survived some craziness. Maybe she could too.

She opened her eyes and looked up at Margaux. Speaking from the floor was definitely not a physical power position. Laurel rolled to her knees and stood up, leaning against the door of the lab for support. "I know this doesn't look good."

Margaux arched an imperial eyebrow as she crossed her arms, still looking down her nose at Laurel. "Our specimens are not for entertainment."

"It's for Zinnie."

"For Dr. Fazail?" The question dripped doubt.

"It is! Zinnie's mother has not been well."

Margaux looked down at the jar of deformed lamb and slowly raised her eyes to Laurel's face.

Laurel plowed on, determined to do her best. "Zinnie has a new roommate who is a disaster – someone she found online to be live-in help for Ursula. This woman is truly horrible. She may be responsible for credit card theft and some of Zinnie's things are missing." Laurel pointed at the jar. "By law Zinnie cannot do things to make a tenant uncomfortable — but I was thinking I could pop in with something ugly and hang out."

"I see."

"Sounds stupid, but we're worried about Zinnie," Laurel said.

Margaux's clear blue eyes looked thoughtful. "Who is this roommate?"

"May Belle Pope. Supposedly experienced in eldercare. Only I can't find her online at all. She has an eyeglass case with a monogrammed 'K', so there's a chance she's using a pseudonym."

Margaux uncrossed her arms and leaned in. "Does she have any pets?"

"Yes! She has two little dogs. They bark constantly."

"Mabel Knight," Margaux said grimly. "A woman by that name stole from a couple I know — friends from my bridge club. The woman had two little dogs and an excuse for everything."

"She was a live-in helper?"

"On a week's trial. My friends' elderly mother died at the end of the week. My friends said the presence of the dogs made a bad situation worse. They realized jewelry was missing a week after the funeral. By then Mabel Knight was long gone."

"She may be the same one then."

"Has Zinnie reported the thefts to the police?" Margaux asked.

"I know she reported the things bought on her credit card," Laurel said. "She was working through an inventory of the house and garage when I left."

"And how is Ursula?"

"Unusually sleepy this morning."

Margaux looked down at the heavy specimen jar and said, "I suggest we use the new cart from the custodian's closet and take the freight elevator at the back of the building."

"I don't think my badge gets me into those spaces," Laurel said.

"Oh, but mine does."

Chapter Twenty-Four

Donnie entered the looming barn and shuffled to a dark corner. He picked up a portable wire kennel pen. It was one of a dozen puppy pens he had purchased with hope. Now the pen was like his life, a distorted sad mess. He bent the wires into place and took the pen outside. He set the wire cage in the back of his truck.

The truck was too distinctive. He knew that. It was a maroon classic with the kennel name stenciled on the door. He'd added the after-market high-beam headlights for a bad-boy vibe.

He had to use the truck. May Belle was using her van, and Sherry's Toyota needed a new engine. They should have replaced the timing belt when the mechanic said, but the repair was nine hundred dollars they didn't have. After the timing belt broke, they realized nine hundred was a bargain. A new engine would be nearly three grand, and the car's blue book value wasn't much more.

If he had to use the truck, then he'd better be efficient.

The daylight was rapidly fading. He went back into the kennel barn and ignored the waves of barking from a trio of Jack Russell terriers. The mother and her two offspring kept up the barking, while a deeper bark from a Labrador bitch occasionally boomed along. The terriers were now almost a year old. They had lost their puppy appeal, and they were unsocialized, savage little beasts. He'd be lucky if they ever sold a single one.

It was the Labrador puppies he wanted tonight. Stella, their Lab bitch, had produced four black puppies now past the big potato stage where they rolled around at her feet. At eight-weeks old, the pups were adorable.

Donnie picked up two of the puppies and cradled them in his arms. "We're going for a little field trip," he said. "You be cute, and we'll get this job done. If May Belle can pick up thirty-three thousand for us, our lives will be a hell of a lot better."

The pups squirmed, and one clawed his way up to lick Donnie's face.

"Come on, sweethearts," he said. He carried the pups to the truck and put them in the pen in the truck bed.

"Sack. I need a sack." Donnie returned to the barn and rummaged through a corner littered with leftovers from seventy years of farming. Although the farm had never hosted a potato crop, one previous owner had returned from a farm auction with a stack of long burlap bags meant to hold a hundredweight of potatoes.

May Belle had said her troublemaker was a skinny teenager. A bag over her head and a fast wrapping of rope ought to be enough to keep her contained.

Donnie found the stack of bags and pulled off the top one. It nearly disintegrated into dust. He threw it down in disgust. "Mold's been at these."

He moved through the pile rapidly and came up with one bag with some fiber integrity. It stank. He didn't care.

The sack and a length of rope went in the truck. He'd take the girl out to Capital Forest. It was quiet out there. Quiet enough.

* * *

Allie read a dozen recipes for brownies online before choosing a simple one. She checked Marvin's pantry and found he had cocoa, sugar and flour. There was baking soda and vanilla, but no nuts. That was fine. Nuts weren't necessary.

Her father came in. "Baking?"

"*Ja.* I thought I'd make brownies for next door." The closer she kept to the truth, the more likely she would succeed. Laurel was too timid. It was time to address the May Belle problem directly.

"I'm going to the hardware store," Marvin said. "I think we should replace Zinnie's locks tonight."

"Great." The tone was deliberately bored. She wanted him gone.

Marvin looked at her, eyebrows lifting.

Allie cleared her throat. Bored was not the right tone. She went with, "It's a good idea. She'll feel more secure. Makes total sense."

Her father looked at her with the full strength of his green eyes. It was unnerving. It was as if her own eyes were studying her for flaws. "*Mist!*" she thought. She had to remember he worked with students every day. His bullshit meter was fully functional.

"What's happening besides brownies?"

"I'm waiting for Laurel." There. Partial confession.

"And?"

"We're going to talk when she gets here." This was true, although Allie didn't let her mind wander to the concept of lying by omission. It was better to focus on truths that were paternally palatable. She worked to look irritable and a bit defiant, which was a combination her father expected.

Marvin studied her for another moment. "I won't be gone long."

"Okay." Allie picked up a pan and said, "I'll bake brownies while you are gone."

"I look forward to having a taste. I'll be back in an hour."

Finally, her father left, pulling a rain jacket over his cardigan. Moments later the car reversed out of the driveway, and Allie was alone.

"*Mist!*" This time it was out loud. "*Verdammt!*" She'd have to make two pans of brownies now. One for May Belle and one to share with her father.

She found a second pan in the pantry and moved quickly to her father's tablet. She watched a short You-tube video on greasing a pan. Allie found a stick of butter in the refrigerator. She peeled the paper off one end of the bar and rapidly mashed the butter around the bottom of each pan. She tossed the rest of the butter stick into the trash. Wasteful, but she had no time for niceties now.

Allie checked the recipe. It called for half a cup of melted butter. Damn. She looked in the trash for the butter stick she'd just thrown in. It had landed on coffee grounds in the bin.

She rinsed the stick of butter. Most of the coffee bits rinsed off. She set the warped bar into a cup and set it in the microwave. She studied the choices listed on the keypad and decided five minutes on high ought to melt a stick of butter.

She mixed the sugar and cocoa. The butter in the microwave sizzled and popped like popcorn.

Allie looked through the door of the microwave just as a blob of butter exploded onto the window of the door. "Oh, *Nein!*" She rammed her fingers against the control pad of the microwave. The door sprang open, revealing an interior spotted with butter blasts.

The sizzling butter went into the mix along with four eggs, producing an omelet smell as the raw eggs hit the hot butter.

Allie continued, adding vanilla, baking soda, flour and salt.

It was time to divide the batter into two. She poured off half the batter into one pan and set down the bowl. She checked the kitchen clock. Ten minutes had passed! Cooking was a total time suck.

She ran up the stairs to her bedroom and reached under the bed for the shoebox from Charlie's closet. Tucking the box under her arm, she leapt down the stairs, three at a time.

Back in the kitchen, she took another look at the clock and then at the recipe.

"*Sheisse!*" She had forgotten to turn the oven on. The brownies took twenty-five minutes in a preheated oven. She was running out of time.

Allie turned the oven dial as far as it would go. That should preheat the oven faster.

She set the shoebox down on the counter and pulled off the top, revealing two bags of marijuana. How much should she use?

"It's old. Might as well use it all." Allie poured in the contents of the first bag and reached for the second baggie. Under the second bag was a third bag, filled with dried mushrooms.

"Huh." Allie studied the mushrooms. She didn't know what they were, but from the stories she'd heard about Charlie, these were almost certainly something recreational.

There wasn't time to look up information on recreational mushrooms. How much was a dose?

Allie sniffed the dried mushrooms. They smelled slightly earthy.

Shrugging, she crumbled the mushrooms into the brownie batter. After a few swipes of a spoon, Allie had the marijuana and mushrooms poorly incorporated into the batter.

Allie filled the second pan with augmented brownie mix. She carried the two batter-filled pans across the kitchen. She opened the oven door and slid both pans into the rising heat of an oven set to 500 degrees.

Chapter Twenty-Five

Zinnie looked at the faded square on the wall in the upstairs bathroom. Her breath came in short, jagged inhalations. The hummingbird picture was gone. She placed a hand on the tiled wall of the master bath to steady herself through a piercing pain of loss.

Her husband had found a tiny, lichen-covered nest in one of the backyard rhododendrons. He and Charlie had spent hours cautiously building a blind, and they had perfected a stealthy slink-and-crawl into the blind where they colluded to obtain the perfect photo. Dinnertime conversations revolved around "depth of field" and "focal points." It had been a joyous reprieve from a winter of juvenile delinquencies.

That summer Charlie had surprised her with the best of presents. Not only did he remember her birthday, he also gave her a beautifully framed print of their best photo. It showed the tiny female hummingbird snuggled in the nest with her babies' adorable faces popping up from under her — every feather and every lichen in crisp focus. Charlie had proudly instructed her to turn the picture over. On the back of the frame he'd written the scientific names of the lichens the mother bird had used to build her nest. Charlie had also inked in his names for the babies, "Buzz and Bloom."

Now tears streamed down Zinnie's face as she lamented the loss of her picture.

Her cell phone chimed. Zinnie took a moment to blow her nose before answering the call from Marvin.

"Hey," he said, "I'm standing here looking at a colossal row of door lock choices."

"Are you suffering from analysis paralysis?" Zinnie asked.

"Definitely. I know your fixtures aren't chrome or oiled bronze, but what the hell are they?"

Zinnie felt a smile tug at her lips. Marvin sounded irked and overwhelmed by shopping. Having recently purchased bras, she could relate. She said, "The door knobs are brass."

"Bright brass or semi-bright brass? Antique brass or polished brass? Tarnished or satin-tarnished? Weathered or lacquered?" He chuckled and said, "Don't answer. It's impossible. We should take off a lock and bring it in for a match."

Zinnie felt a watery smile rise as she noted Marvin's "we." She said "That sounds smart."

"How's the inventory going?"

"Not well. I think I'm missing a chainsaw, but I honestly can't remember the last time we used it or the last time I saw it." She sniffed, unable to hold back her tears. "And she took my hummingbird picture." Zinnie plucked a tissue from the box on the bathroom counter. "It was a gift to me from my son."

"Oh, man. I'm so sorry."

Zinnie mopped her face. "Me too." She took in another ragged breath and said, "But it's the kick in the pants I needed. Now I'm ready to stop kidding myself. I'm being ripped off. My mother is being drugged. I need to quit pussyfooting around and get serious."

"Good. I'm headed home. Why don't we order a pizza and carb out?" Marvin added, "Allie's baking some brownies."

"Yum! I need to lose some weight, but right now pizza and brownies sounds great."

"I don't know why you'd want to lose weight. You're perfect."

"You may need to visit your optometrist, but thank you."

"My vision is fine. See you soon."

Zinnie tapped off the phone only to have it chime again almost instantly with an unidentified number. She tapped the phone to answer.

"Hi. This is Jennifer Boyer. I was given this number by a vet clinic. I'm trying to reach Dr. Zinnie Fazail about a Cocker Spaniel."

"Speaking! Are you Biscuit's owner?"

"Biscuit was my grandmother's dog. Do you have her?"

"Yes, I do. She's downstairs watching television with my mother who is in her eighties. They seem to get along very well together."

"I see. And, um, are you wanting to *keep* Biscuit?" Jennifer's voice rippled with tension.

"I am interested," Zinnie found herself dropping into the brisk, professorial mode where she could be frank with a frightened and failing student. She might as well name the challenges and see if a path forward appeared. She said, "I am in the middle of being ripped off by a horrible woman named May Belle Pope — who may have another last name — and I am working to stop her. However, she brought Biscuit into our lives, and I would like to provide a home for Biscuit." She paused. "I would take care of Biscuit's medical expenses."

Jennifer burst into sobs. "Thank you," she hiccupped. "Excuse me. I have to find a tissue."

"Join the club," Zinnie said. "I wish I could pass you my box over the phone. I've just learned a favorite picture is missing."

"I don't want to hate anyone," Jennifer said between hiccups. She sniffed, long and wet. "But I hate Mabel Knight. I really do."

"Mabel Knight. That fits. We know she has an eyeglass case with a monogramed 'K.' Tell me about Biscuit and Mabel, please."

"My grandmother passed away at the end of September. Mabel Knight was her live-in caregiver who took so many things." Jennifer sobbed. "She took jewelry. Momentoes. Even my grandmother's cookie jar."

"She took a *cookie jar?*"

"It was a collectible — in pristine condition." Jennifer sniffed. "A school bus jar." After a hard swallow, Jennifer said, "And she took Biscuit. Grandmother died, and my mother is in hospice, and I was about to have a baby, and that horrible woman took Biscuit."

Zinnie held the phone to her ear, mesmerized by the grief in Jennifer's voice.

Jennifer blew her nose again and said, "She said she was going to have Biscuit's cataracts dealt with, but our vet says he never did the surgery. When I started going through my grandmother's bank records, I saw there was a monthly pet insurance payment. I called the company and they said the policy was changed from Biscuit to a dog named JoJo. Mabel has a dog named JoJo."

Zinnie closed the lid on the toilet and sat down in disbelief. "She stole your grandmother's cookie jar and stole Biscuit's pet insurance?"

"It's crazy, but that's what happened." Jennifer's voice shook as she added, "The cataract surgery is expensive. I looked it up before I called you. It's like two grand an eye. Sometimes more."

"Ye Gods."

"And it should be done soon." The wail of a newborn came through the phone.

Sitting on the toilet and staring at the faded square where her beloved hummingbird picture used to reside, Zinnie came to a decision. She stood up and said, "It sounds like you're needed, and I should go check on my mother. If you'll call the vet and get the surgery scheduled, I'll pay for it. Then we'll make a plan for Biscuit. Maybe you want shared custody?"

Jennifer laughed as the wailing baby sounds increased. "Not on your life. If you'll take care of Biscuit, I'll come visit."

"Deal." Zinnie said goodbye and stepped into the master bedroom, wondering what other surprises were in store. *Passports*, she thought. *I should see if they're in the file drawer.*

Checking on her mother came first. Zinnie left the bathroom with a strong stride and lowered brows. She crossed the bedroom and was almost to the door when a bright light bounced through the wide upstairs window. Intrigued, Zinnie turned back and watched as a vehicle with blazing headlights turned into Marvin's driveway.

"Life is bristling with thorns . . ."
Voltaire (1694-1778)

Chapter Twenty-Six

Allie rinsed the mixing bowl as she thought about the dried mushrooms in the brownies. She should research mushrooms. She didn't want to kill May Belle. Not really. She wanted to defang her, with some humiliation added. May Belle drooling in the corner, stoned. Out of the way.

The doorbell buzzed, startling her into almost dropping the bowl. Her eyes flew to Charlie's shoebox. She set the mixing bowl down with a thump and grabbed the shoebox off the kitchen counter. She dumped the box into the recycling bin as she yelled "Coming!" She charged down the hallway to the front door. She'd keep whoever it was at the front door just in case the visitor smelled more than chocolate and vanilla.

She opened the front door and said "Hello" through the screen. A large man stood on the stoop, holding a black puppy.

"Hey. I'm Donnie Knight of Good Knight Kennels. I'm . . . a friend . . . of May Belle's. She told me that you might like to have one of my puppies."

Allie processed the name "Knight" immediately. This was May Belle's family, either a husband or a brother or a cousin. Something was up. The puppy was seriously adorable.

"Wow," she said, cautiously. Allie inhaled and added, "How kind of her." She assessed the man in the fading light of the day. He was big in the sloppy American way of ponderous belly bulging under his T-shirt and jacket like a broad mushroom cap emerging from the forest floor. She wouldn't want to be pinned down by him. She could easily outrun him. He didn't seem dangerous. She could look at the puppies and gather some intelligence. This was Order of the Silver Shield work. She could do this.

The streetlights came on, illuminating the road. A vintage maroon pickup sparkled in the driveway.

"Cool truck. Yours?" Allie asked.

"Yeah. There's another puppy in the back. You want to see him?"

"Sure." Allie lifted her black leather biker's jacket from the coatrack by the front door. She shrugged into the coat and spoke through the screen. "My Dad will be home any minute." There. The guy was warned not to mess with her.

He gave her space. He turned and went down the steps, as if trusting she would follow. Allie thought briefly about grabbing her phone. It was in the charger in the kitchen. It was so far drained she probably couldn't get a photo of the puppies. She should leave the front door ajar so she could hear the oven timer. She pushed open the screen door and followed the man to the truck.

* * *

It took just moments for Zinnie to descend the staircase of her home, intent on checking out the vehicle with the bright headlights in Marvin's driveway. Ursula called out from the family room, "I need to go to the bathroom."

Zinnie raced to the kitchen door and noted another vehicle was coming down the road. It might be Marvin, returning from the hardware store. Zinnie backtracked to the family room to lift Biscuit off Ursula's lap and to help her mother down the hall.

Ursula, of course, took her time. Zinnie's cell phone chimed. She was surprised to see the caller was May Belle. "Hello," Zinnie answered with as much frost as she could manage.

"Hi. It's May Belle. I just wanted to apologize for any trouble my dogs have caused."

Zinnie heard barking in stereo. There was yipping traveling through the cell phone speaker and barking from the direction

164

of her driveway. JoJo and Toad were excited, even by their normally barky standards.

"Where are you?" Zinnie asked.

"I'm outside your house in the driveway. I thought I should apologize before I came in."

"Don't come in. The jig is up. I know what you've taken, and you are not welcome here another minute."

"We have a contract! I have seven days!"

"Consider the contract null and void. I'll see you in court if you like. I'll bring my attorney and my credit card statement and my list of missing items."

"What's happened?" May Belle's voice came across with a sweetness that repulsed. "Has someone been telling you lies about me?"

"More like truths. You really should not steal a grandmother's cookie jar!"

"What? You've been talking to Jennifer. She's a habitual liar! She teaches a Zumba class, and she likes to fat-shame big gals like me."

The sound of the toilet flushing drew Zinnie out of the exchange. The bathroom door opened, and Ursula looked at Zinnie with some confusion. "Who are you? Why are you in my house?"

"I'm the pest exterminator," Zinnie said. "Your dog is waiting for you."

"*Hündchen!*" Ursula smiled and agreed to be led back to the family room.

"Hello?" May Belle's voice came through the phone speaker in a tinny whine.

"Just a minute." Zinnie set the cell phone down, helped her mother descend safely onto the sofa and restored Biscuit to her mother's lap.

"I'm thirsty," Ursula said.

Swallowing a scream of frustration, Zinnie raced to the kitchen where she filled a glass with water and ran back to the family room.

"It's warm," Ursula complained.

"I'll get some ice in just a minute," Zinnie promised. She picked up the cell phone and said, "May Belle, you are not welcome in this house."

"I can't believe you are doing this to me. Where am I supposed to sleep tonight?"

JoJo and Toad continued to bark in high hysteria.

Zinnie moved to look out the kitchen door window. May Belle's van sat behind Zinnie's station wagon. The bright lights truck was in Marvin's driveway, visible through the flattened row of rhododendrons.

It was hard to see with the kitchen light on. Zinnie reached out to turn off the kitchen light as May Belle continued to complain.

"I have to come in and get my things," May Belle said.

"I'll pack them for you. Give me half an hour." Zinnie's eyes were adjusting to the dim light of the driveways. She could see Allie's slim silhouette standing next to a large man and the old truck. They were focused on something in the back of the truck. Where was Marvin?

"You stay out of my things!" May Belle shouted.

"I'll just touch them long enough to fill your bags," Zinnie said. "Then I'll set them on the porch."

"I need to pick up the Cocker Spaniel."

"Biscuit does not belong to you. She now belongs to me."

"You're stealing a dog? I'll call the police!"

"Go right ahead. In fact, I think that's a great idea. I want my hummingbird picture back!"

Zinnie could see JoJo and Toad bouncing like tennis balls as they barked at Allie and the man in Marvin's driveway. Whatever was in the truck interested the little dogs.

The next moment took Zinnie's breath away. Allie leaned forward to pick up something from the truck bed. The large man reached through the open window of the truck, seized a long sack and threw the sack over Allie's head and torso. She tried to twist away as the man grabbed her into a hug, wrapping Allie and the sack with a rope. He then picked up a kicking, hooded Allie and threw her into the bed of the truck. He turned and yanked open the door of the truck and heaved himself onto the high bench seat.

"Hey!" Zinnie yelled. She jerked open the kitchen door and ran down the steps as the man started the truck. She yelled again as she ran across the driveway, threading between the back of the station wagon and the front of May Belle's van as the man shoved the truck into reverse and roared the truck backwards down Marvin's driveway.

Zinnie tripped halfway through the rhododendrons. She fell out the other side of the bushes, dropping her cell phone. The truck driver shifted into drive as Zinnie scrambled up from the ground.

The truck picked up speed. Zinnie sprinted after it, her tight jeans binding as she ran. She knew her one chance of catching the truck would be in front of the Chens' house when the driver should slow for the speed bump. Would the driver brake? It was possible to take the bump at a high speed if the driver didn't mind risking damage to the undercarriage.

This driver apparently valued his truck. He braked in front of the speed bump, and Zinnie managed to grab the top of the tailgate. As the driver eased the truck over the obstacle, Zinnie got a foot on the bumper and hoisted herself up. The rear wheels of the truck rolled up and over the asphalt hump, sending Zinnie flying into the bed of the truck where she landed heavily, next to a wire dog pen and on top of Allie.

Allie thrashed and rolled as Zinnie scrambled to her knees. The flash of a headlamp suggested Mr. Chen was coming down his driveway for the mail. Zinnie frantically waved her arms as the truck picked up speed and left the subdivision.

* * *

"I'm terribly sorry, officer," Marvin said. "I didn't realize it's a school zone after dark."

"It's a school zone any time students are present."

"Yes sir." Marvin gripped the steering wheel of the Prius and tried not to look or sound impatient. Being pulled over was his fault. He knew there was a speed trap next to the soccer field of Capital High. The remains of a C team practice squad were out on the field completing a touch-and-go exercise in the fading light. It was highly unlikely any of the lanky fourteen-year-olds would vault the six-foot chain link fence and wander into traffic. Marvin refrained from pointing this out to the officer.

"I need your license and registration, please."

"Of course. The registration is in the glove box, but I would like to get home soon. My teenage daughter is there alone."

"Well, I'll write the ticket fast as I can, but you need to drive home within the speed limits."

Chapter Twenty-Seven

Laurel turned into Zinnie's subdivision with the Cyclops lamb in its heavy formalin-filled jar belted into the front passenger seat. She squinted as a vehicle came her way with blazing high beams.

"For Pete's sake," she swore. "If you're going to upgrade to Xenon bulbs, at least take the time to adjust the shields properly." She lectured to the lamb beside her, "There's supposed to be a shield on the bottom of the light. That's because the human eye reverses things."

She looked to the right until the vehicle roared past. Laurel slowed down for the speed bump and turned into Zinnie's driveway. She parked to the left of May Belle's van. Now that the rhododendrons were shattered halflings, there was room for her small Nissan.

There was a whiff of baking chocolate in the air as Laurel climbed out of her car. Two little dogs barked at her from inside the silver van. May Belle came out of the house, carrying two duffel bags.

"Is Zinnie home?" Laurel called.

"She's gone. I'm gone in a minute."

"You're moving out?"

"You don't have to sound so happy about it." May Belle opened the sliding door on the van and shouted at her dogs. "Get back!"

JoJo and Toad ignored her. They leapt out of the vehicle and ran up the porch stairs and into the house, barking.

"Shit!" May Belle threw her bags into the van and slammed the slider door shut.

Laurel walked around the back of the van, straining to get a look inside the back.

"What the hell do you want?" May Belle snarled.

"Just making sure none of Zinnie's things are in your van by accident."

"Accident, my foot. You think I'm stealing."

Laurel's stomach lurched. She was an academic. She didn't do brawls. In fact, she wanted to burst into tears and call her mother. She was no match for May Belle, and May Belle knew it.

Laurel inhaled and said, "Let me just get out of your way then."

"Damn straight." May Belle turned and stomped up the stairs to the house.

Laurel trailed behind. She might not be able to take on May Belle in a physical confrontation, but she could at least hang about like wallpaper. Her presence might keep some bad behaviors in check.

Ursula! Where was Ursula? Was she with Zinnie? Laurel's heart rate quickened.

Laurel jogged up the steps and nearly crashed into May Belle who was exiting with a dog under each arm.

Thank goodness. May Belle must be ready to leave.

May Belle opened the passenger side front door of the van and pitched in her two dogs with a fierce instruction, "You behave."

The dogs leapt to the driver's seat and began barking as May Belle shut the door.

Laurel closed the kitchen door behind May Belle and locked it. Zinnie wouldn't mind if she waited inside. If May Belle wanted back in, she could come when Zinnie was home.

The kitchen doorknob rattled.

"Open this! You let me in!" May Belle's face loomed at the window in the door.

"Just go!" Laurel shouted.

May Belle charged the door, her eyebrows lowered in rage. Her shoulder hit with a thud, and the door flew open. May Belle staggered through, wind-milling her arms. She regained control and advanced.

Laurel stepped back and collided with the kitchen table. Gasping, she pushed away from the table and saw Ursula asleep on the family room sofa with Biscuit in her lap. The old woman awoke with a startled jerk and looked about in confusion.

May Belle stomped past Laurel and said, "That's my dog."

Ursula's frail arms encircled Biscuit. *"Das Hündchen gehört mir."*

Laurel stepped into the family room. "Leave her alone!" She was too late. May Belle had yanked Biscuit out of Ursula's arms and now marched for the exit.

Laurel was no match for a woman twice her size. May Belle shouldered past her, sending Laurel crashing into the coffee table with a bounce that took her to the floor. The impact took her breath away.

"Hündchen!" Ursula struggled to stand.

Laurel put her hands on the coffee table and took a shuddering breath. Her side ached as she moved to her hands and knees. With one hand on the coffee table, she pushed upright, finding herself face-to-face with Ursula. The old woman shook as tears streamed down her face.

"I'll get Biscuit back," Laurel said. "Wait here."

Laurel hobbled to the kitchen door, each step bringing a jolt of pain from her right side. It felt like she had a broken rib.

The pain ebbed as she stepped through the doorway and saw May Belle reversing her van down the driveway, Biscuit in her lap.

"That's not safe!" Laurel cried as she crab-walked down the steps. "She should be in a dog crate!" She tried to run to her car. She shuffled and hopped, then yanked open the door to the vehicle and flung herself in, causing the jar of Cyclops lamb to rock in the passenger seat.

Laurel's hands shook as she started her car. She bit down on her tongue and focused on fastening her seatbelt. She'd overtake and block May Belle's van. It should only take a minute. Then she'd call the police.

She slammed the Nissan Leaf into reverse as Ursula stepped out onto the porch. A smoke alarm in Marvin's house set off an ear-piercing wail.

* * *

May Belle rolled the van over the speed bump and accelerated. JoJo and Toad barked liked small hellhounds while Biscuit leaned into her chest. The van careened into the middle of the street, and May Belle overcorrected, almost clipping a dark-haired man standing at the community mailbox. She swerved left and then right, taking the exit from the subdivision like a rocket and leaving the dark-haired man scowling in her wake.

Henry Chen shook his head. It was his wife's bridge club night and that was misery enough. He'd spent the afternoon setting up tables and chairs and prepping crudités platters. His excursion to the mailbox was his one escape from his wife's eagle-eyed supervision.

He adored his wife. He didn't adore the chaos arriving in his life with her monthly bridge club hosting. His trip to the mailbox was meant to be the evening's nourishing moment of solitude.

The subdivision had been quiet for years. But tonight, they were back to the days of Wild Charlie and his friends. First a truck had gone roaring by, headlights blinding the world, with some crazy woman in the back. Now he was nearly sideswiped by a woman in a minivan full of dogs.

Wasn't there a law against driving with animals in your lap? Distracted driving. It was definitely distracted driving.

His line of thought erased with a mental "Holy Shit!" as he leapt back from a blue Nissan Leaf careening down the road. He was wearing a headlamp, for Christ's sake.

The young woman at the wheel didn't even wave an apology as she sped out of the subdivision.

He should call the police. This crazy driving had to stop.

Hands trembling, he pulled his cell phone out of his jacket pocket. He paused, hearing the scream of a smoke alarm.

Henry dialed 9-1-1 as he registered the scent of something burning.

"What's your emergency?" a flat voice asked.

Henry Chen took a deep breath, surprised to find his throat constricting. He said, "I think we have a house on fire."

Rusavskia elegans

Chapter Twenty-Eight

The vintage truck had vintage springs. Zinnie bounced as she waved her arms. She slid sideways as the truck made a hard-left turn. She crashed into the end of the dog pen. Inside, a young black Labrador barked and climbed the wire walls in excitement.

The pup's littermate barked from inside the cab. Zinnie could see the back of the driver's head and shoulders. He was huge.

Allie was kicking, squirming and coughing beside the crate.

"Hold still!" Zinnie crawled over to Allie and tugged on the knot holding the potato sack closed.

Allie coughed harder.

"The hell with this." Zinnie grabbed the fabric near Allie's head and dug her fingers into the burlap, creating a hole. She jammed in more fingers and ripped the sack apart, revealing Allie's face, shining like a pale moon in the shadows of the truck bed.

"I can't breathe," Allie croaked.

Zinnie ripped the bag further. She pulled the opening over Allie's shoulders. She helped Allie sit up against the cab. They bounced to the left and right as the truck sped down the road. Zinnie kept low. She didn't want the driver to know he'd picked up an extra passenger.

The whipping cold air worked to revive Allie. She sneezed, then said, "Thanks."

"Who is this guy?" Zinnie asked.

"He came to the door with a puppy. His name is Knight. I think he's related to May Belle. He said she wanted me to have a puppy. I am such an idiot. I thought I could look at the puppies and be okay."

"Do you have your phone?"

"No."

"Me either." Zinnie looked down at Allie. Underneath the potato sack wrap, Allie was in her usual all-black. She practically disappeared against the dark bed of the truck.

Zinnie's arms prickled with goose bumps. Forty-five degrees, in damp and windy conditions could trigger hypothermia. She looked down at the truck bed, searching for a weapon or a blanket. Her Northwest Lichenologists T-shirt glowed with its giant depiction of *Letharia columbiana*. It was an especially handsome lichen with chartreuse spindly arms and dark brown buttons of apothecia. Zinnie always felt daring in this dramatic shirt. Unfortunately, the shirt was nowhere near bright enough to signal for help, and it did little against the cold of the encroaching night.

"Can you get me out of this sack?" Allie wiggled and frowned. "It smells."

"I'm not sure I can get the knot undone," Zinnie said. "It's tight."

"We could jump out anyway. Maybe when the truck stops at a light."

Zinnie looked over the side of the truck bed. "We're on Evergreen Parkway. There are no stoplights – except if he turns onto Mud Bay. Then there's a light at Delphi Road."

"Where do you think he's taking us?"

"Good question. I don't think he'll take us downtown. I bet we go the other way."

"Toward the Shipwreck Café?"

"Yes. Out to the countryside."

"We better jump."

"No. It's too dangerous. Give me a minute. We'll think of something."

* * *

Marvin turned into his subdivision clutching the traffic citation in his hand. He didn't want to set the ticket down in what he called his "rolling office." The backseat of the car held books, his briefcase, free samples from educational vendors and an assortment of jackets, shirts, and shoes. He'd emptied the passenger seat when Allie arrived, thus depriving himself of a priority paperwork filing spot. If he wasn't careful about where he put this citation, he stood a good chance of forgetting to pay it.

He still had the citation in his hand as he neared his driveway. A middle-aged Asian man in a green Goretex jacket and a headlamp stood at the foot of the driveway and waved his hands, indicating Marvin should not turn in.

Marvin rolled down his window and heard the wail of the smoke alarm. His front door stood open, and a small stream of pearly gray smoke lifted out of the doorway.

"What the hell?" Marvin shoved the Prius into park, and tossed the speeding citation into the car clutter in the back seat as he exited the car.

"A fire truck is on its way," said the man in the green jacket, his headlamp bobbing as he spoke. "I just called it in."

"My daughter's inside!" Marvin raced up the drive with the man behind him.

"I shouted in there," the man called. "No one answered."

Marvin tore up the steps and through the open front door. He ran down the hall, prickling in sweat. He shouted, "Allie! Allie!" as he ran through the living room. He saw smoke billowing from the kitchen as the smoke alarm shrieked out its warning.

Smoke poured out of the oven in a great stream of gray clouds.

Marvin saw the dial setting and quickly turned the oven off. He could see two pans of burning brownies through the oven window. Coughing, he backed off. He grabbed a kitchen chair and positioned it under the fire alarm. With a smooth motion he stepped on the chair, pulled the cover open and unplugged the 9V battery. His ears still rang even as silence descended.

Marvin climbed off the chair and turned back to the doorway. He saw Allie's cell phone plugged in on the counter.

He picked up the phone and dashed upstairs to check the bedrooms of the house, shouting for Allie. Convinced she was not inside, he ran out the front door and down the stairs, nearly colliding with the man in the green raincoat.

"She's not in there?"

Marvin coughed and shook his head. "No. She was making brownies when I left. I think she may have gone for a walk."

"Ah." The man frowned. "But she hasn't returned?"

"Apparently not." Marvin scrubbed his eyes, still stinging from the smoke.

He put out a hand. "I'm Marvin Armentrout."

"Henry Chen. I called the fire department."

"I'll call to cancel." Marvin brought up the cell phone and stopped. "This is her phone," he said. "She never goes anywhere without it."

Henry's eyebrows steepled with concern. "Your front door was open."

"Let me cancel the truck, then we'll take a better look around." Marvin pulled his own cell phone out of his cardigan pocket and dialed 911.

"I need to cancel a fire alarm call." Marvin recited his address. "My daughter was baking brownies. At 500 degrees." He answered the operator's questions and put Henry Chen on when requested. Marvin's foot jiggled as he willed the call to come to an end.

"I will cancel the truck response." The operator's voice came across as unimpressed by cooking adventures.

Marvin ended the call and spoke to Henry. "I know she's not inside. If she went next door, you'd think she'd have heard the smoke alarm."

"The old lady is out on the porch. We could ask."

"Ursula?" Marvin looked across the driveway to Zinnie's house. The porch light illuminated Ursula's slim form standing at the top of the porch stairs.

"She shouldn't be out by herself," Marvin said.

The two men crossed through the battered rhododendrons and came to a halt at the base of the stairs as Ursula stiffened.

"It's me. Marvin. Have you seen Allie?"

Ursula didn't answer.

"Is Zinnie home?"

Ursula's face contorted, and she began to cry.

"Oh, man." Marvin didn't know whether he should try to get closer to her or stay where he was. To Henry, he said, "She's been having some health problems."

"I heard. I helped look for her the other day." Henry looked up the stairs and said, "You know my wife. You know Tilly Chen? We live in the house with the red door."

Ursula wiped her face. Slowly she nodded.

"Super. My name is Chen too. I'm Henry Chen."

"*Hündchen!*" Ursula came down the steps, hands flapping. "*Hündchen!*"

"That's her name for the dog," Marvin said.

She put a hand on Marvin's arm and pulled, pointing at his car.

"You want to go in the car?"

"*Ja. Ja.*" Ursula nodded. "*Wir müssen meinen Hund abholen.*"

Allie's cell phone rang. Marvin fished it out of his pocket and answered, "Hello? Allie?"

"It's Laurel."

"Do you know where Allie is?" Marvin tilted the phone so Henry could hear.

"She's not with you? Or with her phone?" Laurel's voice sounded tinny.

"No. She's not at home. I'm in Zinnie's driveway. Zinnie's not here either, but Ursula is, and she wants us to get in the car and fetch her dog."

"I'm on it. May Belle came to Zinnie's and grabbed Biscuit. I tried to stop her, but she knocked me down. She's in her silver van. Now I'm just following her. I'm at a stoplight. She just turned onto Evergreen Parkway."

"Be careful," Marvin said. "I'll get a jacket for Ursula, and we'll drive around the neighborhood to look for Allie. Can you call again in a few minutes?"

"I'll try. I don't usually use the phone when I'm driving."

"Right. You're in the blue car?"

"Yes. It's a Nissan Leaf."

"Stay safe. Talk to you soon." Marvin clicked off and opened the rear door of his car. He shoved his belongings to one side and emerged with a puffy down jacket. He shook the coat and held it open for Ursula.

She stared at the coat, and looked up at Marvin. She transformed in a moment, from a frightened old woman to a dignified lady. She straightened her stance, lifted her chin and extended one arm.

Marvin slid the coat onto her arm. She rotated for him to help her into the coat. Marvin breathed a sigh of relief as Ursula gracefully slid her other arm into the jacket. He lifted the neck of the jacket, folding her into the warmth of the coat.

Henry said, "When I started out to the mailbox, a truck with high beams went roaring by. There was a woman waving in the back. I thought it must be a teenager, but now I'm wondering if it was Zinnie. A minute or so later a silver van and a blue Nissan almost clocked me."

"The silver van is May Belle Pope, and the blue Nissan Leaf is our friend Laurel. I don't know who owns the truck. Maybe Allie took a truck?"

"Shouldn't we call the police?"

"And tell them what? That a fifteen-year-old girl left her phone in the charger and burned some brownies? Let's check the neighborhood and make sure Allie isn't doing something obvious, like talking to someone and losing sense of time."

Marvin opened the passenger door to his car. Ursula sat down inside the Prius, knees together, ankles close. She rotated her legs inside with the grace of a long-ago movie star. Her arm came up and her hand curled in a charming beckon to the men. "*Wir gehen jetzt.*"

Marvin raised his eyebrows. "I think that means we're going now. Would you care to come?"

"Absolutely," Henry said as he shut the car door for Ursula. He opened the back door and climbed in, saying, "It's bridge night, which means I wash dishes, but I think you need more help than my wife does."

Cladonia fimbriata

Chapter Twenty-Nine

May Belle floored the gas pedal. The van's aging and cruddy fuel injectors refused to deliver much in the way of fuel. Meanwhile, Biscuit anxiously circled in her lap.

This was ridiculous. Donnie had done his job. He was getting the snotty teen out of the way. If he had Zinnie in his truck, he could just keep driving, keeping both females out of May Belle's way.

It was time to think about her own task. She was supposed to be at Zinnie's house, figuring out how to transfer Ursula's money from the credit union. She'd only managed to grab Biscuit. She'd let herself get rattled.

May Belle slowed down as she came to Evergreen Parkway. She rolled up to the stop sign and used the halt to set Biscuit in the passenger's seat next to JoJo and Toad, saying, "Stay."

Biscuit behaved better than JoJo and Toad, who both leapt into May Belle's lap.

"You idiots." She rubbed JoJo's head as the headlights of a car came up behind her. She needed to move. She also needed to think.

May Belle put her turn signal and turned right onto Evergreen Parkway.

She thought about Zinnie running out of the house.

That was a missed opportunity. When Zinnie ran out, she should have run upstairs and at least tried to log in to Ursula's account.

Laurel had tried to fight for Biscuit. She might still be at the house. Ursula was not a challenge.

Could she lure Laurel away?

May Belle drove two hundred yards down the divided parkway to a crossing point, scanning for traffic. She moved to the left lane and made a U-turn to return to Zinnie's house.

Behind her, a blue Nissan Leaf did the same.

* * *

Laurel knew she excelled in math and understanding ecological concepts. She had no talent for rollerblading or karaoke. It was now apparent she also had no skills in tailing a vehicle. May Belle's face contorted with recognition, then rage, as she finished the U-turn and sped past Laurel, giving her the finger.

Heart pounding, Laurel braked to a stop in the crossover zone. She scanned for traffic and saw none in either direction. With trembling fingers, she called Allie's number.

The phone rang, and Laurel willed Marvin to pick up. Eventually a voice said, "Henry Chen answering Allie's phone while Marvin's driving." The calm voice helped Laurel focus.

"It's Laurel. May Belle just made a U-turn, and she's headed back up Evergreen Parkway. She saw me for sure."

"She's coming our way?"

"I think so."

"Any sign of the truck?" Henry's voice was calm and clear, like an air traffic controller directing flight traffic.

"What truck?" Laurel hated the vibrato in her own voice. She took a deep breath and tried to calm her systems. Heart and respiration rates responded, barely.

"There was an old truck with super bright high-beam lights barreling down the street when I was getting the mail," Henry said. "I think Zinnie may have been in back. Maybe Allie too."

"Oh! I saw that truck earlier." Laurel thought of the roads around the campus. "Gosh. There's no telling where they went."

"Then we need to get some information out of May Belle." Henry's voice was smooth and confident.

Laurel had the odd sensation that Henry was enjoying the excitement. She asked, "How's Ursula?"

"She was upset at first but she's seems okay for the moment — she's watching out the front seat window. I think she's looking for her dog. Do you want to speak to her?"

"No. I'll call again if May Belle stops."

"Please keep in touch," Henry said.

Laurel tapped off the phone and put the Nissan Leaf into drive. She completed the U-turn and started back to Zinnie's house. Within minutes she caught sight of May Belle's vehicle. The van sped past the turn off to Zinnie's subdivision and then stopped at a light.

When the light changed to green, the silver van turned right onto Cooper Point road, moving away from Zinnie's subdivision.

Laurel shoved down the accelerator pedal on her car and took the turn to follow the van. Why the U-turn? Why not return to Zinnie's? Where was May Belle going now?

* * *

Zinnie and Allie bounced and slid as the truck sped down Evergreen Parkway, high beams blazing and no other traffic in sight. The normal five-to-six traffic vanished when college students and staff were on Thanksgiving break.

"My head hurts." Allie squirmed. She wriggled her right hand up and out of the wrapped sacking. Zinnie helped her push the burlap down until both arms were free. Now Allie wore the frayed potato sack like an outsized cummerbund.

"Did you hit hard when you were thrown in?" Zinnie asked.

"*Ja.*"

Zinnie tried to see Allie's eyes — an impossible task in the flickering dark. "You may have a concussion. We definitely don't want to be jumping out of the truck if there's any chance you have a concussion."

"What?"

Zinnie repeated herself, yelling into the wind and road noise. The black Lab puppy in the wire cage barked.

"Ow!" Allie covered her face with her hands "Make him shut up!"

"Shh." Zinnie soothed the puppy through the wires. The little dog licked her fingers and wagged his whole body in excitement.

"What are we going to do?" Allie shouted. "We don't have a phone!"

"We're going to think!" Zinnie hunkered down next to Allie. "He's not going into town. He can't be."

"Do you think he'll stop at the café?"

"No. But there's the big hill down to Mud Bay." Zinnie sat up. "It's November 24!"

"Okay."

"There's a party tonight at the tavern! I saw flyers for it on campus. It's *All Our Uncles Are Monkeys* Day."

"What?"

"*All Our Uncles Are Monkeys* Day!" Zinnie yelled into the wind. "November 24. The anniversary of the publication of Darwin's *Origin of the Species*."

"So?"

"There will be a lot of people at the tavern." Zinnie rocked to her knees as the pickup veered right and took the ramp to Mud Bay Road.

"What are you doing?" Allie called as Zinnie crawled to the back of the truck bed.

"I'm signaling." Zinnie pulled off her T-shirt. She stripped off her brand-new tangerine No Sag bra. "I'm about to signal with everything I've got."

Chapter Thirty

Donnie's body pumped out sweat as his heart rate soared. He was beyond wet armpits. His t-shirt was soaked, and the sweat now seeped through to his flannel shirt.

He felt like he was in a sweat shower.

He was screwed. Again. He was in a highly recognizable truck. It was a beautiful classic truck. The high beams were totally kickass get-outta-my-way bad boys. Everybody commented on his truck

So screwed. He had his name on the door, for Christ's sake. *Good Knight Kennels* in a size legible from fifty yards away. With a street address.

And now he had two women in the back, one of them half-naked.

What had he been thinking? Hero stuff. Stupid. He'd wanted to be the guy who saved the day. He wanted to solve May Belle's problem at her target house. Getting the mouthy teenager out of the way sounded manly, and he wanted to impress Sherry.

Sherry. She'd gained some weight. Who wouldn't, being in pain and home all day? She was such a good gal. She deserved better than his sorry ass, and he knew it.

Donnie was nearing the end of Evergreen Parkway. He could go straight and take the on-ramp to downtown Olympia. No way.

He could take the right lane and then turn left onto Mud Bay. It would take him by the mega-church where May Belle and Sherry had taken him to services. They had prayed for salvation and good health and decent paying jobs.

The ten weeks of church-going had helped May Belle several eldercare jobs.

Until the assistant pastor followed up with his parishioners.

The previously trusting congregation started passing the word around, and the coffee hour got cooler and then downright cold. Sherry cried after each social slight.

May Belle hadn't taken that much from the church clients. Not really.

Screw them.

He'd go right, like he had planned.

It would take him past the aquatics center where the physical therapist had encouraged Sherry to sign up for hydrotherapy.

Seventy-five bucks a month. Right. That wasn't going to happen.

Sherry had applied for disability and had been denied. Chronic pain sufferers on internet forums told her to appeal with the help of an attorney.

That wasn't going to happen either. An attorney was two hundred an hour.

His racing thoughts weren't helping. Focus.

The Lab puppy came wriggling across the bench seat and into Donnie's lap. She climbed up Donnie's chest, gaining traction by digging in with her sharp little puppy claws. She licked Donnie's chin, no doubt getting a taste of salt.

He loved dogs. He'd turned into a crappy owner of a rundown puppy mill. Sherry didn't see it. She didn't get out of the house to see the barn, but he knew. He saw the dogs stepping in their own shit and not getting out of their kennel runs.

He knew.

Donnie took another look in the rearview mirror. His unwanted passenger was waving her arms and her naked chest at a car passing on his left. The driver of the car honked enthusiastically, and a passenger flashed a "thumbs-up" as they went roaring by.

They must think this was a party truck. The gals in back were party girls. No need to worry.

The thought momentarily buoyed Donnie's mood, but the feeling evaporated as the final decision point arrived at the road split. He drove the truck down the exit lane to the right.

He couldn't stop for the turn at Mud Bay. That would give the women in back a chance to bail out of the truck. He could tell the teenager was free. She wasn't moving a lot, but he could see enough to know the older woman had gotten the kid partway out of the sack.

It'd been easy to sack up the girl. He was surprised how well that went.

Now he'd go to jail for kidnapping. He'd be butt-fucked by guys bulging with muscles and connections.

A new river of sweat came pouring off his neck and back as he accelerated down the ramp.

He careened the truck onto Mud Bay, going west. He knew he was damn lucky he wasn't T-boned by cross traffic. A giant tow truck came from the left, but there was space for a merge. Donnie floored the gas pedal and roared around the stop sign, sending the puppy in his lap sliding across the bench seat and into the panel of the driver's door.

The women in the back and the dog cage all went careening to the left. The topless one disappeared for a moment as the tow truck driver tapped a beep on his horn.

Donnie drove his truck down the long hill, praying there was no cop at the bottom. It'd been a favorite speed trap for years until locals complained that the giant hill made it entirely too easy to be nabbed.

He hadn't seen a cop there in a long time. With his luck, there would be one now.

All he had to do was get to the farm.

Donnie cursed himself for his stupidity. What would he do with two women out there?

The shirtless woman was back up on her knees, waving a bright orange bra and screaming, "Help Me!"

Donnie had never seen underwear in that color. It was eye-catching, for sure. Even in the dark of the fall evening, the tangerine bra glowed.

The tow truck driver was taking her seriously. Swirling lights went on as the driver jabbed a finger toward the road edge. The man's face looked like a cross between a bull and an avenging angel.

Donnie swallowed. Hard.

Was he supposed to stop for a tow truck? Was it the law?

The tow truck driver made the decision for him. In an incredibly ballsy move, he moved his rig alongside Donnie. The driver turned on the cab-top lights and motioned for Donnie to pull over.

They were roaring down the hill with no exit in sight.

The tow truck pulled forward and began to move in. The message was clear as the giant size EVERGREEN NORTHWEST TOWING inscription came within inches of Donnie's face. The tow truck driver was ready to run Donnie off the road.

Faced with near certain annihilation, Donnie stood on the brakes. The truck bucked and skidded.

Donnie rode the truck brakes down the hill as the tow truck driver shepherded him to the right. Donnie knew he could be pushed into the pond at the bottom of the hill. Normally a quiet resting place for small ruddy ducks and buffleheads, the pond was plenty deep enough to swallow his truck.

Donnie put on his emergency flashers as a signal of compliance and a weak prayer for options.

The tow truck driver stuck with him. They were past the pond. Now Donnie was going to have to stop or he would be pushed into a giant cement-rimmed planter box paralleling the road.

That left the parking lot at Buzz's Tavern.

Donnie stood on the brakes and cranked the steering wheel to the right, shooting the gap between the pond and the planter box. The tow truck braked hard before following, scattering gravel as the big truck narrowly missed a parked car.

Donnie's brain scrambled for options. Where could he go from here?

His desperate brain thought of the archeological site in the news a decade before. The dig had been up the right side of the bay from Buzz's Tavern. If he could get there — up to Munro Farm — he could get out to south of the college and call May Belle to pick him up.

It wasn't drivable. He'd have to go on foot.

Donnie shoved the truck into park. He flung open the driver's side door and heaved himself out. The Lab puppy scrambled to follow.

Either the dog would keep up or he wouldn't. Donnie started to run. The puppy leapt into the game, tangling into Donnie's feet.

Donnie stumbled around the puppy as a gaggle of college students emerged from a van. Two of the girls wore fake gray beards and three others wore headbands with plush monkey ears. One wore a full monkey costume with a four-foot brown tail. The monkey-suited girl carried a sign with "Evolve" written in rainbow-hues.

"Oh, cute dog!" she said.

Donnie reached down, grabbed the puppy and handed the wiggling fur-ball to the student. "You're a prizewinner!" he said as the November air turned his sweat into a cold vapor layer.

He turned away from the girl and ran into the night.

Chapter Thirty-one

Zinnie scrambled to pull on the tangerine bra and her *Letharia columbiana* t-shirt. The colors fluoresced under the shine of the tavern's lights. The colors were alive and so was she.

She was decently covered by the time the tow truck driver climbed down from his rig.

"You okay?" The driver called as he jogged over.

"Yes. Thank you. Thank you so much! You rescued us, and I am so deeply grateful."

"You looked like you were in trouble."

In the dark shadows of the parking lot, it was hard to tell if he blushed at her thanks, but he might have done.

"I had my dispatcher call the police," he said.

"Could you call for paramedics too?" Zinnie pointed at Allie. "I'm concerned she may have a concussion."

"On it." The driver pulled a cell phone from his pocket and turned away from the road noise of traffic streaming down Mud Bay Drive.

The puppy in the wire cage sent up a barrage of barks as the monkey-costumed students came close.

"Dr. Fazail?" A dark-haired student walked over, holding the Lab puppy awarded by Donnie.

"April! Where did you get the dog?"

"A big guy went running by. He was tripping over this pup. I said, 'Cute dog,' and he grabbed the puppy and handed it to me. He said I was 'a prize winner,' but I don't think I want a dog. I'm more of a cat person."

"Why don't we park your puppy with this one? I think they go together." Zinnie knee-walked to the wire pen and managed to help the student get the second puppy penned with the first. The two dogs wiggled and licked each other.

"Are you going to give my prize a good home?"

"We'll think of something. May I use your cell phone?" Zinnie infused her words with good cheer. Relief endorphins were sweeping her body, but she wasn't going to make any promises about re-homing puppies.

As an ambulance and a police car arrived, Zinnie managed to make a phone call to Marvin.

She said, "We're in the parking lot at Buzz's Tavern. A big guy who may be related to May Belle grabbed Allie and threw her into the back of a truck. I jumped in and managed to wave long enough to get some help. The big guy pulled off at Buzz's Tavern. He parked and ran off. Allie bumped her head. I think it's just a goose-egg, but the paramedics are here to evaluate her. The police are here too." Finishing the update left Zinnie out of breath.

"I'm on the way. Please tell Allie to hold on." His voice vibrated with tension as Marvin added, "Ursula is with me in the car, and we've got our neighbor, Henry Chen too. Laurel is following May Belle, who took Biscuit."

"May Belle took Biscuit?"

"Yes. I am afraid so. Laurel peeled out after them, and apparently May Belle turned back. Laurel called and said they may be headed back to your house. If I see May Belle, I'm going to stop and put the fear of God into her."

"Sounds good."

There was a mumble. Marvin came back on. "Actually, Henry says he called his wife. She's going down to your house with her friends to make sure no one gets into your house. We'll be with you shortly."

Zinnie's head swam as she returned the cell phone to the college student. Ursula was with Marvin. That was good. May Belle had Biscuit. That was bad. Laurel was following May Belle. That was good. Or was it? Henry was . . . Who was Henry? Right. Tilly Chen's husband. Her neighbors in the house with the red door. Right.

She stretched her neck, hearing a pair of pops as her mind settled. She remembered when Charlie painted white dots on the

Chen's black cat. The Chens had not been happy about it, but Henry had talked his wife out of pressing charges. He was a nice man.

Zinnie joined Allie at the tailgate of the ambulance. Allie was enduring an inquisition from a paramedic.

"Did you lose consciousness?"

"No."

"Any vomiting?"

"No."

"Any bleeding or leakage from your ears or nose?"

"No."

"Look at the light please."

Allie sighed and looked at the paramedic's penlight.

"Do you feel irritable?"

"Duh."

The paramedic grinned and said, "Let's try again. Are you feeling more irritable than usual?"

A smile tugged at Allie's lips. "I'm about usual. My head hurts here." She pointed to the front of her forehead. "I don't like it when the puppies bark."

"Okay. Do you have a parent or guardian here?"

"My friend, Zinnie."

"That's me. Her father is on his way."

"Great. Let me go start my report, and I'll talk to your dad once he's here."

Zinnie shivered as she sat down next to Allie. The bumper step of the ambulance made for a tight fit. "You okay?" she asked.

"I think so."

"Dr. Fazail?" A tall college student detached himself from the student group. "Would you like my sweatshirt?" He held out a heavy, dark green college sweatshirt.

"Thank you!" Zinnie slipped on the sweatshirt and rolled up the sleeves, drinking in the heavy scent of aftershave. Her son Charlie had worn a sweatshirt like this for years, and his youthful experiments with aftershave had been equally enthusiastic.

She smiled at the student and said, "I can have it for you at the Biology Department after the break."

"No problem." He flashed a smile which demonstrated a parent's large investment in orthodontia and returned to his friends.

Each student had a cell phone out and was busily photographing or videotaping the truck or Zinnie and Allie sitting on the bumper step of the ambulance, or the patrol car turning into the graveled lot.

Zinnie suddenly realized a topless professor arriving at a tavern would trend on college social media. She had no idea which platform was in favor this week, but she was confident there was one — and she could believe Yousef Berbera, her department head, or Margaux, his formidable assistant, would be tracking the hot campus news of the day.

She was about to be highly popular or fired or both.

Zinnie was still digesting this as a policeman left his vehicle and approached the ambulance.

"Good evening. I'm Sergeant Martinez. Are you the ones who called in?"

"The tow truck driver called, but we're definitely the people who need help," Zinnie said. "Allie, are you up to saying how this started?"

Allie nodded, gingerly. "A big man came to our house. He rang the doorbell. I answered. He was holding a puppy. He said he was a friend of May Belle's. He said I could see the puppies in his truck. Like an idiot, I went to look, and when I was reaching for the puppy in the pen, the big guy threw a sack on me."

Zinnie said, "May Belle is a woman who recently moved into my home to help with my elderly mother."

Sergeant Martinez's eyes narrowed, and he tilted his head back. The lights from the tavern side cast his face into shadows. "May Belle?" he asked, carefully.

"She told me her name is May –then- Belle and said her last name is 'Pope.' I've been told by another theft victim from Oakville that May Belle may be 'Mabel' and her real last name may be 'Knight.' She's known to have a monogrammed case with a 'K' on it."

Allie jumped in. "It was a sunglasses case. I saw it in her van."

Sergeant Martinez turned to Allie. "Tell me more about the man in the truck with the puppies, please."

"He's a big guy. He put the sack over me. He was very fast. Then he tied a rope around me. The sack was horrible. Very smelly and I couldn't breathe."

Zinnie took up the story. "I saw the guy throw Allie into the truck bed from my kitchen. I ran after them. Thank God, there's a speed bump in our neighborhood. I was able to catch up when the truck slowed. I grabbed the tailgate and managed to climb in the back."

"This's the truck?" Martinez pointed to the maroon truck, still sitting, driver-side door ajar, with its high beams on, illuminating the rising tide. The faded sign on the open door could just be made out in the lights of the parking lot. *Good Knight Kennels.*

"Yes."

"And do you know what this party is about?" Sergeant Martinez's thumb flicked at another carload of tavern-goers, emerging from a vehicle in an assortment of homemade costumes.

Zinnie nodded. "Yes. I saw some flyers around campus last week. November 24 is *All Our Uncles Are Monkeys* Day. It's the anniversary of the publication of Darwin's *Origin of the Species.* I think there's a prize for longest-beard and best-looking monkey."

"O-kay." The policeman surveyed the parking lot as the college students streamed into the tavern. "Sounds about right for late November. Not as nutty as Halloween, but nutty enough."

The tow truck driver stepped in, saying, "Sergeant Martinez, I'm actually on a call. I should get going."

"All right. Let me get your business card." To Zinnie and Allie, he said, "I'll be right back."

Zinnie nodded, then blinked as Marvin drove his Prius into the parking lot, Ursula at his side, and Henry Chen in the back seat.

Marvin was here. The world felt better.

"If your opponent is of choleric temper, irritate him."
Sun Tzu (545 – 470 BCE)

Chapter Thirty-two

The cool air of the November evening nipped at Zinnie's ears as she watched Marvin park. She saw the worried look he threw at Allie, still seated with Zinnie on the rear step of the ambulance, but he took the time to circle his car and open the door for Ursula. He offered Ursula his arm. She gracefully tucked a hand under his forearm, and he guided her carefully through the rough parking lot to the ambulance.

Henry Chen emerged out of the back of the Prius, sketching a wave at Zinnie.

Marvin asked, "Are you okay?"

Allie nodded. "My head hurts a little. I'm sorry, Dad. I let a guy *with puppies* grab me. How stupid!"

"Don't worry about it. I'm glad you're safe." He squatted down, reached out and patted her knees. "Your brownies didn't survive."

"Oh, my God! The brownies!"

"Burnt to a crisp. Which is a good thing. The smoke alarm went off. It got the attention of our neighbor. He came over, and the two of us figured out you weren't there."

Allie eyed her father. "The brownies are in the trash?" Her tone was oddly hopeful, triggering Zinnie's parental sensors.

Marvin was oblivious. "The brownies are still in the oven, but they aren't salvageable. Don't worry. We can make some more. Just not at 500 degrees."

"Okay."

Henry Chen arrived with a pilled cardigan pulled from Marvin's trunk. Henry offered it to Allie. Her face lit up with a smile as she slid her father's cardigan on over her black leather jacket. Henry pulled out a cell phone and stepped away to make a call.

Zinnie stood up and spoke to her mother. "Why don't you take my seat?"

Ursula sat down on the ambulance back step without speaking. She looked warm enough. She looked at the arriving vehicles with worry on her face.

"It's all right, Mom."

Ursula eyed the swirling lights on the police car and pulled herself down into a silent hunch. Zinnie patted her mother's shoulder.

She had to admit it was a poorly lit tavern parking lot with people in homemade monkey costumes streaming into the bar — and then there were the swirling lights from a police car casting red and blue shadows. No wonder her mother was confused.

"How'd you get the truck to stop?" Marvin asked her.

"You don't want to know." Zinnie snorted.

"Actually, I do."

Zinnie looked at his shadowed, grim face and relented. He must have been terrified by the screaming smoke alarm and his missing daughter. He could use a laugh. She smiled and said, "I stripped off my shirt and my new bright orange bra and waved everything — I do mean *everything* — and a tow truck driver decided we were in trouble. He forced the truck to pull over. The kidnapper bailed out of the truck and took off running up the Sound, leaving me topless but victorious."

Marvin burst out laughing. "All this I would've liked to see."

"You may. There were kids from campus in the parking lot when we arrived. I may be trending on social media."

"Oh, my God. How is your supervisor with this sort of thing?"

"I'll find out. Yousef usually has a pretty good sense of humor."

Henry Chen tapped off his cell phone and rejoined the group.

The paramedic approached them and spoke to Marvin. "You the Dad?"

"Yes, sir."

"Your daughter received a bump on the head, which we never like, but she didn't lose consciousness, she's not vomiting. Her pupils are normal. I'm thinking she can go home and have a quiet couple of days. You definitely don't want a second injury, and you absolutely don't want to waste any time getting her seen if there are any changes. If there's lethargy, confusion, throwing up — anything at all — you take her in. Okay?"

"Yes."

"All right then. Give me one more minute, and we'll have some paperwork. Then you can go home."

Marvin turned to Zinnie. "This may get snug. My car is my office. Henry built a tower of books and paper to get space to ride in the back seat."

Henry shrugged. "This is much more exciting than helping with chairs for bridge. I just spoke with my wife. Tilly knows about Mabel Knight from a couple in her bridge club. When I told Tilly you had been targeted, she said she'd take the whole bridge club down the street to protect your house until you get home."

"How kind!"

"It's a nice night for it — and they have a bone to pick with Mabel."

Henry was right. It was a beautiful autumn night. The air was crisp with wisps of fog rising from the bay.

"I could call Tilly back and ask her to send someone from the bridge club," Henry said.

"Couldn't we get an Uber?" Allie asked.

Three sets of senior eyes looked at her with uncertainty. Ursula wasn't part of the conversation. She withdrew into the puffy coat as she stared at yet another new carload of party-goers.

"I've never called for an Uber," Marvin said. "It's a thought."

"Do we have to download an app or something?" Henry asked.

Allie rolled her eyes.

One of the puppies caged in the maroon truck yipped.

Still perched on the back step of the ambulance, Ursula sat up. She began to rock. "*Hündchen!*" Tears leaked out and ran down her face.

"Oh, Mom." Zinnie dropped to her knees and tried to take her mother's hands. Ursula pulled back.

Zinnie looked up at Marvin. "I wonder where Laurel is."

* * *

Laurel was parked behind May Belle at the Safeway gas pumps. She knew there could be distinct differences between intellectual understandings and practical realities for many issues. It had not occurred to her that there were times when the Bad Guys needed gas.

May Belle glared at her as she exited the silver van and clicked the locks down with her key fob.

Biscuit's sweet face appeared momentarily when she put her feet on the passenger door panel, and she stretched her head to explore the window. Biscuit dropped out of sight after a few sniffs.

JoJo and Toad bounced around the interior of the van, barking as usual.

Laurel heard her cell phone buzz. Her eyes took in the text message from Marvin. He was with Allie and Zinnie. Good!

Laurel took a steadying breath as she watched May Belle stab in her zip code and phone number. It was rather astonishing how many taps were required to get the gasoline flowing.

This was no time for sympathy. Biscuit belonged with Ursula. May Belle was a thief and a jerk. Laurel opened her car door and stepped out into the cool night air.

"I'm here to collect Biscuit," she called.

"Fuck off!"

Heads swiveled from other pumps. A sour frown creased the face of a young mother filling a Toyota Highlander with a kid rubbernecking out the back window.

"I'll call the police!" Laurel shouted. "You just wait!" The "wait" came out with tremor. She wanted to sound forceful. The wobble in her voice betrayed her. She'd never actually spoken with an emergency operator. Did they take calls about dog-napping?

"Go away! You're harassing me." May Belle turned her broad back on Laurel and stared at the gas pump.

"Harassing?" Laurel inhaled. She found herself slamming the door of the Nissan Leaf and marching over to May Belle while ignoring the twinge from her bruised ribs. "I'll show you harassment!" Laurel said.

She stomped toward the pumps, stopping just a few feet from May Belle. Laurel saw the high whirling numbers on the gas pump.

"My God," Laurel cried. "How much gas do you use?"

"Leave me alone!" May Belle pulled the nozzle from the gas tank and slammed the handle down at the gas pump. She whirled back to the van and cranked the gas cap on before slamming the cover door shut.

"We don't have to live this way," Laurel began.

May Belle flung open the van door and heaved her bulk in.

"Haven't you heard about global warming?" Laurel shouted as the van roared to life, and May Belle shifted the vehicle into drive.

Chapter Thirty-three

Donnie's side hurt. His breath came in ragged bursts as he did his best to keep walking. He'd given up running along the shore of the inlet after his left foot slid into a muddy slough. It was hard to keep moving with a waterlogged shoe. He moved inland, where the ground remained rough.

He gave up the idea of making it to the college. He stumbled upon a narrow deer trail and took the path up a hillside.

The fine visibility rendered by the clear fall evening diminished once he was under the canopy of firs and cedars. He ran into a long, ropey lichen that he frantically slapped away. He thought about spiders and felt his heart rate soar higher.

Donnie stopped for a moment to see if he could hear any sounds of pursuit, but his pounding heart and the noise of his own heavy breaths made it difficult to hear. The hot sweat drenching his body quickly cooled in the November air, raising goose bumps and increasing his agony.

He'd lost his truck. The police would be after him.

For kidnapping.

The two Lab pups would be taken. No money to be gotten there.

He had to get home. He and Sherry should leave town. Tonight.

His sister would have to pick him up. First, however, he needed to know where he was.

God, he hoped May Belle had gotten to the old lady's bank account.

They could start over.

Arkansas. They could go to Arkansas. Sherry had some family near Little Rock.

They could do some eldercare or maybe some more puppy-raising. They just needed to get there. Shit. They needed a stake of money to make a fresh start.

Donnie plunged through the darkness and worked to keep up a steady stream of positive thinking. That's what got him through high school. Thinking positive. Moving forward — which was better than thinking of the skinny girl in black he had grabbed this evening. She must hate him now — and who was the half-naked woman who jumped in the truck and got him run off the road? Who the hell was she?

The deer trail widened. Donnie gulped air and kept going. A porch light beckoned. He must be near one of the side streets off Delphi Road. Maybe he was at Fifth Street. He was still too close to Buzz's Tavern. He needed to get farther from the truck.

Donnie followed the trail to its end at a paved road. Chest heaving, he tapped his cell phone and called his sister.

* * *

Laurel was getting the hang of tailing a vehicle. It helped that she was no longer trying to be discreet. She followed May Belle up Cooper Point Road past the high school. May Belle's van sped past the Goldcrest subdivision and then past the 28th street turnoff.

"You're going back to Zinnie's *now*?" Laurel kept May Belle's van in sight until it turned left on Kaiser. May Belle had to know she was being followed.

It didn't matter what May Belle knew. What mattered was keeping track of the van and Biscuit.

Dognapping. Clearly May Belle was a woman with no limits to her depravity. She probably ate deep dish pizza with a fork.

Laurel's lips firmed as she took the turn onto Kaiser. She returned her hands to the proper position of ten and two on the steering wheel. She muttered, "Allie made me a member of the Order of the Silver Shield, and you are not going to defeat us. I have you in my sights, May Belle Pope, or whoever you are."

It looked like they were returning to Zinnie's neighborhood, having made a large loop of west Olympia.

May Belle had gas. She had her luggage. She had Biscuit.

Why would May Belle be returning to Zinnie's now?

"Well, I'm going to follow you, you horrible thing," Laurel vowed. She recalled there was a group called "vagrant lichens" which specialized in moving with the wind. She even knew the German name for them: *Wanderflechten.* These lichens rode the wind across steppes and plains and deserts, halting only when they blew against a rough surface. There they would lie in wait for months or years, until there was enough moisture to unfold and live.

"The leafy part of the fungus dries around the algae," Laurel lectured an imaginary student as she accelerated down Kaiser Road. "It turns into a little ball. The two parts are stuck together, just like I'm sticking to May Belle Pope!"

Vagrant lichens lived a rather monk-like existence in the arid lands where they were common. A vagrant lichen rarely put any energy into creating reproductive parts.

"Kinda sad, like my dating life," Laurel acknowledged as she followed May Belle into Zinnie's subdivision.

Hands still tightly gripping the steering wheel, Laurel's mind galloped through lichen trivia, seeking something inspirational. Vagrant lichens had the special charm of adventurers, she recalled. They were hardy. They were mobile. They were adaptable. She needed to be hardy and adaptable.

"The Order of the Silver Shield shall endure!" Laurel followed her proclamation with an "Oh, shit!" as a car turned onto the road in front of her, requiring a fast foot on the brake.

Laurel was able to keep May Belle's van in sight. This was hard work. Her stomach rumbled. Her thoughts again turned to lichens.

The vagrant lichen *Leconora esculenta* might be the "manna" of the Biblical book of Exodus. Certainly country people trying to survive famines in Armenia, Turkey and parts of ancient Persia had eaten this bitter-tasting lichen.

May Belle's van made the turn into Zinnie's subdivision. Laurel clicked on her turn signal to follow.

Of course, both botanists and Biblical scholars debated the un-prove-able. The sweet tasting "manna" that was "white like a hoar frost" might be a mycelium of a ground-dwelling fungus.

She would be an academic until her death. It was not possible to stop her brain from making connections even as her heart was pounding and her armpits were wet with stress sweat.

She really hoped Zinnie was home now. Or Marvin. She should call Zinnie. Or Allie. Or her mother. Her mind careened around a list of possibilities for comfort and rescue. No. It was best to see where Biscuit was going. She might not get another chance at Biscuit if she spent time on the phone. She'd call Zinnie soon.

Laurel thought of the artic lichens that almost saved Admiral John Franklin. The artic explorer and his crew ate cructose lichens dotting the rocky, cold coasts they navigated. Laurel recalled that the polar explorer and his hundred-plus shipmates had starved to death after their wooden ships were caught in the ice. Artic lichens weren't high-calorie foods.

Her stomach rumbled. It was dinnertime.

How could she think about food right now? It was up to her to save Biscuit. She could eat later. Her stomach growled in defiance.

Laurel clung to her steering wheel as she stabbed the brakes before rolling over the speed bump in front of the house with the red door.

Chapter Thirty-four

May Belle cursed her rotten luck. The dashboard had lit up with the "need gasoline" signal at the worst time. She should have gone straight back to Zinnie's and dealt with the old woman, gotten the bank funds transferred and then filled the van with gas.

Instead she'd let the dashboard icon for low fuel interfere with her plans.

Hindsight.

In truth, she was terrified of running out of gas. Walking down the road with JoJo and Toad would be a nightmare. She really should get a pair of leashes for emergencies.

Now she had a blue Nissan riding her butt, and she had just finished an upsetting conversation with her brother.

She had been turning into the subdivision when her cell phone rang. "Kinda busy, Donnie," she'd answered.

"You gotta help me! I lost the truck!"

"What happened?"

"I got the girl sacked, and I threw her in the back — but then an older gal jumped in. We got onto Mud Bay Road, and the grandma peeled off half her clothes. I had a naked woman in the back, and she was waving and screaming and throwing her boobs around. A guy in a tow truck saw her and forced me off the road."

"My God. That must be Zinnie. She ran out of the house and didn't come back. Short, dark hair. A little heavy?"

"Yeah. That's her. I pulled into the parking lot at Buzz's, and I took off on foot. I left the truck at the tavern."

"Shit."

"I ran through the woods. I'm over on Fifth — off Delphi — at the end. Can you pick me up?"

"Not now. I'm going back to Zinnie's to see if I can get on the computer — and there's a friend of Zinnie's in a blue car, and she's riding my ass. She's been following me — even to the gas station. She wants the little Cocker."

"What'a you goin' to do?"

"I'm not sure. Did you call Sherry?" May Belle asked.

"Not yet. I didn't want to upset her."

"Well, maybe you should call one of your bowling buddies. I need to get on Zinnie's computer. That's going to take a while."

"Sis, we gotta pack up and leave. The cops will be out to the house soon. The kennel name is on the truck, and my papers are in the glove box. They'll be coming quick."

"You should call Sherry. She needs time to pack. I'll call you as soon as I'm finished. See if you can find somebody to get you a ride home."

"Okay." Donnie paused, then said, "A Prius has a pushbutton start, right?"

"I think so. Zinnie's neighbor has a Prius. Hell, half of Olympia drives a Prius. Donnie, I just don't know."

"There's a woman who just pulled up to a house in a Prius. She's got her garage door open, and she just put her purse down on the workbench. Now she's hauling in groceries. If the key fob is in the purse, I should be able to start the car."

"Go! Let's get this done." May Belle looked across at the dogs as she tapped off the phone. JoJo, Toad, Biscuit and her purse made for a full load in the passenger seat. JoJo took exception to being crowded and scrambled through the slot between the front seats, barking. Toad followed, leaving Biscuit, who looked at May Belle with soft Spaniel eyes clouded with cataracts.

May Belle rolled over the speed bump and slowed to make the turn into Zinnie's driveway.

The driveway swarmed with people. There were visitors on the porch too — all of them in Northwest "evening out" wear. They wore rain jackets or fleece pullovers in black, blue or green, along with jeans, and rubber-soled sandals with wool socks. Three had sensible hats and four had headlamps set on 'high' even as visibility was fine. The streetlamps were on, lighting the road and the driveway through rising wisps of fog.

Who *were* these people?

She stopped the van at the foot of the driveway and gasped as she recognized one couple. The Silsbys! Her former clients didn't know all she had done. She'd taken some jewelry, and they knew about that. They had figured out some details when the senior Mrs. Silsby had died. They had been vehement in their accusations and yet they had no proof. That was the beauty of eldercare thieving. When things disappeared, it was hard to prove where items had been.

May Belle was pretty certain the couple didn't know about the credit card account she'd opened at a department store using Mr. Silsby's recently deceased mother's name. Sherry was supposed to go shopping and return the items for cash, but Sherry hadn't been feeling well enough to go.

Whoever these people in the driveway were, they were friends of the Silsbys.

May Belle ignored the jeers of the people who yelled as she shoved the van into reverse. Forget Ursula's savings. She'd go home to the farm and help Donnie and Sherry get out of town.

She yanked the gear shifter into drive and steered the van to the right. She'd circle around the backside of the subdivision and get back on to Evergreen Parkway. If she was lucky, Laurel wouldn't see her. Biscuit slid off the passenger seat and fell into the footwell with a yip of dismay.

May Belle didn't care.

* * *

Laurel drove to Zinnie's house and was mystified by the crowd standing in the gravel driveway. She recognized Margaux, who waved and walked down to the street.

Laurel tabbed down her car window, and Margaux leaned in.

"This is my bridge club," Margaux said. "We got a call from the husband of our hostess that Zinnie's house needed protection from Mabel Knight. We voted to come down and stand guard. She showed up and we ran her off!"

"Great!" Laurel said. "Where's Zinnie? Is she still with Marvin?"

"I don't know Marvin. Zinnie's with the teenager she rescued out of a kidnapper's truck." Margaux smiled. "Apparently it was dramatic and ended at Mud Bay in Buzz's parking lot. Zinnie's 'trending' on social media."

"Wow. And Ursula? Is she back now?"

"No. She's with Zinnie. They're speaking with the police at the tavern. They should return home soon, I hope."

"Okay. Where did May Belle go, then?"

Margaux pointed. "Around the long backside of the loop. At a fast clip."

"I should go after her," Laurel said. "May Belle has Ursula's dog. I think I can catch her on Evergreen Parkway."

"Go!" Before stepping back, Margaux added, "Laurel, could you throw something over that jar?"

"Right!" She'd forgotten about the jar in the passenger seat. It could be upsetting for some to see — and Margaux almost certainly did not want to answer questions about how a specimen had escaped the Biology lab. Laurel reached into the back for her raincoat. She draped her purple jacket over the jarred one-eyed lamb before easing the car into a sweeping turn as Margaux commanded her friends to stand back.

It wasn't until she was navigating a turn around the back of the subdivision that Margaux's words really registered.

She'd said, "Laurel." Not "Dr. Baumgarten."

Laurel grinned and went in pursuit of Biscuit.

Chapter Thirty-five

The Labrador puppies barked. Ursula's head swiveled toward the maroon pickup, parked haphazardly in the tavern's gravel lot.

"Want to see the puppies, Mom?" Zinnie stood up and offered a hand.

Ursula nodded and accepted the help. They began a slow shuffle toward the maroon truck.

Marvin joined them.

He said, "Henry just got a call from his wife. Tilly's friends were standing in your driveway when a silver van pulled up. It was May Belle — when she saw the crowd, she reversed and left at high speed!"

"Hallelujah." Zinnie guided her mother to the side of the truck so Ursula could see the puppies leaping about in the wire cage.

"There's more," Marvin said. "Henry was told that Laurel is still following May Belle."

"Oh, no. That doesn't sound safe."

"I was thinking I would take Allie home. Then I can come back for you and your mom. I'll keep an eye out for May Belle and Laurel."

"Can we call Laurel?"

"I'll ask Allie to call, but it may not do any good. Laurel may not answer when she's driving."

"Right." Zinnie blinked her eyes, feeling a wave of exhaustion sweep over her.

"Hang in there. I'll be back soon." Marvin gave her a peck on the cheek.

Zinnie processed the miniature smooch and found a smile erupting just as the police sergeant came jogging over.

"There's been a carjacking nearby," Sergeant Martinez said. "It may be our kidnapper. All units are responding. I'll be back eventually."

"I hope you catch him," Zinnie said.

"We will. He took a baby." Sergeant Martinez took off at a run.

Zinnie felt the world move out of focus. A baby taken! How awful.

"You okay?" Marvin was with her as she put a hand out to steady herself on the truck.

"Yes. You go. I think Mom and I will sit in the truck."

"Good idea. The wind's getting a bite." This time Marvin swept her into a fast hug before he left, taking Allie and Henry.

Whines from the puppies caught her attention. Ursula was trying to pet them through the wire. The little dogs leapt up and licked her fingers. One sat down and shivered.

Marvin was right. The rising evening breeze delivered a chill. Zinnie reached into the truck and unlocked the wire cage. The puppies wiggled out. "You poor things. I'll bet you haven't had your dinner yet." Carrying a puppy in each arm, Zinnie moved to the passenger side of the truck and managed to get a finger under the door handle. She opened the door and said, "In here, Mom. You can hold the puppies."

Ursula looked at her. After a long pause she stepped forward and stood in the open door of the truck.

"Up you go," Zinnie encouraged her.

Ursula put a hand on the cab door and another on the dashboard and hauled herself up onto the high bench seat of the truck.

Zinnie set the puppies in Ursula's lap. Her mother smiled and began to stroke the two velvety dogs as they scrambled to lick her face. After a few licks, one of the puppies sat down and yawned. A moment later the second puppy did the same. Ursula arranged the two little dogs on her lap as their eyelids began to close.

As Zinnie closed the passenger door to the old truck she saw keys hanging from the ignition slot on the steering column.

Zinnie walked around the front of the truck and studied the open driver's side door with its sign, *Good Knight Kennels. 1300 Old Olympic Highway.*

She reached in and took the keys from the ignition. She definitely did not want her mother getting an idea to drive the truck home. She said, "Mom, I'll be right back." Zinnie walked to the door of the tavern and stopped a young woman in a monkey hat and a college pullover.

"I teach at the college," Zinnie said.

The young woman's eyes enlarged. "Dr. Fazail! You're Dr. Fazail! Oh, my God!"

Zinnie swallowed. Well, if she had a new claim to fame, she should use it. "I don't have my phone, and I'd like to visit a website for a moment. Would you be able to help me out?"

"Oh, Absolutely!" The young woman handed over a gleaming smart phone easily worth a family's monthly grocery bill.

"Thanks." Zinnie leaned against the wall of the tavern and read rapidly about the *Good Knight Kennels.* She returned the phone and jogged back to the truck.

She opened the driver's side door and climbed in.

Ursula's eyebrows went up and then down, signaling fear and confusion. Her fingers tightened on the two sleeping puppies. One pup wiggled and sighed.

"Mom. It's me. Don't you know who I am?"

Ursula studied Zinnie, taking in the dark green college sweatshirt. The air was thick with the smell of a young man's aftershave.

Finally, Ursula said, "I know you. You are Charlie's mother."

* * *

Donnie crouched behind a large cedar, hands unsteady as he tapped his cell phone. His voice shook as he whispered, "Answer, Sis. Please, please. Answer."

May Belle answered with a harsh bark. "What?"

Relief coursed through his system. "You gotta help me," he croaked. He cleared his throat and said, "Sis, I need some help."

"Donnie! Where are you?"

"I'm back in the woods near Evergreen Parkway. I screwed up. I screwed up big time."

"Did you get the car?"

"Almost. I ran over to the garage." He inhaled and said, "The lady went inside with more groceries. Hell, she must shop for an army."

"Busy, here . . ."

"Okay, okay. I grabbed the purse, got in the car, pushed the start and put the car into reverse — only there's a kid in the car. A baby!"

"What?"

"There was a kid in a car seat in the back."

"You took a baby?"

"No! I didn't! I was backing the car out of the garage, but then I saw the cars seat. I put the car in park on the street. I was getting out of the car, and that's when the mom came back." Donnie's breathing went ragged. "Justa minute. I'm gonna faint."

"Put your head between your knees."

Donnie sat down, hard, on the needle duff of the woods. He dipped his head down, hearing a whoosh and a roar in his ears. The tree trunk bark, a foot from his eyes, blurred and then sharpened into the vertical striping of a Douglas fir. He turned his head to one side and threw up.

"Donnie?"

"I think I'm having a panic attack."

"Breathe. Think of sunshine." May Belle knew the right thing to say.

"Okay. Better. Sweet Jesus."

"Tell me about the kid in the car."

"The baby was asleep. She had a big pink bow on her head. She was tiny. Really tiny. That's why I didn't see her at first. She was in the back seat, and she was facing the back. That means she was, like, a newborn or something."

"Where is she now?"

"How the hell do I know? I ran away from there as fast as I could."

"Were you seen?"

"Yeah. Oh, hell yeah." Donnie sniffed back tears. "The mom started screaming. She was so loud."

"You didn't hit her or anything?"

"God, no!" Donnie inhaled again, his voice settling. "I wouldn't hit somebody's mom!"

He sniffed. "I'm sure she called the cops. I ran for the woods. I found a trail back to the parkway, but I've seen a couple cop cars go past with their lights swirling. You gotta come get me."

"I'm on the parkway right now. I'm just passing Seventeenth."

"I'm south of there on the Munro Meadow trail. I'll run across, and you can get me."

"I've got that girl in a blue car following me. We're going to have to do something about her."

"Just get me out of here," Donnie said. "We can deal with her later."

"Realize that everything connects to everything else."
Leonardo DaVinci (1452-1519)

Chapter Thirty-six

May Belle swore as she thumbed her cell phone. As usual, it was up to her to deliver bad news to Sherry.

Her brother was a good guy. He really was — but he never caught a break. Now the cops were looking for him as an almost baby-napper. Being sought for grabbing a teen was bad, but being a baby-napper brought out every cop and every parent in the universe. Anyone who ever watched the evening news knew that.

Sherry answered. "Hey."

"Hey. We need to leave town. Right away."

"What?"

"I don't have time to talk right now. Donnie's in trouble. I'll pick him up in just a minute, but the police may be out to the farm before long, and we need to be gone. It's serious, Sherry."

"But . . . what about the dogs?"

"We'll call one of Donnie's pals to take the dogs to the shelter."

"The shelter!"

May Belle gritted her teeth. Stupid. She should've remembered. Sherry hated the idea of the animal shelter.

"Not little Sweetie," May Belle said. "Sweetie goes with us. And maybe Donnie's buddies will take over the farm."

"I don't know about this," Sherry said. "When will you get to Donnie?"

"Hang on. I think I see him." May Belle slowed the van as the headlight's illuminated Donnie's lumbering form on the walkway paralleling the parkway. The wisps of mist were congealing into a thicker bank of fog, but Donnie's size topped the mist layer. She brought the van to a halt, and Donnie ran to meet her.

The blue car following the van also came to a halt.

May Belle swore some more as she pulled Biscuit into her lap. JoJo and Toad barked like maniacs as Donnie opened the van door and boosted himself onto the passenger seat. His pale face and haunted eyes paired with a body smelling slightly of vomit.

"Here." May Belle handed Biscuit to Donnie as soon as he'd fastened his seatbelt. To Sherry, she said, "I've just picked up Donnie. He's in rough shape. Sherry. Listen. You need to pack us each a small bag. Two sets of clothes for each of us. You can do this. Hang on."

May Belle thrust the phone at Donnie. "Talk her into it."

"Hey, baby," Donnie said. "Don't worry. We can come back for our stuff. It's just for tonight and maybe tomorrow night. We gotta go away for a few days — just until things settle down."

May Belle pulled the van away from the curb and accelerated. "Tell her to bring her meds and extra glasses."

Donnie passed on the message.

"We'll need a few things to turn into cash," May Belle said. "Tell her we need the laptops in a carryon — and the shotgun."

Her brother turned to study her, his eyebrows rising with a silent questioning.

"Go ahead. Tell her." May Belle looked at the lights in her rear-view mirror. The blue car was still behind her. "We may need to look tough."

"Baby," Donnie said into the phone, "We want to travel light for a few days, but we'll need some cash. Put the laptops in a suitcase." He paused. "And get the shotgun out of the front closet."

He held the phone away from his ear as his wife began a shrill round of questions.

"Baby," Donnie spoke quietly. "We'll sort it out when we get there. We won't have a lot of time. Just do your best. I love you." He hung up and sniffed, dragging the back of his hand under his nose. "God, what a fuck up I am."

May Belle saw no point in agreeing. The fog thickened as May Belle turned from Evergreen Parkway onto Mud Bay Road. It would be thicker still at the bottom of the hill.

May Belle flicked her eyes to the rearview mirror. It was unlikely she'd lose the girl. It was a straight shot past Bay Mercantile and Buzz's Tavern at the bottom of the hill. To get home to the farm, she had to cross the freeway and turn right on Old 410, which wound through rural country. If the girl in the blue car kept up for another few minutes — and she likely would — it would be impossible to lose her. There would be no dodging off a side road with the lights off. Not on a night like this.

"Donnie, that girl is going to follow us to the farm. We need to have a plan."

* * *

Laurel's side hurt. She should take some Ibuprofen. Or some acetaminophen. She had both in the glove box of the car. She took her eyes off May Belle's taillights and darted a look at the glove box. She'd have to lean too far. It wasn't safe to open the glove box while driving. Her cell phone chimed. With a stab of guilt for even taking a quick look, she glanced at the screen. Allie was calling.

Her eyes caught movement at the side of the road, and Laurel's foot shot to the brake pedal. A doe and her almost-grown fawn emerged from the fog and lowered their heads to graze at the road edge.

Swallowing hard, Laurel edged around the deer and sped carefully to catch up with May Belle's van, now veering right to merge onto Mud Bay Road.

The potential of hitting a deer resolved things for Laurel. Now was no time to talk to Allie. She couldn't make a call while keeping up with May Belle in the thickening fog. It was too dangerous.

Laurel mentally scrolled through scenarios as her fingers tightened on the steering wheel for the run down the hill to Mud Bay. The road curved, giving a driver the swoop and drop of a roller coaster. She'd never liked this stretch of road.

Scenario Number One would be some sort of lovely ending. May Belle would stop — in a well-lit, civilized place — and would listen to reason. Biscuit needed expensive surgery. Ursula loved Biscuit. May Belle might be in trouble with the authorities for taking the dog.

The last justification was weak, Laurel decided. May Belle clearly lacked the respect for law that one wanted to see in citizens.

What did May Belle respect?

Money.

She could offer May Belle money.

Which could be a problem. She didn't have much cash. She had her cell phone, and the cellphone cover cleverly held her debit card. Phone apps and a debit card were all she ever needed. How did one offer a bribe in a cashless society?

Maybe May Belle had a payment app on her cell phone and took cards?

Unlikely. Time to rethink.

Scenario Number Two. May Belle and the big man were headed to some sort of home lair. How smart would it be to follow them there?

It would depend on the details. Some addresses were safer than others.

She could see where they went. Then she could back off and call the police. Or she could stop to call Allie and see where her friends were. They could coordinate their actions.

An academic review and analysis made her feel better. She could do this.

Laurel followed the van down the hill, intent on rescuing Biscuit.

Chapter Thirty-seven

Zinnie's stomach rumbled with a plea for dinner. The mist over Mud Bay thickened with each passing minute. The view from the interior of the truck was narrowing to the concrete barrier at the end of the parking strip. She could no longer see the dark water of high tide sweeping in to cover the mud flats.

She thought about taking Ursula into the Tavern for a chicken-fried steak or kimchi on noodles, two specialties at Buzz's. She glanced at her mother who gently stroked the two sleeping puppies.

The back door of the tavern opened and a couple stepped out, enveloped by loud voices and even louder music.

Zinnie shook her head. She couldn't think with music that loud, and Ursula would certainly be unhappy. The hip hop sounds blared with a brutally prominent beat, a far cry from the cheerful bounces and gentler swings in Ursula's beloved musicals.

A large pickup turned into the parking lot and cruised slowly, the driver seeking a space to park. Zinnie realized she could straighten the old truck to a better fit. It would be a kind thing to do as trucks, vans and economy cars were increasingly packing the lot with arriving party goers.

Zinnie turned the keys in the ignition. The old truck came to life with a click and a purr. Ursula turned to look at her, a question on her face.

"We're just adjusting."

Ursula reached down and fastened her seatbelt.

Zinnie smiled. Her mother had always had a thing for seatbelts. Zinnie fumbled for the belt end that had fallen off the bench seat. The old vehicle didn't have a shoulder belt. There was only the lap strap.

Uncomfortable with the notion of no shoulder seat belt, Zinnie carefully put the truck into reverse and rolled the truck backward a few feet.

Another large pickup swung into the parking lot, the driver clearly eager to get at the wide space that Zinnie was supposedly leaving.

"Okay. You can have it," she muttered. She'd park the old truck across the road at the Bay Mercantile. When Marvin returned, he would have his cell phone. She could call and tell the police where she parked the truck.

She should remember to take the keys, and she should tell the police dispatcher she had them.

Zinnie inched the truck through the crowded parking lot. She turned into the exit at the end of a giant raised bed, ready to shoot across the busy road to the mercantile.

She peered to the left. Two vehicles were descending the hill.

There was no traffic from the right.

She checked left again. The headlights of the two vehicles were approaching fast.

She would wait.

A silver van went flying by. A large man sat in the passenger seat and Zinnie caught a flashing look at the blonde Cocker Spaniel in his lap. Biscuit! Moments later a blue Nissan Leaf sped by, in hot pursuit of the van. Laurel.

Biscuit and Laurel.

"Hang on, Mom!" Zinnie turned on the headlights and swung the truck onto the road.

* * *

Laurel had a moment of relief as she reached the bottom of the big hill at Mud Bay. She flexed her fingers before tightening her grip on the steering wheel once again as May Belle drove on, roaring past a small, deep pond just to the right of the road and then barreling past Buzz's Tavern.

Laurel swallowed hard as she followed May Belle's van, praying no party-goer would exit the tavern parking lot in front of her. Her quick glance to the right showed no swirling lights and no sign of a police car.

May Belle took the curve and the overpass. Laurel followed, allowing a distance to open up between them.

She felt hot and cold at the same time. Laurel felt damp in the armpits and crotch and numb at her fingertips and toes. Interesting. Her sympathetic nervous system was being stimulated by her vagus nerve into a "fight or flight" mode. If she could take a few minutes to meditate, she might be able to bring her body temperature into a steady state.

Meditation. So easy to contemplate, so hard to do. Impossible at the moment.

Her style was to analyze.

"Analyze, then," Laurel said as she followed the silver van.

May Belle turned right onto the Old 410 highway.

Laurel let the gap between them widen. She turned after the silver van, deciding to follow with some caution. She'd been on this road once before. The road climbed and circled a vast hillside of big-leaf maples. Eventually the road came out on Highway 8. She should be safe if she stayed on Old 410.

The fog diminished as the road elevation rose from the waters covering the mud flats. A long rusting guardrail appeared on the right, giving Laurel a small perception of safety as she drove on. She could see the taillights of May Belle's van several hundred yards ahead. The road curved, and she lost sight of May Belle's taillights. They reappeared a curve later.

The winding rural road was taking her far from town. She should find a place to turn around.

She saw May Belle take a left turn onto the Old Olympic Highway, which was no highway at all. It was a narrow country road. The Cyclops lamb sloshed in the jar as Laurel braked hard, careening into the turn.

How stupid. If May Belle was watching her rearview mirror, she'd know she was still being followed.

Swearing a heartfelt "Fudgecicle!" at her incompetence in stealth car stalking, she closed enough distance to see the brake lights of May Belle's van winking as the road narrowed and the van slowed for a curve.

Laurel stopped her car and studied the road. The damp paved road shone like a winding black snake in the shards of light broadcast from a few houses set well back from the pavement. The shadows of the looming trees made the road-snake glisten ominously.

She'd go just a little farther. She might see where May Belle turned off, then she could decide whether or not to turn around.

Decision made, she eased the Nissan forward just as bright headlights lit up her rearview mirror. The lights flicked off and then flashed back into a retina-bleaching brilliance.

Laurel gasped. She knew those lights. It was that truck that she now knew had been carrying Allie and Zinnie. She was sure of it. Zinnie and Allie may have escaped, but, she, Laurel, was now sandwiched between May Belle and the kidnapper.

"The condition of man . . . is a condition of war"
Thomas Hobbes (1588-1679)

Chapter Thirty-eight

"Donnie," Sherry whispered into the phone. "I can't do this."

"Don't worry, baby. All we're going to do is scare the girl off." Donnie wished he felt as confident as he sounded. He held Biscuit in his lap as he crooned into the cell phone. "We're almost home. She might not turn off. I hope so, but if she follows us to the house, we need to be ready."

"My nerves can't take this."

May Belle steered the van around another tight curve, driving near the center of the road as the woods closed in on each side.

"Tell her to get the suitcases outside, ready to load," she said.

Donnie relayed May Belle's instructions, and added, "You just set the laptops out there too. If they don't fit in a suitcase, then in a box is fine . . . No. Not your spinning wheel . . .Yes, baby. I know it's a family heirloom."

He swallowed hard and said, "I think we'll run down to Arkansas. Go see Cousin Ed. You don't like dark and wet winters, so we'll go get a little sunshine and eat some biscuits and gravy."

May Belle interrupted. "Donnie, we're almost there. She's got to put the shotgun out." May Belle's eyes flicked to the rearview mirror. "Damn that girl."

"Sherry," Donnie said, "Just take the shotgun and take it to the barn corner. Do that last. Like I said, we only need to scare this girl off."

"Make sure she sets out the box of shells," May Belle directed.

"I can't do that," Donnie hissed. Into the phone he said, "I'll call you right back." He tapped off the phone and told May Belle, "She's not going to touch a box of shotgun shells. An empty gun is one thing. Live ammo is another. She won't do it."

"She needs to grow a backbone." May Belle arrived at the *Good Knight Kennel* sign and turned the van onto the long rut-filled drive to the farmhouse.

"Sherry's not well. You know that."

"I know, I know. There were shells in the shotgun last time I had it out. Last spring when we had those raccoons in the barn, remember?"

"Yeah. I was stupid to leave the dog food out." Donnie hunched over, owning another failure.

"You got the stuff binned up. It worked out. But there was one night when I heard some screechy noises in the barn — maybe just those raccoons getting it on. I took the shotgun out with me. I know it had shells in it then."

"Christ. Sherry shouldn't be carrying a loaded gun."

"All guns are loaded, right? We're supposed to act that way!"

"Well, Sherry doesn't — and you said we're just going to scare this girl off. Why do you need shells?"

"What if she won't leave?"

"We tie her up. Her friends can come get her in the morning." Donnie caressed Biscuit's ears. "Or we can give her the dog. It's going to be crowded in here with Sherry and Little Sweetie and our luggage."

"Think, Donnie! We're going to need cash. The laptops are worth something. They'll get us gas money to go south. But we need a rent deposit and food. We need to cash in on the little spaniel."

"We could take the girl's car. Sell the car."

May Belle glanced at her brother. "How much would we get?"

"Depends. What kind of car is it?"

"Blue. Looks new. Electric, I think."

"Hey, electric is expensive. We might get real money for it. A couple thousand easy. Maybe more."

"Even without a title?"

"Sherry could make one up. Or we could get something off a website. Price it right with a good story and sell it a hundred miles from here. Yakima maybe, with a change of plates. For cash."

"All right." May Belle chewed her lower lip. "Call Sherry back. Tell her to be at the corner of the barn with the shotgun. We'll stop in the parking area. I'll get the shotgun from her, and you load our things. I'll tell the girl we're taking her car. Sherry can ride with me, and you can drive the electric car."

"Okay." Donnie shrugged. He swiveled his head to look over his shoulder. "It's hard to tell with all the curves, but I think she turned out her headlights and is still following us."

* * *

Zinnie groaned. Laurel had not understood her headlight signaling, which made sense. Laurel couldn't know who was driving behind her. Honking wouldn't be any better.

She watched as Laurel turned off the road at the signboard labeled *Good Knight Kennels,* still following the silver van. She saw the headlights on the Nissan go off.

"Mom," Zinnie said, "I'm not sure what Laurel's thinking."

Ursula didn't respond.

Zinnie glanced over at her mother.

Ursula sat wedged in the angle between the truck door and the back of the bench seat with two sleeping puppies in her lap. Her eyes were closed. She seemed to be napping.

"All righty then. You're not worried."

Zinnie sat, studying the turnoff for a moment. She ran through her options. She didn't have her cell phone. It would take twenty minutes to drive back to her house. It was ten minutes back to Buzz's Tavern. She could try driving to a nearby house. That didn't seem wise. It would take time to explain who she was — and it would take more time for help to arrive.

What was she worried about? Her biggest fear was that Laurel would confront May Belle over Biscuit, putting Laurel at risk.

Sitting here did no good. If Laurel was driving into trouble, then the action would take place in the next few minutes.

May Belle was amoral, but would she actually attack Laurel?

"If there's anything I've learned from life with Charlie," Zinnie mumbled as she swung the truck onto the rutted drive, "It's to anticipate the arrival of unintended consequences." She turned off the headlights. No point in broadcasting her arrival.

She threw another glance at her mother who bounced slightly when the truck slipped into a rut. Ursula slept on, the two pitch-black puppy shapes barely visible in her lap.

Zinnie slowed the truck to a crawl. It would be best if Ursula slept through whatever was about to happen. Zinnie gripped the steering wheel and eased the truck down the long drive, hemmed in by Douglas fir trees and high huckleberry bushes. She could barely make out the road ahead.

"First I'm topless and then I stole a truck. Now I'm trespassing, and if I go off the road, they may never find our bodies. My last meal might be raw puppies." Zinnie's mental review didn't stop there. "I finally have a new bra that fits, and I'm gonna die before it gets appreciated by anyone other than me."

The truck rolled down the road, and Zinnie reached a conclusion.

"If I survive this, I am going to schedule a good time. I'm buying new panties, new jeans that fit, and, by God, I am going to figure out how to find reliable help. No more beating myself up. I'm going to anticipate more changes and get this done right."

Jaw set, she stared into the night. Her conclusions felt right. She'd take the time to study the ecology of dementia. Early stage, middle stage, late stage. Just like a lichen lifecycle. She'd study what was known, and she'd make a management plan.

Craving her mother's approval and hoping for peace were normal, but she needed to create a structure instead of just living with hope that the day would work. She'd study, plan, and activate.

She, by God, would not let May Belle keep her from this.

All she had to do was find Laurel and Biscuit and beat a hasty retreat. The rest would unfold with her hearty embrace of reality. No more denial about the new rapidity of Ursula's decline.

A field of stumps emerged from the darkness on her right, signaling a landowner's need to clear-cut timber for cash. The road curved ahead and disappeared into the darkness. May Belle's van and Laurel's Nissan had vanished.

Zinnie let the truck roll forward, around the bend. The road ahead turned again. Two Douglas firs leaned over the road, one festooned with long ropy lichens.

"Great. If we die out here, at least our last breaths will be in a location with excellent air quality."

Ursula responded with a light snore.

"An army marches on its stomach."
Napoleon Bonaparte (1769 -1821)

Chapter Thirty-nine

Marvin gently eased his car over the speed bump and continued down the street to home.

"Look at all the people in Zinnie's driveway!" Allie said

From the backseat Henry Chen said, "That's my Tilly. She doesn't do anything by half measures."

Marvin turned into his drive and parked next to the battered rhododendrons. A merry party of seniors gathered around a portable fire pit blazing in the middle of Zinnie's driveway.

Tilly Chen emerged from Zinnie's kitchen door bearing a tray filled with steaming mugs. "Oh, they're home!" she cried.

One of the firepit crowd detached from the perimeter of the party and took the tray from Tilly. She slid around the group and through the rhododendrons to Marvin's driveway.

When Marvin and Allie stepped out of the car, Allie was immediately swept into a hug by the small force of nature that was Tilly Chen.

Tilly said, "Oh, you are such a brave girl!" while patting Allie's back. "I am so glad you survived. We are so proud of you!"

Allie managed a stunned smile. "I mostly was an idiot," she said. "Zinnie saved me."

Tilly patted Allie's arm again. "And you're modest too. What a sweetheart."

Henry Chen emerged from the backseat, and said, "Don't I get a hug?" I provided important ballast."

His wife left Allie and hugged her husband. "I am so glad to see all of you." To Allie, she said, "Come meet my friends. We ran off Mabel Knight, and we're celebrating — but you're the real talk of the hour. Everyone wants to meet you."

Allie's eyes widened. "They do?"

"Easy, Tilly," Henry said. "She has a mild concussion. She may want to lie down."

"I'm fine," Allie insisted. "I could use a drink. Is that cocoa?"

"Lattin's cider," Tilly said. "We broke into Zinnie's house to use her stovetop. Her door locks are terrible."

"Working on it," Marvin said.

"Oh, right. You're the one who's sweet on Zinnie," Tilly said.

Marvin started to speak, but nothing came out.

"Get used to it," Henry laughed. "Tilly knows everything."

"I should get back," Marvin said. "Zinnie and Ursula are still at Buzz's Tavern."

"Come do a fast fuel up," Tilly suggested. "You can gulp some cider and pick up some food. Our sandwiches and hors d'oeuvres are arriving. . . now." She pointed at three people coming down the road. One pushed a wheelbarrow loaded with plastic bins topped by a large tray of sandwiches. "I sent Margaux to supervise moving the bridge party food."

Marvin's stomach rumbled. "Thank you. If you don't mind, I'll also take some sandwiches with me for Zinnie and Ursula."

"Please do!" Tilly smiled. "No sense in going hungry. Not with the weather changing." She turned to her husband and said, "The forecast says to expect a temperature drop after midnight. This is our last lovely evening of the fall."

"You're telling me this to let me know I will be cleaning up the remains of this driveway party in freezing fog tomorrow morning?"

"Henry, you are a brilliant man. You absolutely read my mind." She turned to Allie and said, "We're going to enjoy the cider and sandwiches and then go back to my house for bridge. Would you care to join us?"

Allie blinked. "I'd like to." She looked at her father. "This is fine?"

"Sure. If you feel up to it." Marvin found the November outdoor party a bit surreal, but it was also comforting to have caring neighbors. He looked at his daughter and said, "I would rather you were around people until I can fetch Zinnie and Ursula."

"*Ja.* I'm good." Allie looked at Tilly and said, "I don't know how to play bridge."

"Darling, it's outwitting evildoers by working with a competent partner. You'll be a natural."

A white car came down the road, slowed for the speed bump, and then rolled past the community mailbox to stop at the foot of Zinnie's driveway.

The passenger side door opened. A long-legged dark-haired man emerged. He spoke words of thanks to the woman driver as he opened the back and extracted a large rucksack and a black guitar case.

With a fluid ease, the new arrival donned the daypack and shouldered the guitar case. As he strode toward Zinnie's house, he smoothly lifted a sandwich off the tray in the wheelbarrow as it trundled by. He did so with an impish smile that earned him a laugh and a faux slap from Margaux.

"Well, well," Marvin said. "Charlie, welcome home."

Good Knight Kennels

Sherry felt her heart pounding. She kept going, depositing a third and fourth suitcase at the edge of the gravel where May Belle usually parked. The laptop computers, still in their cardboard delivery boxes, were stacked next to the suitcases. Donnie was going to be impressed at how much she had done in the twenty minutes since he had first called. She hadn't stopped for a single cigarette. She started back inside for another load.

She wasn't stupid. They were over-extended. They had done their best. Now it was time to go, and she needed to hold up her end.

It wouldn't do to think about her things. She'd just keep pretending they were going to go away for a night or two. It was a fantasy to tamp down her anxieties.

That and four lorazepam tablets. She gobbled those down, first thing. Maybe she'd be snoring before they drove out to the mailbox. That might be a good thing. She hoped she didn't fall asleep, quit breathing, and die. That would be so horrible for Donnie. He wouldn't do well with the police after him and a dead wife in the van.

Maybe she should go put a finger down her throat and throw up the medication into the toilet. Sherry climbed the stairs to the porch of the house and stopped. Her stomach heaved with uneasiness.

Things were upsetting enough without throwing up. She wasn't dainty with vomiting. If she threw up the lorazepam, she'd have to change clothes, and she might not be able to get the loading finished. Even with the drug coursing through her system, the fear-crazies were lurking at the edge of her eyes. She could feel them.

Sherry swallowed hard and beat back the urge to heave. Best to get on with it. She'd packed clothes for all three of them. Extra shoes too. She had her medicines and her extra eyeglasses. Leashes. What else?

Dog crates. Little Sweetie wasn't often crated. But who knew what lay ahead? It'd be smart to get the dog crates out.

Sherry moved into the house and spoke to her white mop-head of a dog who scampered to her and rotated in circles of excitement.

"Sweetie, just a minute. We'll make this easy." She moved as rapidly as she could to the kitchen. The little dog followed her, ears perked. Sherry opened the refrigerator and took out an aged roll of liverwurst. "Phew. I knew this was ripe. It's really gone."

Sweetie danced at her feet and yipped.

"I hear you. I know you want this."

Sherry shuffled back to the front door, sliding the liverwurst into her cardigan pocket. This time she allowed the dog to exit the house with her, confident Little Sweetie would stay close to the liverwurst. A short tower of small dog crates leaned against the back of the house. Sherry moved three to the gravel parking strip and opened the wire door on one. Thumbing a large gob of liverwurst out of the wrapper, Sherry spoke to Little Sweetie.

"I'm going to throw this into the dog crate and you're going to jump in and get it."

Whether or not the little dog understood, Little Sweetie did as she instructed. As soon as the liverwurst splattered on the back of the plastic crate, the dog raced in to claim the stinky prize. Sherry shut the door and latched it.

She propped open the wire doors on the two remaining crates, and again used her thumb to bait each crate with a glob of liverwurst. Packing the van would be distracting enough without JoJo and Toad jumping around.

"Ugh. I need to wash my hands."

As she started up the steps, she thought about her husband and her sister-in-law and herself. Donnie worked hard. She did what she could on the computer. May Belle was the tough one, keeping an eye on tomorrow and making sure they survived. They'd get through this. They were an interlocking trio, all right.

"Positive self-talk," she murmured. They'd seen this discussed on Oprah. Or was it on Ellen or Dr. Phil? Donnie believed it kept the heebie-jeebies away.

She made it up the steps, breathing hard. She didn't want to put liverwurst on the doorknob. If the door hadn't latched completely, she might be able to open the door with a tap from her hips. She turned to try.

A flicker from headlights caught her eye as a vehicle made its way along the twisting road in the woods above the farm house. A fog-shrouded moon gave just enough light for Sherry to make out a dark car with no lights trailing behind the first vehicle.

"Oh, no! They're here already." Sherry's heart rate soared.

She seized the doorknob, greasing it with liverwurst. She fumbled the door open and half ran to the front closet. Pushing past a curtain of old coats, she found the shotgun, propped in the corner of the closet.

Donnie had said she was to take the shotgun and wait in the shadows at the edge of the barn.

She would do so — if her heart didn't explode first.

Chapter Forty

Laurel slowed her car and watched the taillights of May Belle's van as the vehicle emerged from the trees and descended the drive to a barn and house. A porch light illuminated a gravel parking area and part of the barn.

The truck behind her had turned off its blazing headlights, but she knew it was still behind her, coming slowly. She'd seen its dark shape in the rear-view mirror before the last curve.

Fog surrounded the evergreen huckleberry bushes, and the banks of sword ferns next to the road. The plants of the thick underbrush appeared like dark lace on darker satin. Visibility was better once the road turned away from the trees.

Laurel braked to a stop. She leaned over to the passenger-side and ran her hand over the seat until she found her cell phone. It was time to let someone know where she was.

She tried Zinnie's number. It went to voice mail.

She called Allie.

"It's so nice," Allie babbled. "The people are so kind. We're eating sandwiches at a bonfire."

"Where are you?"

"Zinnie's house. In the driveway. The neighbors chased off May Belle, and we're celebrating. I hit my head earlier, but I'm okay. I feel fine. Well, mostly. My forehead still hurts."

"Um." Laurel thought rapidly. Allie sounded jazzed and jangly. Laurel asked, "Is your Dad there?"

"He went inside. I think he's in the bathroom. He's going back to the tavern in a few minutes to pick up Zinnie and Ursula. He's taking them sandwiches. Do you want me to have him call you before he takes off?"

"No. I'm at the Good Knight Kennels. I'm going to see if I can get Biscuit."

"Oh." Allie put worry into the word. "By yourself?"

"I'll be really careful. I'm not going to get too close to the house. I'm going to park behind a big barn and see if I can grab Biscuit."

"Be careful!"

"I will. Tell your Dad where I am. I'll call soon."

"Okay."

Laurel clicked off, feeling uneasy. The bad guy in the truck was behind her. May Belle and Biscuit and a big man were in the van in front of her and were now almost to the farmhouse.

There wasn't a good place to turn around. She could make out a row of cattails to the left, a sure sign of wet ground.

The bright-lights vehicle behind her should be coming out of the woods any moment. "Be bold," Laurel whispered. "It's just a little dognapping."

Swallowing hard, she flipped the slide toggle for the interior light so the car would remain dark when she opened the door.

She'd park by the barn. She'd get out of the car without the dome light going off. If she was lucky — really lucky — she would be able to dart out and grab Biscuit as the people from the van unloaded. She could hotfoot it back to her car and make an escape with her headlights off, hopefully dodging around the bright-lights vehicle. She wasn't tougher than May Belle, but she was faster.

Laurel inhaled. Her ribs still hurt from the fall at Zinnie's house. She pushed gently on the accelerator, rolling the car down the last hill to the homestead.

* * *

May Belle flexed her shoulders. The muscles of her neck ached with tension, sending stabs of pain up to her skull and down her spine. She kept a white-knuckled grip on the steering wheel and took the last ruts of the road to the farmhouse as smoothly as she could.

She hated know-it-alls. She hated smug people who told her how to improve herself. She hated those slender, casually-but-expensively dressed, highly-educated millennials like the girl in the blue car. Someone like that had no idea how hard it was to make a living when you had no assets and no safety net.

There was too much to worry about. The dogs. The laptops. Their health problems.

They should be able to get Sherry loaded and be on their way quickly. The real challenges would be in a day or two when Sherry began grieving for her things and her anxieties kicked in.

That's what you got with sentimental, artistic sorts.

Donnie would do his best to keep his wife happy. He'd do as much driving as his bad hip and aching back allowed.

May Belle knew it would be up to her to make the hard decisions. Getting to Arkansas with little cash would be the first hurdle. To Donnie, she said, "We should get you to reach out to one of your bowling buddies. Let's see if one of them will come out to the house and take some things to sell."

"Sherry won't like that."

"I know." She pulled in her chin, stretching the tight muscles on the back of her neck. She said, "We need to go as many miles as we can tonight."

"I know."

"Do you think you can drive that blue car all the way to Yakima?"

"I think so. Sherry's got some oxycodone. One of those will help."

"Once we're in Yakima, we can get a motel room and get some sleep."

"If the police are looking for us, aren't they going to be checking motel parking lots?" Donnie asked.

"You're right. We need to change the look of the van. How fast will the cops be looking for the blue car? Maybe we should tie the girl up so she can't report it stolen."

"Or we could cruise through Chehalis and pick up somebody's license plates. If we swap out ours for theirs, the car owner might not even notice for a week or two. Do that for both vehicles."

"Donnie, that's brilliant." May Belle chewed her lower lip. "We should look for somebody who's got a magnetic door sign on their vehicle. If we took that, the van would look like a business van."

"Nah. People got video cameras on their work vehicles. We'd get busted. We can just stop at Walmart and get a stack of military stickers. Get some more at a truck stop. Get an American flag and stick that on. We'll look like we're proud folks with nothing to hide."

May Belle smiled. "That's smart. We'll stop in Chehalis."

Donnie ran his hands over Biscuit. "You ready to give the girl this dog?"

"No. That dog is worth two grand. And I'm not taking any shit from Dr. Ms. Fancy College," May Belle said.

She parked the van on the gravel parking pad in front of the farmhouse, her headlights illuminating the row of dog crates at the edge, one closed and two open.

Donnie said, "Let me put JoJo and Toad away."

"I'll help." May Belle chirped to her dogs, who came bounding up to the front seat. She tucked JoJo under her arm and opened the van door. Donnie grabbed Toad. He pushed open the passenger side door with Toad under one arm and Biscuit under the other.

JoJo and Toad were happy to charge into the liverwurst-spattered crates. Sherry called from the barn's shadow. "I'm over here."

Donnie set Biscuit down on the gravel and went to his wife. "You done good, baby."

"Here. Take this." Sherry offered him the shotgun.

"Better let me," May Belle said, walking to the couple, Biscuit slowly trailed her, peering blindly into the night.

May Belle said, "Donnie needs to load things." She took the shotgun from Sherry. "We're going to take the girl's car. That'll give us seed money."

Sherry's face went white with worry as they heard Laurel's car crunch on the gravel behind the barn and come to a stop.

Peltigera
membranacea

Chapter Forty-one

Laurel sat in her car, studying the layout. She could see part of a gravel parking strip, poorly lit by a dim high porch light from the farmhouse. May Belle's van had turned left in front of the barn and had disappeared.

The barn loomed large on Laurel's left. She heard a dog barking from inside. It was a deep, desperate and constant barking.

Laurel licked her lips, her mouth suddenly very dry. This was not a nice place. She should start the car, back up, and get the hell out of here before the blazing-lights vehicle arrived. Still, it would be smart to let someone know where . . . to find her body.

She rapidly tapped her cell phone and called Allie. "I'm here," she reported in a rush. "I'm just outside a big barn. I'm going to get out and peek around the corner to see if I can see Biscuit."

"Be careful!"

"No kidding. Don't worry. I can outrun these guys. If I have to run into the woods, I will." Laurel surprised herself with her firm statements.

"Okay." Allie accepted Laurel's pronouncement of competence as gospel. Allie said, "I'm waiting to tell my dad about you."

"You haven't told him?"

"He was in the bathroom."

Laurel closed her eyes. She needed to get moving. Did it matter where Marvin was?

"Laurel? Are you there?"

"Yes. I need to get going."

"Okay. Dad just came out of the house. I'll go tell him right now!"

"Thank you."

Allie said, "I'm walking over to him right now. He's talking to a guy and packing some sandwiches."

"Super. Just tell him 'Good Knight Kennels.' That's where I am."

"Okay." Allie swallowed, and said, "Are you sure you are safe? Maybe that place is not so good."

Laurel exhaled. She had assured Allie that she could run to safety, and, acting as a supportive, but young, friend, Allie assumed she was right. Now even Allie's bumped, distracted mind was sending up warning signals.

"I'll be all right."

"This cute guy just showed up," Allie said. "He has a guitar. He could rescue you. I mean, not that you need rescuing. He could back you up maybe."

"I've got this," Laurel said. "Just tell your dad where I am. If I don't call back in an hour, then he should call the police."

"The police?"

"It shouldn't be necessary. It's our backup plan." Laurel tried to infuse her words with confidence. "I'll call as soon as I've got Biscuit." She tapped off the phone and released her seatbelt. It was time to get this done.

She opened the car door and slid out as quietly as she could.

A dark truck emerged from the woods. It rolled down the hill toward the barn with no headlights.

"Oh, Damn," Laurel whispered.

She crept forward to the corner of the barn as the dog inside kept up its deep barks of despondency. A cascade of high, shrill barking joined in.

Laurel frowned. The barn must be full of dogs.

May Belle stepped out from the corner and pointed a shotgun at Laurel's middle. "Welcome to our humble abode," she said.

* * *

Zinnie stood on the brakes. She'd been gently rolling the truck forward, trying to keep Laurel's taillights in sight. When Laurel drove around the curve and descended to the barn, Zinnie had stopped the truck and watched. She whispered a plea for Laurel to her senses and back up.

Finally, Laurel had stepped out of the car, her slender form disappearing into the dark shadow of the barn. Zinnie eased the truck down the hill, headlights off, desperately hoping that she could come up to Laurel and insist they depart.

Then, to her horror, she saw May Belle step out from the front corner of the barn with a shotgun, her round body silhouetted by the light from the farmhouse.

To Zinnie's amazement, Biscuit came into the light, slowly sniffing her way toward May Belle.

Zinnie debated turning on the headlights. It was too risky. She might startle May Belle into pulling the trigger.

The squeak of the truck brakes notified May Belle of Zinnie's presence. May Belle stepped to the right. The shotgun barrels still covered Laurel, but now May Belle had a wider field of fire.

Biscuit started to follow, then stopped and turned toward the truck, cocking her head.

Zinnie rolled down the truck window and yelled, "Don't shoot. We can make a deal."

"Get over here!" May Belle called back. "Get out of the truck and get over here, or I'll shoot the girl!"

"I'm going to turn the lights on so I can see where I'm going," Zinnie yelled back.

She flicked the truck headlights on before May Belle could object, flooding the barn wall and the gravel parking area with light.

Ursula sat up. "Good morning," she said in clear, bright English.

"Mom. Wait here. I've got a situation going." Zinnie spoke as quietly and as firmly as she could. To May Belle, she called, "I'm coming."

Zinnie opened the truck door and stepped out. She put her hands up in the air, and walked down the road, coming to a stop a few feet to the right of Laurel.

"Sorry," Laurel said. "I thought I knew what I was doing."

May Belle motioned with the shotgun. "This way."

Before Laurel and Zinnie could move, they heard the squeak of the truck door.

Ursula stepped out of the truck.

She started down the rutted drive with a surprisingly strong stride. Biscuit's tail began wagging. The blonde cocker spaniel took on a silvery cast under the intense truck lights. Biscuit's feet did an arthritic dance, and her tail became a blur of motion as Ursula moved closer.

"Get back!" May Belle shouted. "Get back in the truck."

Ursula flicked a hand at May Belle, shooing her off like an irritating fly.

Zinnie's hands were still in the air. She slowly lowered them and said, "My mother's not in her right mind. You know that."

"We just want the dog," Laurel said. "We don't want any trouble. Let us go."

Ursula kept walking.

"You need to get back!" May Belle commanded. "I'll shoot!"

Biscuit dashed forward, and Ursula knelt to sweep the little dog into her arms. "*Hündchen!*"

Sherry stepped out of the shadow of the barn. "Don't shoot, Mabel. We can't be shooting grannies."

Donnie followed his wife. "We don't want that."

"I'm sure we can work something out," Zinnie said.

Ursula stood up, teetering a bit with the effort of lifting Biscuit, who did her level best to wash all of Ursula's face. The old woman smiled as she stroked the dog and crooned baby names in German.

Ignoring Donnie and Sherry and the howls of the dogs in the dark barn, Ursula crossed the gravel parking lot, carrying Biscuit. She followed the lights of the truck to the ragged

Cypress tree, stopping at the far edge of the parking area where wisps of grass invaded the gravel. She knelt down to the ground and spoke softly to the dog as she pointed at something in the grass.

"Get her back!" May Belle swung the shotgun toward Ursula. "You get her back in the truck, or I'll shoot her."

Chapter Forty-two

"Charlie, I'm headed out to pick up your mother and grandmother from Buzz's Tavern," Marvin said. "Do you want to come along?"

"Mom and Grandmom are at a tavern? How'd that happen?"

"It's a bit of a story."

Allie walked over from the bonfire and said, "Laurel called. She said to tell you she's at the *Good Knight Kennels*. She's going to rescue Biscuit."

"By herself?"

"*Ja.* She said she'd run into the woods if there was a problem." Allie smiled at Charlie. "If you are Charlie, your mother is fantastic. She saved my life by waving her breasts at a tow truck driver."

"I am Charlie, and that does not sound like my mother."

Marvin turned to her, "Does Laurel want us to come out to the kennels?"

"I'm not sure. She said she'd call as soon as she has Biscuit. If an hour goes by, we should tell the police. She sounded like she is okay, but I am some worried."

"Stop a minute," Charlie said. "The police? And who's Laurel?"

"A colleague of Zinnie's," Marvin said. "She went after May Belle Pope, who took a dog that your grandmother loves. If Laurel is confronting May Belle, I think it could be dangerous."

"Laurel is really nice," Allie offered. She looked at Charlie and said, "I think you should rescue her."

Marvin stared at Allie. "Are you okay?"

"*Ja.* Well, maybe a little tired."

Tilly Chen was nearby, and Marvin waved to her, calling, "Can you help us?"

"Of course!" Tilly slid through the merrymakers and arrived at Marvin's elbow.

He said, "I'm supposed to pick up Zinnie and Ursula, but I'm thinking I should take Allie to the Emergency room. She's not her usual self."

"Noooo." Allie's face contorted. "I want to stay here. I'm just a little tired. I'm okay."

Tilly scanned Allie's face. "Let's get you down to my house." She turned to Marvin, "I'll put her on the sofa in the family room. It should be quiet. I'll keep a close eye on her."

Marvin checked Allie's eyes by the light of a streetlamp.

"The pupils look the same size," Marvin concluded.

"I'm good. I'm going to take a nap and then maybe play some bridge. I will tell Tilly if something changes. You should go." Allie's voice was fierce. "Zinnie and Ursula need to come home — and you should check on Laurel."

Marvin turned to Charlie and said, "She's right. We should get moving."

"Let's do it." Charlie weaved through the party-goers to take his guitar into Zinnie's house. He returned quickly, grabbing a second sandwich and his rucksack before folding his long frame into the passenger side of the Prius.

Marvin backed the car into the street and said, "Let's hope we're done with adventures."

"Wha 'appen'd?" Charlie's mouth was full of tuna fish. He swallowed and tried again. "What happened?"

"Your mother brought in an eldercare helper named May Belle Pope. Only she's not an eldercare helper — she's a rip off artist. She started stealing things right away."

"Including my mom's credit card?"

"I'm afraid so."

"Why didn't Mom just throw this witch out on her ear?"

"It took Zinnie a while to realize what was going on. I mean, we knew right away that things were weird, but you don't want to jump to criminal complaints until you're certain."

"Thieves don't need long if they're good."

"Good point." Marvin eased the car over the speed bump and accelerated. "Give us some credit for making progress. May

Belle's gone now, the neighbors are unified in protecting your mother and grandmother, and we've learned that May Belle has at least one assistant. Earlier this evening a large man grabbed my Allie and threw her into the back of his pickup. Your mother jumped in and managed to signal for help."

"Doing a strip routine?"

Marvin smiled. "Yes, indeed."

"I think you'd better drive faster," Charlie said. "I'm an expert on the topic of impulse control, and it sounds like my mother has lost all of hers."

Good Knight Kennels

Zinnie's eyes flashed around the group, seeking a path to defuse tensions. She said, "I'm sure we can work something out."

May Belle stared at her. Zinnie lowered her eyes and turned her palms up. May Belle jerked her head toward Laurel's car. "Donnie, pull the car up."

To Zinnie, she said, "We're taking this car." May Belle's eyes darted toward Ursula's kneeling form and then back to Zinnie. May Belle's face firmed into flat planes of anger. She said, "Go stand next to your mother. Both of you." She pointed the shotgun at Laurel.

Zinnie stood fast, but held out her hands, palms up, and said, "Let's see what we can work out. I can tell this has been very stressful for you."

Laurel rocked back on her heels and made eye contact with Zinnie, who gave her a small nod.

"I'm so sorry I caused you stress this evening," Laurel said, taking a small step to the left, away from Zinnie. "I wasn't my usual self."

"You were a pain in the ass." May Belle trained the shotgun on Laurel's midsection. "Get over there."

"Physics," Zinnie said gently. "You can't shoot all three of us with two barrels of a shotgun. Not when we're separated like this. We'd be crazy to go stand next to my mom. We're not going to do that, but we don't want any trouble. Let's work something out."

May Belle swung the shotgun toward Zinnie. "Don't boss me!"

"You can take the car," Zinnie said. "Go. Go quickly. The police are on their way."

"Ease up, Sis." Donnie edged past May Belle. Laurel stepped back to let him pass. Zinnie took the moment to move a few inches farther from May Belle.

Donnie opened the door to the Nissan. He turned to put his rear down on the driver's seat, but then he couldn't get his legs in. He reached under the seat to pull the adjustment lever. The seat remained forward.

"Where's the seat adjust?" he called.

"The back seats are folded down," Laurel told him. "You have to remove the headrests from the back seats, and then you can move the front seat. I'm sorry it's so complicated."

"We're not stupid," May Belle shouted. The dogs inside the barn had fallen silent. May Belle's loud voice triggered another round of barking.

"Sis," Donnie said. "Come on. Let's just get going. He levered himself out of the driver's seat. He stooped to look into the back of the car.

"Let me, Donnie." Sherry came out of the shadow of the barn. "I'll fit."

She slid into the driver's seat, leaving the car door open. She spoke to Laurel. "I need the keys, dearie."

"It's an electric car," Laurel told her. "With a button start."

"Oh. That's why it's so quiet!" Sherry looked around the car interior in wonder. "There's no dome light?"

"I turned it off." Laurel turned to speak to May Belle. "You can have the car. No problem. Let me show her the switches."

May Belle grunted. Laurel stepped over and pointed at the slider at the base of the ceiling light.

Sherry reached up and tabbed the light on. "Oh. Wow. Look at this dash, Donnie. There's a computer screen!"

May Belle interrupted. "We're not car shopping, Sherry! We've got to get going."

"All right. All right." Sherry put on the seatbelt. She reached to pull the car door closed just as the wind picked up, swirling leaves across the parking strip.

"May I have my jacket please?" Laurel said.

"Sure." Sherry reached for the purple rain jacket. It stuck as she pulled.

Sherry leaned toward the passenger seat and pulled harder.

The jacket came off the jar, leaving Sherry eye-to-eyeball with the Cyclops lamb.

"To see things in the seed, that is genius."
Lao Tzu

Chapter Forty-three

Sherry screamed. She fought the seat belt latch with a flurry of her hands before hitting the release and fighting her way out of the driver's seat. The purple jacket came with her, empty sleeves flapping like bat wings.

Donnie swept his wife into his arms as Laurel grabbed the jacket and slid behind Donnie.

Zinnie felt a flood of relief. If May Belle shot at Laurel now, she'd be shooting her brother and sister-in-law too.

Sherry kept screaming.

"What did you do to her?" May Belle shouted. "Make it stop!"

"It's a biological specimen in a jar," Laurel shouted back. "It won't hurt you." Inside the barn, the barking dogs picked up the pace, now sounding like machine gun fire.

Zinnie stepped over to pat Sherry's back. "I recognize that jar. It's from the biology department's collection. It's a silly thing. It's not going to hurt you."

"Get away from her!" May Belle moved closer.

"Don't hurt Donnie and Sherry." Zinnie's voice came out firm and clear. "I read about Donnie and Sherry on your kennel website page while I was waiting at the tavern. I only had a few minutes on a borrowed phone, but I could see Donnie loves dogs, and Sherry loves crochet."

May Belle's stopped. Her eyes narrowed. She thrust the shotgun out.

"I'm a biologist," Zinnie said. "I study ecosystems and how parts work together. Donnie is a producer. He works hard. He shares what he has."

Donnie swallowed hard and stared at Zinnie.

"I read your blog, Donnie. You were a truck driver until your back and hip gave out. Truck driving is hard on the body."

He nodded and tightened his hug around Sherry, who rained tears down his shirtfront.

"Your body responded to its environment," Zinnie said. "Too many hours sitting can cause muscle groups to tighten and atrophy, particularly the psoas muscles which can shorten and pull the lower spine forward. It can be very painful."

Zinnie kept her eyes on May Belle and the shotgun as she continued in reasonable tones. Zinnie said, "I spend too much time at the computer, and it causes neck and shoulder muscles to move out of alignment. It's worse for Sherry."

May Belle's eyes cut to her sister-in-law.

Encouraged, Zinnie said, "Sherry writes on her blog about her fibromyalgia. We've learned that a person's nervous system can go on 'high alert' so pain sensors are always screaming. Despite her pain, she keeps up the kennel website. I know she spends a lot of time on the computer because it's a beautiful website." Zinnie kept a hand on Sherry's back as she added, "I'm not surprised to see that Sherry is a textile artist."

"Textile artist" was a generous term for Sherry's crochet, considering the photos of neon-colored scarves posted on Sherry's blog, but now was a time to stir in cream and sugar. Zinnie took a breath to keep up her patter.

"Creating art and loving animals can calm the nervous system," she said. "So can collecting things." Zinnie personalized her next comment, "May Belle, think how destroyed Sherry and Donnie will be if you go blasting our bodies with a shotgun. There will be blood and guts and brain bits everywhere."

May Belle's eyes narrowed. The barking of the dogs inside the barn mercifully subsided.

"It would be such a mess," Zinnie said. "No matter where on the property you take us, Donnie and Sherry will hear the shots. Or if you take us off in the woods and come back alone, they'll still know you left us bleeding and broken."

Sherry burst into a fresh rain of tears. Donnie stroked her back and said, "She's right, May Belle. I couldn't bear it. Sherry neither."

"Let's come up with an alternative that works for everyone," Zinnie said. She needed to strengthen the connection with Donnie. He seemed to be reachable. She said, "I've been frantic and overwhelmed. I'm anxious, and I haven't been having much fun. Driving Donnie's old truck is wonderful fun. It's a marvelous truck."

There was a brief smile from Donnie, which disappeared as Ursula called to them. *Kommen Sie and sehen Sie die blauen Schwammal!"* She pointed while Biscuit's tail wagged like a rapid-set metronome.

May Belle swiveled. She pointed the shotgun in Ursula's direction, putting Zinnie's heart rate into high gear.

Zinnie said, "She's just looking for the blue mushrooms again. She's no trouble."

"I think she's *found* them," Laurel said. "Look!"

A trio of mushrooms stood a few centimeters tall, sprouting from the needle duff. The bright lights of the truck illuminated them beautifully. They were a handsome navy blue, fading to black at the edge of the light.

"My God." Zinnie whispered. "Do you see? There really are some blue mushrooms."

"Oh. They are so pretty!" Sherry wiped her eyes and stared. "Donnie, look."

Her husband nodded. "I see, baby. They're really nice."

Laurel pointed. "There are more in back."

Sherry slowly started moving. She pulled Donnie along, holding his hand. "I want a closer look," she said.

The pair stopped next to Ursula and marveled.

Donnie called to his sister, "These are *amazing*. You should come see."

Zinnie spoke to May Belle with an added urgency. "Please go take a quick look. We're not your enemies. We're just people trying to live and learn. You don't want to kill us. The police will be out here sooner or later. Let's take paths that don't lead to jail."

May Belle swallowed. Her voice came out raspy, but firm. "You're not going to just let us go."

"Yes! I am!" Zinnie nodded. "May Belle, I'm a lichenologist. I see Donnie as the green algae — the producer layer of a lichen. I see Sherry as the yeast of the lichen that provides color. Now, don't take this wrong, but I see you as the fungus — which doesn't sound nice, but it means you are the tough one. You provide shelter and protection. The three of you can travel and thrive in another location. Lichens break off and travel in the wind and rain all the time."

As if on cue, the breeze rose again, swirling leaves across the gravel.

"Take your dogs and your family," Zinnie urged. "Take those laptops. I'll put the keys back in the truck, and you can get a friend to deliver it or sell it. But you need to get going!"

Donnie heard them. "Come on, Sis. Take a look and let's go." He still held Sherry's hand and now he tugged her hand, moving toward the silver van. "Sis, she's right. If we're gonna have any chance, we gotta go."

"What about the blue car?" May Belle's chin thrust at the Nissan.

"Takes too much time," Donnie said. "Sherry's not going to drive it, and I'm too big. We gotta go, Sis. Now."

May Belle looked at Zinnie and said, "You stay there. The girl stays still too."

"No problem," Laurel said.

May Belle broke open the shotgun and draped it over her arm before walking across the gravel to stand next to Ursula, who still knelt in the grass.

Ursula looked up and smiled. Biscuit wagged her tail.

May Belle smiled back and said, "Those are pretty mushrooms. I didn't know there were blue ones."

Ursula's smile widened. "*Ja*," she said. "*Sie existieren.*"

The wind freshened and blew the drift of leaves farther. Zinnie stood still, mentally straining to be calm. She wanted to race to her mother and make sure Ursula was not too cold. She wanted to go home. She wanted Marvin.

That last thought surprised her. She didn't take time to mull on it. Donnie helped his wife into the van and began loading the dog crates. JoJo and Toad barked as they were ferried to the van. Answering barks came from inside the barn.

"Feed the dogs?" Donnie called. "Find them a home?"

"Yes. I promise!" Zinnie said.

May Belle waited until Donnie heaved himself into the front passenger seat of the van. With a rocklike face, May Belle carried the shotgun to the shadow of the barn. She looked at Zinnie as she extracted two shells, unloading the gun.

"I don't want this gun in the van if we get pulled over," May Belle said. "So, I'm leaving it."

"Thank you," Zinnie said.

"I'm taking the shells. You won't be able to shoot this."

"Understood."

May Belle closed the shotgun and leaned it against the barn. She strode to the van and took her place in the driver's seat.

Zinnie closed her eyes in relief as the van started. May Belle drove past, grimly navigating around Laurel's car and Donnie's truck. The vehicle slowly moved up the dirt road, taillights shining a red-eyed farewell. Zinnie waited until the van was a hundred yards down the road before exhaling a sigh of relief.

Laurel beat her to Ursula. The young woman knelt down next to the old, speaking softly. "Wow. You did it. You found blue mushrooms."

Ursula smiled.

Zinnie joined them. She squatted down, reaching to fondle Biscuit's ears. "You are quite a pair. Come on. Let's go home."

Ursula shook her head. "*Nein.*"

"Mom. It's late. Clouds are moving in. It'll start raining after a while, and I think it's going to get a lot colder. We haven't eaten. We need to go home."

"*Nein.*"

Zinnie stood up. She rubbed her eyes and exhaled. She did not want to manhandle her mother. She looked over at Laurel in her jacket, now a deep, radiant purple in the rays of the truck high beams. Zinnie said, "Got any ideas?"

"I've got a granola bar in the car. Food as a lure?"

"She hates granola bars. She says they taste like sawdust. We could offer her some of your pickled lamb."

Laurel burst out laughing. "Let me call Allie and give her an update."

"Okay. Maybe they can talk in German." Zinnie smiled at her young colleague and said, "Thank you. Thank you for risking your life to find Biscuit and helping my mother and me."

"Glad to. We members of the Order of the Silver Shield need to stick together."

"And I shouldn't mention this to your parents?"

Laurel's snort of agreement was interrupted by another round of desperate barking from inside the barn.

"I think we should feed those dogs," Laurel said.

"Right. And we should move the puppies in from the truck."

"What about your mom?"

"Until we come up with a workable lure, I think she's not moving." Zinnie rubbed her face. "We're not done yet."

Chapter Forty-four

Marvin said, "When I last saw them, they were sitting in an old truck, and your grandmother was holding a pair of puppies." He steered the car through the narrow strip of gravel remaining at Buzz's Tavern. The parking lot was now filled to overflowing.

"I'm having a hard time picturing that, but okay." Charlie's head swiveled as he spoke. "I don't think they're here."

Marvin braked as his phone chimed. He stopped by the front door of the tavern and tapped his phone. "Laurel! Are you all right?"

Charlie arched an eyebrow as two young women came out of the tavern. One grinned at him and waved. Charlie waved back, a dimple forming as he smiled. He tabbed down the car window and said, "Hey! Ashley and Ashley! How are you?"

"Great! We're headed over to Skip and Skein next. Wanna come?"

"Thanks, but we're here to pick up my mom and grandmom. You haven't seen them, have you?"

"Here?" The Ashleys giggled. "No."

Charlie heard their opinions on the local party scene until one Ashley pulled back, saying, "Getting cold. Catch you later." The two women waggled fingers and sauntered off, arm in arm, the rhinestones on rear jeans pockets flashing in the dim light.

Charlie enjoyed the view.

Marvin punched his upper arm and hissed, "Focus!"

"What?" Charlie rubbed his arm. "You were on the phone. I can't enjoy the scenery?"

"That was Laurel. She's with your mom and grandmother and they need our help."

"Remind me. Who's Laurel?"

Marvin put the Prius into drive and spoke as he pulled out of the tavern parking lot, turning right onto Mud Bay road. "A young instructor at the college. A friend. A very brave friend.

She followed our thief, May Belle, to her lair! It sounds like Laurel's managed to get Biscuit back — that's the dog your grandmother likes."

"Is she cute?"

"Adorable. Shaggy blonde hair and soulful brown eyes. I think. She has cataracts, so it's hard to tell about the eyes. I'll bet they're brown. Lovely personality. Loves to cuddle."

"Laurel has cataracts and loves to cuddle?"

"Ah, no. Biscuit does."

"Okay. And Laurel?"

"Down, boy. Laurel is a friend," Marvin said, "I'm rather certain your mother feels protective of her. Laurel's twenty-four and a newly minted Ph.D. who is working very hard."

"Twenty-four and a Ph.D? Jesus, I'm twenty-eight and just starting mine."

"She's smart. When she comes across as young, it's because she is."

"Hmm."

"She followed May Belle to an old farmhouse off Highway 410. She said May Belle had a shotgun out, but your mom talked her out of shooting."

"What?" Marvin had Charlie's full attention.

"From what Laurel just told me, your mom delivered a lecture on lichenology and the bad guys left," Marvin said.

"The lecture I can believe — but Mom's okay?"

"Mostly."

"Whad'ya mean 'mostly'?"

"Ursula found some blue mushrooms. She's sitting with Biscuit and refuses to get up. Laurel said they were going to feed some dogs in the barn and then try again with Ursula. I said we'd come help."

"Hmm. Blue mushrooms this time of year might be a late *Leptonia*. They can grow in disturbed sites. Cool." Charlie rummaged in his rucksack. "I'll bet I can get Grandmom to move."

* * *

Laurel clicked on the light switch, activating a row of wan bulbs set high overhead in the rafters of the barn. The lights triggered a scramble of paws and waves of barking.

She did a quick scan. Most of the noise was coming from a trio of terriers whose barking sounded like machine gun fire. A black Labrador retriever with two puppies joined in with a deeper, more desperate voice.

"Quiet!" she yelled. The Labrador subsided. The terriers ignored her and yammered on. They charged their pen fence, snapping.

Laurel left the barn. She went out to the parking strip, easily navigating by the porch light and the light cast by the truck's high beam headlights. She could see Ursula was still kneeling on the ground, holding Biscuit and admiring the mushroom patch. Zinnie stood up from her squat next to her mother and came to join Laurel.

"What's it like in there?" Zinnie asked.

"Not as bad as it sounds. There're three barky dogs that are wild little beasts. They may be vicious, but they are in a secure pen, and there's a black mom dog with two more puppies. Stinks a bit."

"Let me give you a hand." They walked up to the truck where Zinnie opened the truck passenger door and picked up a puppy, who roused and yawned. She passed the pup to Laurel.

"Ooh, so cute!" Laurel cuddled the puppy. "I can carry them both."

"Good." Zinnie handed her the second pup. "I want to keep an eye on Mom. If she wanders off at this point, I think I'll lose my mind completely."

"I'll put these two with the others, and I'll see about getting the dogs fed." Laurel carried the pups into the barn and set them into the pen with their delighted mother.

Laurel picked up the bowls in the pen and found two bins of dog food. One looked like puppy kibble. Unsure of feeding quantity, she went for a generous filling of each bowl, hoping she wasn't going to make a dog sick. The happy Labrador family went into ecstasy overdrive when she returned with the full bowls.

That left the terriers.

These three charged the pen gate, snapping. Laurel studied them and decided against retrieving the dog food bowl from their run. She fetched a scoop of kibble and reached high over the pen gate to pour the dog food onto the floor of the pen. It wasn't sanitary, but it was better than being bitten.

The terriers fell into muffled growls as they snapped up the kibble rolling across the dirty floor of the pen. In the bark-free quiet Laurel heard a car door slam.

Marvin. He must have arrived.

Laurel stepped through the open door of the barn She noticed the shotgun propped against the outside wall.

"That should be put away," she murmured. "Even unloaded, it's not something to leave out." She carefully picked up the shotgun and pointed it to the ground as she walked out of the shadow of the barn.

"Marvin said to be nice to you. Since you're holding a shotgun, I think it's really good advice."

The voice came from Laurel's right. She swung to look, keeping the shotgun pointed down. A tall, dark-haired man stepped out from the corner of the barn. His broad shoulders cast a wide shadow, which tapered to a lean waist and long, long legs.

He smiled, showing a cheek dimple and glorious white teeth. Laurel swallowed hard and stared as he said, "Hi. I'm Charlie. I'm here to rescue you."

Chapter Forty-five

Zinnie felt a wave of relief when she saw Marvin's Prius glide into the light of the farmyard. No matter what Ursula did next, it was going to be better managed with Marvin here.

The certainty rising in her mind calmed and invigorated. She was glad Marvin was part of her life.

Her heart soared with a great swoop of happiness when her son Charlie stepped out of the car. He waved to her and then turned his head toward the barn door. Zinnie could see Laurel framed in the entrance, head down, walking toward the shotgun.

Charlie waggled fingers at his mother and stepped toward Laurel.

Zinnie snorted. Charlie knew his mother would wait.

Marvin was already striding down the rutted drive toward her. Zinnie creaked to a stand and smiled at him. When Marvin reached her, he opened his arms, and she stepped in, embracing him and drinking in his warm, clean smell.

"I'm so glad you're okay," he said into her hair.

She pulled back from the embrace and said, "It was a bit scary for a few minutes."

"Are you ready to go home?"

"Absolutely, but Mom found her blue mushrooms, and she won't get up."

"Charlie said he has an idea," Marvin said.

As if on cue, Charlie and Laurel began walking across the farmyard, with Charlie talking as Laurel's face produced a bigger and bigger smile. They joined Marvin and Zinnie.

"Hi, Mom!"

"Hello, Charlie." Zinnie embraced her son.

"Nice place you've got here."

Zinnie burst out laughing. "Don't get started. I'm cold, and I'm hungry, and I need to find a bathroom. We have to get your grandmother in the mind to move so we can go home."

"Go in the house for the bathroom," Charlie said. "The bad guys are gone, right?" He winked at Laurel. "See how brilliant I am? Social conventions are for breaking, especially when no one is present to complain."

"You know," said Zinnie, "You have a point. I will go find a bathroom. I'm going to look around for my hummingbird picture too."

"They took the Buzz and Bloom picture?" Charlie whistled. "No wonder you had a shotgun out."

Zinnie laughed.

"Go on, Mom," Charlie said. "I'll work on Grandmom."

"All right," Zinnie said. "Laurel, we can park the shotgun inside and hunt for my picture. These guys can figure out how to charm my mother away from the blue mushrooms."

Charlie watched Zinnie enter the farmhouse, his sense of relief mixed with guilt. His mother had survived a confrontation, but she needed a haircut. She'd gained some weight. Clearly, she'd been under stress, and he hadn't been home to help.

Well, he was home now.

He turned to Marvin. "Laurel seems steady."

"Yes, she is."

Charlie nodded. He'd resisted the temptation to take the shotgun from Laurel. He didn't think she would have responded well to his Y chromosome wanting to control the firepower. There was some steel behind the wonderment in her young eyes.

He liked that.

A raindrop hit. Clouds were moving in. The breeze now held an edge of iciness.

"Any ideas to get your grandmother to leave her mushrooms?" Marvin asked.

"Let's go see what we've got." Charlie crossed the gravel parking strip and knelt down next to Ursula who now sat, cross-legged, with Biscuit in her lap.

"Hi, Grandmom."

Ursula looked at him with no recognition. Her eyes swept to Marvin. She huddled down, looking frightened. She held Biscuit close.

"He's okay. We're here to see your fabulous mushrooms," Charlie said. "Mind if I take a look?"

Ursula thought for a moment, then nodded.

Charlie plucked a mushroom and started talking to Ursula. "I'm seeing a handsome navy-blue mushroom. Sorta velvety, don't you think?"

Ursula looked at the mushroom, but she didn't speak. Charlie kept on, "Nice depression in the cap. Looks like someone dented it with a thumb — like when we make thumbprint cookies. Nice straight stipe ending in a white mycelium clump." He tilted the mushroom so the underside was illuminated from the truck's high beams. "Pale, wide-spaced gills. But what really draws my eye is how the gills are attached. Decurrent gills."

He paused, then whispered in a conspiratorial tone, "Shall we tear into this one a bit?"

Slowly Ursula nodded. Charlie pulled the stem of the mushroom apart. "No surprise. A nice white, fibrous interior." He sniffed the mushroom. "Not much of anything. 'Indistinct', if we go for the academic term." He held the mushroom up to Marvin, who dutifully sniffed it.

Ursula watched and leaned in, clearly expecting a turn. Charlie brought the mushroom down to her level. She sniffed and smiled. "Indistinct," she mumbled.

Charlie said, "I'd call it *Arrhenia chlorocyanea*, also known as the Verdigris Navel. I'd like to come out tomorrow and look at these in the daylight. I'm thinking this is more often a winter mushroom, but, hey, we're almost to Thanksgiving, so maybe these guys just got an early start. Worth checking out a bit more, don't you think?"

Ursula listened and nodded her head once more.

Charlie rocked back on his heels and looked up as Zinnie and Laurel came down the steps of the farmhouse, Laurel without the shotgun, and Zinnie with a framed photo under her arm.

"Got a plan?" Zinnie called.

"Yep." Charlie stood up. "I think we're going to waltz."

"Waltz?" Laurel asked.

"Yep. Marvin, can you waltz with my mom?"

"Of course! Marvin said. "I grew up in a Polish neighborhood. I can waltz, I can drink beer, and I can polka."

"Good. Give me a minute." Charlie loped up to Marvin's car and came back with his rucksack. He pulled out a tiny canister. "Portable speaker," he said. He plugged the wires into his cell phone and began tapping.

"I'm not quite following you, son." Zinnie said.

"You're going to waltz with Marvin. I'm going to waltz with Laurel. We're going to ignore Grandmom."

"I get it." Zinnie grinned. "She's going to want a turn."

"If we're lucky. She seems to want to be included."

"I don't know how to waltz," Laurel said. She sniffed her hand. "I smell like liverwurst."

Zinnie laughed. "Me too. This has been the strangest night."

"Which is good," Charlie said. "It can just get a little stranger, and we'll have a nice story to tell." To Laurel, he said, "Waltzing isn't hard. Count to three. For you, one big step back with the right, two little ones. Then a big step back with the left and keep going." Charlie winked. "You'll be in good hands. Hands of someone who likes liverwurst."

He tapped his smart phone and the lilting voice of an oboe sang out from the speaker followed by a staccato burst of brass. Marvin bowed and offered a hand to Zinnie. She accepted, and they were off, swirling across the parking lot.

A flute solo warbled out of the speaker as Charlie extended a hand to Laurel. She saw Ursula turn her head and look up. Laurel smiled at Charlie and stepped into his arms as the *Tales of the Vienna Woods* poured out of the speaker.

They danced in sweeping circles, Laurel's body tense at first before she relaxed to embrace the rhythm and the joy of the music. Charlie was an excellent dancer, leading confidently and kindly until the big crescendos where he firmed his hand on her back and enlarged their circles, moving with speed and grace.

The music ended and they stopped, breathless and smiling.

"Here's where we do our thing," Charlie said. He took Laurel by the hand and led her to Ursula who had watched the entire waltz. Charlie stopped by Ursula and bent down to tap another selection on his phone. The opening bars of *The Skater's Waltz* rang out. Ursula leaned forward, recognition blossoming on her face.

Charlie stroked Biscuit's ears before gently lifting the dog from his grandmother's arms. He handed Biscuit to Laurel, then turned to offer an open hand to his grandmother.

"May I have this dance?" he said.

Ursula took his hand and rose stiffly.

Charlie bestowed his most charming smile, a dazzling event. "Thank you," he said.

Slowly he gathered his grandmother into his arms and they waltzed gently around the graveled parking strip with the high beams of the old truck illuminating their circles as the troop of blue mushrooms gleamed in the background.

Fall leaves whirled and fluttered at their feet as the tall man and his fragile grandmother waltzed with a slow grace. Zinnie stood at the edge of the gravel, holding hands with Marvin as tears streamed down her face.

After all the challenges of Charlie's teenage and the hardship of this last year, this moment was such perfection it left her weeping with love.

As the last bars of the waltz sounded, Charlie pivoted to take his grandmother near to Marvin's Prius. The music ended, and Charlie announced, "Ah! Your carriage has arrived!" He opened the car door, and Ursula sank into the passenger seat, looking fatigued, but also smiling.

Charlie helped her fasten the seatbelt as Laurel quickly brought Biscuit across the gravel and deposited the dog onto Ursula's lap.

"Well done," Marvin said. "Amazing."

Sniffing and smiling, Zinnie said, "We should go before Mom changes her mind and wants a second dance."

"Why don't you ride with Marvin," Charlie said. "And I'll catch a ride with Laurel?" Charlie raised an eyebrow at Laurel, who made no objection.

"Fine." Zinnie retrieved her hummingbird picture from the farmhouse porch. "Will you turn off the truck lights?"

"Okay. Do me a favor?" Charlie said.

"Sure," Zinnie said. "What do you need?"

"See if the police will send an officer out to the house to take a report. They might want the whole story." Charlie grinned. "I know I do."

Chapter Forty-six

9:45 p.m. Monday

"You let them drive away?" Charlie shook his head.

Sergeant Martinez sat at the kitchen table with a notepad and a cup of cocoa. "That was a smart thing to do," he said. "We don't always get a nice ending when a firearm is present."

"But it's not a nice ending if the bad guys get away!" Charlie protested.

Zinnie shook her head. "Think of this ecologically. I didn't at first, and that is what got me into trouble. In *every* ecosystem there are predators and parasites, including the eldercare ecosystem. I was so frazzled and reactive that I didn't keep an eye out for the predator part of the landscape."

"It's hard to do," Sergeant Martinez said. "We don't have enough tools in law enforcement to catch them."

"So, how do you stop them from robbing somebody else?" Charlie's cheeks puffed out with exasperation.

"I tell my story," Zinnie said. "And I keep in mind that May Belle might have turned out differently if she wasn't so overwhelmed. I don't think she was born a predator, but became one."

"This particular group has a guy who kidnapped a teenager and tried to carjack a car with a baby," Sergeant Martinez said. "We know the van they are driving. I'll have an APB out for them shortly." He drained the cocoa cup. "In fact, I need to get on it. Thanks for your help, and the hot chocolate."

Marvin arrived as Sergeant Martinez was leaving. "My daughter's fallen asleep. We spoke for a few minutes and she seems astonishingly normal."

"Good," Sergeant Martinez said. He pulled a business card out of his pocket. "I'd appreciate it if Allie would call in tomorrow and check with our detectives. They may have further questions, and they can update her on our efforts to pick up her kidnapper."

"I'll make sure she calls." Marvin shook the officer's hand and said good-bye. To Zinnie, Charlie and Laurel, he said, "We'll get the locks changed tomorrow too."

"Thank you," Zinnie said. "I'm so glad we're all safe."

"Allie likes the bridge club," Marvin said. "Tilly said she was very charming. I think she'll be her usual self tomorrow." Marvin grinned. "Oh, joy."

Zinnie laughed. "She won't be fifteen forever."

"How's Ursula?" Marvin asked.

"Deeply asleep. Biscuit too. I need to get some dog kibble tomorrow."

"I can research dog food brands for you," Laurel said.

Zinnie eyed her. "Don't tell me there are decision trees with dog food too. The door locks choices are bad enough."

Charlie laughed. "Mom, you're out of date. For dogs there's all sorts of protein-carb mixes. Bison and Duck with sweet potato. Salmon with brown rice. Rabbit and Alligator too."

"Rabbit and alligator? You're pulling my leg."

"Not this time," Charlie said. "There's puppy kibble, weight-loss kibble, and senior kibble."

Zinnie sat back in her chair. "There has to be an evolutionary aspect to this plethora of offerings."

Laurel yawned. "When you figure it out let me know, and I'll be a warm body assistant to get second billing on the paper you write."

"Deal." Zinnie looked at her young colleague. "You were so brave to go after Biscuit. Thank you so very much."

Laurel flushed.

"How brave are you, Laurel?" Charlie's eyes sparkled. "Brave enough to go back with me to the farmyard tomorrow to key out the blue mushrooms?"

Laurel sat back in her chair and thought a moment. "We have to go out there to feed the dogs in the barn, so sure, I'll look at mushrooms too."

She tilted her head to smile sweetly at Charlie. "We actually need to get those dogs to the animal shelter. I can manage the puppies. Perhaps you could help with the terriers? They are a bit lively."

"Lively is my middle name," Charlie said.

Zinnie laughed. "Shame on you, Laurel. You called those terriers 'wild little beasts.' If there's anything I've learned on this adventure, it's knowing the worth of experts. Let's call Sergeant Martinez and have him connect us with an animal control officer."

Laurel smiled and shrugged. "All right. I wanted Charlie to have a memorable initiation into the Order of the Silver Shield, but initiation can wait."

"The Order of what?" Charlie said.

"The Order of the Silver Shield," Marvin said. "We unite as a lichen does, each with a contribution to make, with improved survival for all. Our first mission was to protect Zinnie." Marvin looked across the kitchen table to meet Zinnie's smiling eyes. "I'm sure our Order will grow from here."

Parmelia sulcata

And then . . .

Epilogue

Summit College is launching an innovative summer program, *Natural Sciences for Athletes*. This six-week program will have students immerse in ecosystems in the Puget Sound area, including the Salish Sea, tidal zones, estuaries, forests and alpine habitats. Participants are expected to be physically fit for canoeing, hiking and rock climbing.

In the third and sixth week of the program, students will make individual and group presentations on species or habitats in written, spoken, and art formats. Each presentation week will include one-on-one support from the Writing Center to develop and enhance productions to meet collegiate level standards. Students can earn up to eight credits in biology and two additional credits in either communications or art.

Contact Dr. Laurel Baumgarten for more information.

Ready for another chapter of Fungal-rich fiction? Read on for a sample of *The EvoAngel*

How to help Writers of Fungal Fiction

This is an independently published book. The narrator of wild mushroom adventures is such an odd and rare creature that many (gasp!) have never heard of her.

Please do your bit to support the odd mushrooms of the literary world by sharing a recommendation to friends or <u>posting an online review.</u>

Bugling praises from mountaintops, on-line mentions and dishing newly learned fungal tidbits into the ears of your beloved are also most appreciated.

Learn more about me at www.ellenkingrice.com

Read on for a sample of *The EvoAngel*

"Once the mushroom has sprouted from the earth, there is no turning back."
Luo proverb from Kenya

Chapter One

Tuesday morning, September 15,
Kamilche Peninsula, Shelton, Washington

She could poison the doctor.

Edna's hands trembled slightly as she lifted the latch on the door to her cabin. There was no lock. There had never been a need for one. Edna entered and hung her purse and jacket on the peg row by the front door. She desperately needed a cup of chamomile tea.

Oh, she knew which mushrooms to use. She could kill the doctor dead, dead, dead and, if she was careful, no one would connect the death to her.

Edna crossed her narrow living room, navigating carefully around the edge of the rug. At her age, she didn't need a fall.

She knew where to collect the Death Angel mushroom. There was a disturbed site behind the school bus barn that produced *Amanitas*. Even if the species she needed happened to be growing in a mixture of other fungi, as mushrooms often do, the Death Angel would stand out to her. She would know, instantly, when she had found any specimen of the Death Angels group. Eighty years of mushroom hunting was good for something. She knew her fungi.

Edna made it to her kitchen and rested her hands on the deep enamel sink. She remembered the day her husband had installed it. There was a chip near the drain hole. The geraniums on the windowsill needed watering. Edna blinked back tears. She had bigger challenges now. Her hands continued to tremble as she filled the teakettle.

She knew a Death Angel signaled its presence with a bright white stem erupting from an egg-shaped sac. Then there was the

271

white ring on the stalk, the white spores, the unattached white gills, and the elegant profile that all said *Amanita phalloides* just as clearly as a nametag.

She would have preferred the prettier *Amanita ocreata,* with its brighter cap, but that was a spring Death Angel. She was going to have to make do with the fall alternative.

As the flames of the propane burner licked the bottom of the teakettle, Edna's nerves steadied. She should think this through.

Amatoxins were not affected by heat. Cooked or raw, they poisoned. Surely a casserole would be a better vector than a salad. Who gave a gift salad?

Edna's mind skittered through the details. It would take several hours for the mushrooms in the dish to begin their poisoning of Dr. Band. The vomiting and diarrhea might not be connected with her offering. A day of intestinal agony might be attributed to a passing virus. She could hope. That weasel of a woman deserved all the agony the planet could deliver.

There would be a rebound day. Her victim would feel much better. It would be on the third or fourth day when the kidneys and liver began to fail.

Edna lifted the squealing kettle off the fire and poured the boiling water over a teabag. She made her mind take a step back from thoughts of murder.

She trusted Dr. Patel. He was a sweet man. None of this was his fault. She had made the appointment with him, trusting that her odd condition would be discreetly discussed. And, no, she hadn't been naïve. It was time to tell someone about her changing body.

She had not known there was a visiting doctor at the clinic, an intense, scary woman with a tiny body and ferocious eyes. Dr. Band was a witch of the worst possible sort.

Edna grimaced, a sour taste in her mouth despite sipping the mild tea.

"These days it is 'witch' with a B," she muttered.

Dr. Band was trouble.

As she sipped her tea, Edna considered her options. She could get a dog. A large dog with large teeth. And a *No Trespassing* sign. Her daughter would think her aging poorly, with the fears of old age sprouting like mushrooms after fall rains.

Edna's mind veered back to murder. Weasels sometimes had to be killed to protect a flock. No matter what, she should protect her daughter and granddaughter.

What she had, they might have next.

Feathers. An old woman should be sprouting chin hairs, not feathers. And a feather had emerged on her sternum a month ago and now that odd emergence was adding little friends. Dr. Patel had been kind and soothing. Dr. Band had been . . . fascinated.

Edna had seen the rectangle of a smartphone in the pocket of Dr. Band's white coat. When Dr. Band's hand went snaking into that pocket, Edna had leapt off the examination table and she had fled the clinic. There would be no photographs of her chest. Not if she could help it.

Edna picked up a frame from a kitchen shelf and studied the picture of herself as a bride. Marrying a cousin had not seemed so bad as they had no plans of children. She had been a fifty-year-old bride, for heaven's sake.

"Well, 'oops', as they say." Edna replaced her bridal picture on the shelf and took down a framed photo of Lena. Edna hugged the picture frame to her sagging chest. Her daughter Lena was so much more than they could have ever hoped for. More marvelous, more flawed and in so much danger from the modern world. Thank goodness Lena's husband was such a good man. And their daughter, Piper, had the family cunning to go with the family oddities.

Edna kissed the glass of the picture frame, steering her lips to the glowing halo of bright hair surrounding her daughter's perfect oval face. Edna's stomach swooped down with a wave of worry, then stabilized as the chamomile did its magic.

Edna's jangled thoughts began to settle. There was a better way.

She would protect Lena. She would protect her granddaughter. She would forge a back-up plan in case she needed a speedy exit for Dr. Band. Forget the mushrooms that had sustained and enchanted her all these many years. She needed to get out of the cabin and into the woods. She would collect some water hemlock.

Acknowledgements

I am deeply grateful for the love and support of friends and family. I am blessed with reading friends, writing friends, dog-loving friends and mushroom-hunting friends. My family members live with my passions as they embrace their own. I feel abundantly blessed (and often impossibly slow). Your love and fellowship kept me going through the slogging bits.

I am especially thankful for friends who helped with reviewing this story. Binda Douglas, Johanna Flynn, Cliff Rice, Cindy Levy and Sheila Rodriguez were generous with their time and talents. Members of the Olympia Writer's Group also did their best to clean up my act. The reviewers found clichés and errors in punctuation, grammar, location and logic. Any remaining embarrassments are all my doing and I can only claim insufficient chocolate intake as a weak defense.

Working with illustrator Duncan Sheffels is always fun. His talents bring a special extra dimension to these stories and I am grateful for his art and his insights.

Special thanks to Sally Bennett, Steve Ness and Eric Chandler for your fellowship in learning about the fungi of the Pacific Northwest. Above all, thank you to the Rice Men, including Newton. You make me smile every day.

Thank you, all, for your gifts of time and knowledge and for your words of encouragement.

Titles by Ellen King Rice

The EvoAngel – 2016 Wishing Shelf Book Awards Finalist
Winner, San Francisco Book Festival

Undergrowth – 2019 IPPY Winner

Lichenwald

Under construction:

The Slime Mold Murders

Larry's Post-Rapture Pet Sitting Service

www.ingramcontent.com/pod-product-compliance
Lightning Source LLC
Chambersburg PA
CBHW050233110726
47898CB00007B/2135